CONTAINMENT

CONTAINMENT

NICK THACKER

Bookouture

Published by Bookouture in 2020

An imprint of Storyfire Ltd.
Carmelite House
50 Victoria Embankment
London EC4Y 0DZ

www.bookouture.com

ISBN: 978-1-83888-716-2
eBook ISBN: 978-1-83888-715-5

To my wife, Emily, for the idea and the passion and the support.

CHAPTER 1

Six Days Ago

Canada–US Border

"Liz, put that bloody map away and help me read the signs!"

Liz pouted in the front seat, but she obliged her husband. She could tell Paul was stressed; he was always stressed.

The roads here didn't help, either. She couldn't make sense of where they were, even though everything was in English. They'd taken a wrong turn somewhere south of Abercorn, which itself was somewhere south of somewhere else, and neither of them knew where they were now.

The kids both needed to pee, but the last building of any sort they'd seen was a half-hour ago, and it looked like nothing more than a worn-down barn, empty and devoid of all life.

"Please," Liz said, "let's just pull over and wait for another car."

She knew her husband was doing his best. It was hard enough driving on the right side of the road on the left side of a vehicle, but her cellular service had dropped hours ago, their phone batteries were on their last legs, and they'd somehow found the last stretch of uncivilized country in North America.

"I want to go home," their daughter said, complaining for the twentieth time since they'd left civilization.

"I know, Brooksie. But we need to get back to the hotel, so we can get to our flight tomorrow. Then we'll be home, okay?"

"Yeah," her eight-year-old son said. "*After* a thousand-hour flight over an ocean."

"Peter," her husband snapped, a bit of his Liverpool slant returning to his voice. "Stop with it. You're scaring her."

Their daughter, two years younger than Peter, had a slight phobia of flying, only exacerbated by the fact that a London to Montreal flight was mostly over water.

"Ma, we've been driving for hours. Does Daddy know where we are?"

"No," Paul said tersely. "I do not."

"It's okay," Liz said, putting on her sweetest comforting voice. "We're always close to somewhere."

"Yeah, the middle of nowhere."

"Pete!"

The road turned, then doubled back on itself. Liz checked her phone's signal once again and decided against bringing up the fact that they hadn't rented the GPS unit with their vehicle when the cashier had asked.

The Canadian night was brutally dark, the road diminishing to nothing but a one-lane stretch with no streetlights or lit signs to help them along.

They drove along for another few minutes, then Liz pointed. "There!"

The reflection came off another vehicle's headlights, then the windshield. Then… the lights on top of the vehicle.

"It's a police car," Liz said. "Thank God."

Her husband pulled the rental over to the right side of the road, just past the police squad car. As they passed it, Liz saw the silhouette of a man stepping out.

"He's coming out; he'll be able to help us," she said.

They waited for a minute while the officer slowly ambled up to the side of the car. Her husband's window was down already, the cool fall air quickly dropping the temperature inside.

The officer walked up to the window, his tall frame blocking out the view Liz had of the opposite side of the road.

"Evening, sir. Ma'am."

Paul's hands were gripping the wheel, about shoulder-width apart. He responded to the officer—something muttered that Liz couldn't hear.

"License and registration?"

Her husband frowned, then looked over at Liz. She fumbled through the glove compartment, coming up with the receipt from the rental desk. Paul had his license out when she handed it over to him.

He gave the items to the officer and leaned his head out the window a bit. "We, uh, just need some help finding our way. Took a wrong turn somewhere, I guess."

Liz couldn't see the officer's face, but there was no immediate response. He flipped through the items, then leaned down and looked into the rear window.

Brooks and Pete were silent.

"Where are you staying?" the man asked.

Her husband answered. "Sutton. Small bed and breakfast there."

"You get off the highway?"

Her husband answered quickly. "No, no I don't think we—"

Liz placed her hand on his arm. "We might have. The road narrowed, remember? We tried to get back to something recognizable."

"Right, right," her husband said. "We might have, uh, gotten off the highway."

Liz leaned over. "Can you tell us where we are?"

"Sure, ma'am. You're just outside Richford, Vermont."

"Vermont?"

"Yes, ma'am. Please wait here," the officer said.

Without waiting for a response, he strolled back to his own vehicle. He entered the car, turned it on, then pulled up next to theirs.

Liz saw the man leaning over in his seat to talk to them. "Follow me," he said.

Liz met her husband's eyes. "Honey," she whispered.

"I know."

"What do we do?"

"He told us to follow him. So we follow him."

CHAPTER 2

Six Days Ago

Richford, Vermont

The town of Richford, Vermont, proudly displayed a sign boasting of a population of just over 2,000 people. New England-style houses lined the streets, the lots small and well-kept. But as idyllic as Liz imagined it would have looked in the daytime, it had a dreary, tired cast over it at night.

They crossed a large, green bridge, barely illuminated by a pair of small ground lights. A courthouse, no larger than the houses that led up to it, stood recessed on a city block, and a single-garage fire station stood on the corner just over the bridge.

"Where is he taking us?" Brooks asked.

"I don't know, sweetie," Liz said. "He's probably just taking us to his station, where they can help us find our way back over the border."

"We crossed the border?" Pete asked in hushed tones. "We're in America?"

"I guess," Paul said. "I didn't see a border patrol, or a customs station. Did you?"

Liz shook her head.

This trip was quickly becoming a nightmare. They had landed in Montreal a week ago, planning to see some of the land north of the United States. Liz's parents had raved about Montreal for years, and they had finally scraped together enough money to take a family trip. Convincing Paul to take the time off without worrying about missing an important meeting or coming across as lazy to his coworkers had been a struggle though.

Liz knew that it was less about his work ethic and more about his ability to worry: the man she'd been married to for sixteen years was able to worry about anything. Even now, she saw his whitened knuckles gripping the steering wheel as he drove the rental car through the streets.

"It's going to be okay," she said, keeping her voice low.

"You don't know that." His voice snapped, still quiet, but she could sense his anxiety growing.

She reached over and placed her arm on his shoulder.

The police station was on the opposite side of the street, a block farther down the road from the fire station; they followed the police officer into the parking lot of this tiny one-story building. Liz had seen no one since they entered Richford; it was like a ghost town. A few cars were parked alongside rusting meters on the street, old snow piled and dried out on their hoods and roofs.

The station had a single light on inside, but she couldn't see through the window as it was caked with dirty snow and fog.

Paul pulled the car into a spot next to the police cruiser and Liz immediately opened her door. She shuffled back to the rear seats to check on the children.

"Ma'am," the officer said, standing behind her. "Please come inside with me. We have coffee."

She turned and eyed the officer as Brooks unbuckled her seatbelt and began to exit the rental car. Pete, on the other side, was already out and bounding toward the ice-covered walkway.

"And, uh… tea." He offered a slight smile.

Liz forced a smile in return, then followed her daughter toward the front door of the station.

CHAPTER 3

Present Day

Hudson, Massachusetts

Jacob Parker hunched his tall, athletic body over the wheel of his Toyota Corolla, wishing he were a bit shorter so he could more easily appreciate the scenery. Instead, he was forced to focus on the road ahead, looking for nothing and everything at the same time. This place brought that desire out of him; he couldn't help it. He loved that the land here stretched as far as his eye could see, though his eye could see only from the windshield of his car to just past the first house on his left. The dense and unending Northeastern forest was the cause of that.

In his mind, Massachusetts had three distinct zones, each offering a unique geography: Boston, not-Boston, and the Berkshires. He was driving through the section of the state he called "not-Boston," which was, true to its name, *not* Boston. But when explaining his location to an outsider, this area was just as easily described as "near Boston."

The winding roads in this zone connected nation-old trade routes between farms that existed today only on paper. The houses were sturdy, well-constructed, and while they had the façade of an existence harkening back to Revolutionary times, they were modern, most built or rebuilt within the last fifty years.

The trees that framed the road weren't planted, they were *grown*; most were older than the houses they surrounded. The forest in this zone—the "not-Boston" zone—stretched completely through the middle portion of the state, thick and majestic, making it difficult to pinpoint where exactly he currently was.

But Jake wasn't confused about his location. The destination was on his right, and he pulled off the road, immediately buffeted by the emotions that struck every time he visited this place, yet silently choosing a reaction that was more suited to his newfound love of Stoicism.

Today is going to be a good day.

It was still early, by most citizens' count, but Jake was an early riser and by 8 a.m. most mornings he was finishing his second— and last—cup of coffee for the day. His destination today—the Walden Pond State Reservation—had just opened, and he saw the docent walking the path to the visitor's center as he parked.

The reservation was nothing but a handful of scattered buildings, one of which was a visitor's center and museum, and another the reconstructed cabin of Henry David Thoreau, a man who would have been decidedly unenthused about a state government claiming control over a pond and natural area.

Jake sighed and reached to the passenger seat for his shoulder bag, slung it over his head, then exited the vehicle. *Today is going to be a good day.*

"Here early?" the docent asked.

Jake smiled, a characteristic half-grin that tucked out from the corner of his mouth, a way of smiling without having to truly feel it. "Same time as always, Kurt. Maybe you're a few minutes late."

Kurt threw his head back and laughed, a hearty roar that would have felt out of place even in a noisy bar. "Well, we'll get you set up. Same as always?"

"Same as always," Jake nodded. He followed the docent into the visitor's center to pay for his parking—$8 for residents—and turned to leave just as two more cars entered the lot.

One had non-Massachusetts plates, but both vehicles were full of children and teenagers and ragged-looking parents, one even wearing a fanny pack.

Tourists.

They were here early, and they would no doubt be heading to Thoreau's reconstructed cabin for some sightseeing. There was no need to rush; Jake was heading to a different spot.

He walked across the road and onto the trail that would lead to his destination, a spot on the trail called Thoreau's Path, and a stone commemoration with words written by Henry David Thoreau himself: *Down the road on the right hand, on Brister's Hill, lived Brister Freeman... there where grow still the apple trees Brister planted and tended.*

Brister Freeman, a black man who had earned his freedom during the Revolutionary War, had purchased an acre of land, built his home, and raised a family with his wife. The land had been taken from him by the town's local government, but he had refused to leave, working out his days as a day laborer.

This was the place where Jake would spend the mornings when he needed to find a sense of solitude. The memory of a man so devoutly committed to his goal of living a free life, pushing against the force of society, gave him a sense of hope. It was this place where he had first read *Walden*, and it was in this spot where he felt closest to himself, able to be truly free once again.

The phone in his pocket rang, disturbing the sanctity of Jake's solitude.

He pressed the side button on the phone, declining the call, then took in a deep breath. He held it, reciting his mantra silently. *Today is going to be a good day.*

He let out the breath and sat down on the dirt next to the stone marker. He wanted to just sit and think, to be alone for a while, but there was an elderly couple holding hands, walking by in front of him. In the distance, he could hear the train rolling along, and farther back the sounds of the highway, the incessant droning of faraway grinding and roaring as the commuters made their way to work.

This was as alone as he would get.

It didn't matter. In the three years he'd been coming here, looking for something Thoreau and Brister and countless others had been looking for before him, he'd found nothing and had only ever left with more to search for.

He nodded once at the elderly couple, then pulled out his phone. He opened the calendar app, checking the schedule for the day. As usual, it was empty. He'd made a grocery run earlier that week, and that would last him at least another. His car's tank was filled, and it too would last another week—he had nowhere else to be, nowhere to go. Nowhere he *wanted* to go, and yet he felt trapped.

His one-bedroom apartment, nothing but a converted set of rooms that had been built above a bar and tavern in downtown Hudson, was devoid of all life forms when he wasn't in it, and it was devoid of many things that would imply life when he was. He had always meant to decorate, but after selling everything in his previous home in the downsizing, he'd never gotten around to it. No television, no couch in the living room, no pictures on the walls. He had a single plate and a single set of silverware. He owned a laptop, which was usually with him in his shoulder bag, and an e-reader, so there was no need for books or entertainment devices in the home, either. His gun, a SIG Sauer, he kept in the shoulder bag in a holster.

Most of his cooking was done on a single cast-iron skillet he'd inherited from his grandfather, and he drank water out of the single glass he owned. When he drank beer, it was downstairs in the tavern, where the owner would often spot him a freebie for being such a good tenant, and Jake would reciprocate by helping him close down the bar on some weekend nights, emptying the trash bins and taking out the recycling.

Locals that frequented the bar often gave him a hard time for his car, but his response was always the same. "Corollas run forever." He usually didn't add the fact that he'd personally rebuilt just about the entire engine—replacing worn and broken components with brand-new versions as needed, keeping it tuned-up and well-oiled, and treating the old car like an old friend: giving it attention, love, and respect.

Jake looked up at the trees once again. He understood the draw to live here, to eke out an existence on nothing but hands and knees and lots of hard work, not having to answer to anyone and not needing anything but more work. He wished it were still possible to chase a life like that.

But he knew the truth of it; he understood really that what he wanted was a way to go back, to change things. To make certain things right that were now wrong, to bring back things that were now gone. He liked the *idea* of the life this place hinted at, but he wanted the *truth* of the life he'd had before.

Before he'd had to start coming here.

Before he'd had to change everything.

Before he'd had to give it all up.

Jake flicked through a few more apps on his phone, finally landing back on the calendar app. There was a single event that had appeared, uncompleted, notifying him at the top of the screen.

He knew what it said; he'd read it before. It was a recurring task, one that popped up on this day every year, one he'd put in almost ten years ago. He could delete it; it hadn't been needed for the last three years after all, but it hadn't ever occurred to him to do so.

Anniversary dinner with Mel.

He didn't read it, but he flicked it away, knowing it would simply return a year from now.

CHAPTER 4

Present Day

Washington, D.C.

"Mr. Briggs, you're needed in the conference room."

The woman had hardly slowed as she tossed the statement into Briggs' office on her way past his door. He was already putting on his jacket and reaching for his briefcase, and he shook his head.

Things would have been way different if I'd stayed in, he told himself. *No one would have called me "Mr.," and no one would have rushed by me without even stopping.*

He checked his watch—he wasn't even late. The walk down the hall, into the elevator, and then out a floor down and into the conference room was going to take just over three minutes. That would put him at the head of the table, removing his jacket and placing it carefully over the back of his chair, exactly five minutes before the meeting began.

He rolled his eyes. *All this for just a meeting.*

After eleven years of service in the United States Navy and a relatively quick ascent through the ranks, Derek Briggs had opted for a change in scenery: he now worked exclusively on land. He missed the deployments, the times at sea and the war games, but during the mostly peaceful times he'd served, he had longed for something different.

That "something different" was where he found himself now, eighteen years later. Although, there were just as many—if not more—meetings here. Director of the United States Immigration and Customs Enforcement, Briggs had been handpicked to join the newly formed organization by his predecessor, another Navy man who had also risen quickly through the ranks. Briggs had been groomed for this role, and he was good at it.

But he still hated meetings.

The jacket, a dark-blue heavy denim thing his wife had purchased for him a few years ago, was typically too casual to wear around the office, but he was hoping to sneak out early after the roundtable this afternoon to hit a bucket of balls at the course near his home in Colonial Village. After that, a nice, quiet evening with his wife and a bottle of Merlot.

He reached the conference room on the sixth floor of the seven-story building exactly five minutes before the scheduled start of the meeting—exactly as he'd planned. The years of Navy service had drilled into him a strong sense for punctuality, a characteristic he took pride in.

He folded his jacket and laid it on the chair back, then began working his shirt cuffs up and over his forearms. Since he was first into the room, he went through his notes for the upcoming meeting. And since *that* took all of thirty seconds—he'd written these notes himself, and he had a near-eidetic memory—he used the remaining time to check his secure email account, the one that bypassed the ICE firewall.

He had time to send two responses and archive a few more as people arrived.

Once everyone had entered the room and taken their seats, he cleared his throat. "Well, we're all here," he said, smiling. "Shall we get this going?"

Nods came from the others seated around the room.

His assistant, the woman who had nearly jogged past his office five minutes earlier, sat to his immediate left, a legal pad and pen poised and ready. He liked her; she was old-school, taking notes by hand and then entering the minutes into Word at the end of the day.

The others, five in total, sat around the table, waiting for him to begin. Three were representatives of the two main branches he was in charge of—Homeland Security Investigations and Enforcement and Removal Operations. Two more were executive-level, one from Mission Support Services and another from IHS—Immigration Health Services. He had worked with these two for years, and they had a rapport. There was likely going to be no new information from them this meeting; it would just be business as usual. Anything noteworthy would have been emailed over to him during the month.

His deputy director, who would normally be seated in the chair to his right, was currently overseas, working with one of their attaché offices in Germany on an ongoing transnational investigation International Operations was leading. It was a useful role, but it was an important one to Briggs for another reason—the deputy director was the type of person who enjoyed snooping around other people's work. Lately, Briggs himself had been the target of the deputy director's scrutiny, so Briggs appreciated the opportunity to get some professional work time to himself, without needing to worry about where his coworker's eyes were landing.

"HSI," he began, looking at the woman near the opposite end of the table.

Her head shot up. "Uh, right. Oh. Diane Abernathy, sir."

"Abernathy," he repeated. "Hello—thanks for being with us. You'll have to fill in the rest of your group on what we discuss."

She nodded quickly, no doubt already prepared to do just that. Briggs knew the divisions she was representing—most notably the Intelligence Division—were relying on her update and report on the ongoing missions and projects that fell under the auspices of

ICE. The Office of Intelligence operated similarly to every other intelligence organization on the planet: on their own terms, with as little oversight from their parent organizations as they could get away with.

He turned to the young man sitting next to her. This kid was either a hotshot genius or he'd drawn the shortest straw in his office—Briggs wasn't sure yet. But everyone at the table would know as soon as he opened his mouth.

"Enforcement and Removal Operations," Briggs began, looking down at the notes his secretary had slid over to him. He articulated slowly and spoke the acronym word-by-word. He didn't need to focus on the kid to see his ears perk up. "Everyone's favorite division." There were a few chuckles around the table, but he went on. "Anything we should be aware of?"

The young man looked down at his notes once, then back up at Briggs. "No, sir. Nothing out of the ordinary, anyway. Centers are decreasing in capacity, mostly aligned with the year-to-date plan."

Briggs' eyebrows lowered. "Mostly?"

"Well, sir, there's a beta of .3 on the volatility of—"

Briggs smiled and held a hand up. *Doesn't sound like he drew the short straw,* he thought. "Very well. I understand, I just meant to find out if there's any reason we should expect capacity loads to change in a negative direction."

The kid shook his head. "No, sir. No reason we should expect any major changes."

One of the areas of utmost importance to just about anyone who had Immigration and Customs Enforcement written on their paycheck was the capacity levels of detention centers on US soil. It was not only a hot-button issue and favorite topic of the media outlets; it was also a crucial metric of what their stated mission was. The larger the difference between "Current Residency" and "Overall Capacity," the better. The fewer people being detained on US soil for *any* reason, in the eyes of government officials, the better they were all doing their jobs.

Unfortunately, in the years prior to Briggs' assumption of the directorship, some executives had discovered that by increasing the overall capacity—in other words, building more detention centers—that metric *also* improved.

"Great," Briggs said. He turned to the IHS executive. "Bill, you sent me the charts earlier this week—anything new with you guys?"

Bill shook his head, then spoke. "Nah, not really. Couple of isolated incidents around the country, but we're running by the book with everything. Nothing out of line, that's for sure."

"What type of incidents?"

Everyone looked at Bill. Briggs hated for him to feel like he was in the hot seat. They'd been friends for years, and they golfed together every other weekend when the D.C. weather allowed.

"What do you mean?" Abernathy asked.

"Oh, nothing. I think it's just strange to have a 'business as usual' this time of year. It's boring. I don't want Homeland Security jumping down my throat for cancelling the monthly update, so I figured you'd have something interesting to talk about."

Bill smiled, and Briggs felt like some of the air left the room. Being in charge of a government organization and twenty-thousand employees was a difficult mission, Briggs had come to learn. He always had to be "on," to have an answer, to give people the impression he knew what to do. And in crisis situations he had to remain level-headed and make the right calls.

It was similar in some ways to being captain of an aircraft carrier. So many teams, from cooks to mechanics to flight crews to comms, all doing their jobs and performing well, but often having absolutely no idea of what the others were doing—all relying on their commander to keep them pointed in the right direction.

"Sorry to disappoint, Derek," Bill said. "Nothing exciting. Couple of flus, a few bouts of chickenpox—which I thought we'd already eradicated—but not really anything else. Oh, a measles-like thing, or so we think. It needs far more study, but initial tests seem to imply it's very similar to—"

"Measles?" Briggs asked. "CDC called that 'effectively eliminated' in the United States back in 2000."

Bill seemed confused at first, then nodded. "Yeah, I guess. Sorry, we're thinking it's *related* to measles. Some sort of virus, likely highly contagious since the symptoms seem to be getting worse. We don't know much else yet, but we think it could be considered a similar strain to measles."

"I see. Go on."

"I mean... Sorry, Derek, I really don't have all the details in front of me. Something up north. Vermont, maybe?"

Briggs didn't expect Bill to have the minute details of every potential disease outbreak that could enter the US through their facilities—the number was staggering, and 99 percent of the cases would be eliminated or controlled from the ground-level before it even reached the desks of the local ICE facilities directors. Bill's job wasn't to read these cases; it was to manage the people who ensured none of the cases got out of hand.

"Apologies," Briggs said. "I understand. Not trying to bust your balls." He paused, looking around the table. "Anything else?"

Everyone shook their head.

His secretary was furiously writing notes—on what, he wasn't sure—but she too finally looked up and smiled at him.

Well, he thought. *That was the most boring meeting in the history of meetings.* He knew the captain of a vessel never wished for an attack from an enemy destroyer, but still... It seemed like any action at all would at least be more exciting than the daily grind of non-news and departmental updates. Hell, even the media seemed to be playing nice lately—there hadn't been any ugly reports or Associated Press stories about ICE in over a month.

"I've got nothing else, then," he said. "Good work, all of you. I'm taking off for the rest of the day—weather's nice enough, and it sounds like we've got no emergencies in sight. Have a good one."

They all rose to leave, and the kid from ERO looked over at him.

Briggs glanced at the notes his secretary had placed in front of him once more. *Alan Henderson,* he thought. *Definitely a rising star.*

Henderson nodded once at Briggs, and Briggs returned it. There was an awkward but brief pause between them, but finally Henderson slid back and stood. He left the room.

Briggs sat in his chair for another moment. His secretary looked at him, waiting for him to speak.

He waited until everyone else had left and then he leaned toward her. "Camilla, can you get me more information about that Vermont thing? The measles?"

She looked stunned. "Of course—but, why?"

He shrugged. "It's probably nothing. Just want to read it over. I'm going to have a bit of downtime at home until Amanda's off work, and it sounds like something I should keep tabs on."

She shrugged back at him and scribbled a note. He knew he could count on her to deliver a full packet of information before he left for the golf course.

CHAPTER 5

Briggs had just finished his first bucket of balls when the phone rang. His secretary put him through.

"This is Briggs," he said, holding the phone between his shoulder and his ear. He tried not to sound winded—after all, golf wasn't the most exhausting sport—but he wasn't as young as he used to be, either. He'd played often since taking the job with ICE. It was an easy way to meet the figureheads in counterpart organizations at the federal level, but it was also a great distraction from the job.

Unlike those figureheads, Briggs actually had a passion for fixing the organization—he hadn't taken this job to appease some senator or congressperson on their way to the White House. He wasn't interested in the glad-handing that came with the territory. Golf, and actually focusing on it, gave him respite from those sorts of meetings.

"Yes, hi—uh, sir—my name is Charles Brinkley. I'm up here at Clinton, uh, I didn't think I would be talking to, uh, you."

"That's fine, Charles. What's the update?" Briggs knew the feeling—in the Navy, he had once been asked to attend a standing meeting, during which the Rear Admiral had entered the room and taken a seat near the back. They'd asked Briggs for an update, and he had fallen all over himself stuttering to get the words out. The Admiral had shaken his hand afterward and winked at him, telling him that it gets easier with time. He no longer felt awkward or self-conscious around men and women of rank, but he understood the feeling this ICE employee was experiencing.

"Well, sir, it's… How did you know there was something going on?"

Briggs was taken aback at the change of subject, but he didn't want to dwell on it. "My secretary runs a tight ship. I'm guessing it's not measles, then?"

"No—no, sir. It's definitely not measles."

"What is it?"

Briggs took a swig from the beer sitting on the table behind his spot at the range. His golf bag was standing next to it, and he placed his nine-iron back into the slot so he could hold the phone with his hand.

"We don't know, sir. Not yet. But we're working on it. We think it may be viral from the same strain the measles disease is from, but it's definitely not measles. It's causing elevated blood pressure, and there are visible signs of blood pooling just under the surface of the skin. And it's moving fast. We first noticed it in a family who crossed the border around Richford in Vermont, and the husband-wife couple have been hospitalized since then. The children seem to be fine. I hate to say it, but it's not looking good for their parents."

Briggs almost shuddered. While there were rarely any viruses they hadn't seen before—and therefore didn't have a *plan* for—the word "virus" evoked fear in the hearts of any Homeland Security employee because of one thing: viruses were sorely misunderstood by the common public and the news media.

Anything with "virus" attached to it caused the developed world to go absolutely nuts. An H1N1 outbreak in 2009 nearly halted world travel and killed the economy, even though the CDC had implemented a plan to destroy it years before its run. And that had ended up far tamer than the COVID-19 virus and its related disease.

"Let's hope it's not that," Briggs said. "Are you resourced well enough up there?"

The man paused, and Briggs nearly laughed out loud. *Of course they're not*, he thought. This was Clinton County Jail in upstate New York, just across the water from Vermont. ICE had it listed as a detention center, which wasn't entirely inaccurate. It was just that it was, clearly, a county jail first and foremost, with a few rooms set aside for detainees. He figured this guy, Brinkley, was a part-time county employee who did work as a security guard. And knowing what he did of the area, the guy could also be the highest-ranking employee around.

With its latitude set so far north, Clinton was the only place in 200 miles that Immigration could send someone for temporary detainment.

"Well, sir, we've got Gerald—uh, a doctor—coming in to look at them tomorrow, even though the couple was screened by Dr. Edemza after they entered the country, but we could—"

"Do they need to be moved?"

Another pause. "Well, sir. Perhaps, yes. We can't really accommodate... And if this is viral, we don't—"

"Let's just go slow, Charles," Briggs said. "You've got a professional coming in soon, but I think the smart move is to get them somewhere a bit bigger. What about Albany?"

"Yeah—yes—that would work, fine, sir. Albany's got the staffing for it, I'm sure."

"Okay, Charles. I'm going to get in touch with them and make sure we're checked out, okay?"

"Okay, uh, thank you, sir."

Briggs knew the man was still trying to figure out why the Director of Immigration and Customs was offering to do his job for him, but he also knew the guy had a 50/50 chance of mucking it up. An outbreak possibility like this—measles or not—needed to be controlled. Managed. There were plenty of others in the chain of command who could manage it, but time was of the essence here.

He hung up the phone and dialed his secretary. "I need you to set up an exchange. Albany." He waited for her to write everything down on her trusty legal pad, then continued. "I'm going to fly out Monday."

"You're going? To Albany?"

"Near Boston," he said. "There's someone there I need to connect with. I'll email you the details, then I want to touch base with the Atlantic Group. They're having a meeting at their Boston facility to talk about some new direction. Didn't want to have it in D.C., for whatever reason. Can you set it up?"

She confirmed, and he hung up.

He placed the phone back into his pocket, zipped up the side of his golf bag, and downed the rest of his beer.

CHAPTER 6

Three Days Later

Hudson, Massachusetts

Jake took a sip of coffee from the logo-emblazoned paper cup, then crisped the edges of the newspaper to straighten them, then tried again, then finally gave up and tossed the whole mess down on the table. How anyone managed to read those things was beyond him. His dad used to do it when he was a kid, but Jake had never developed the desire to fight with an inky hunk of flimsy paper. Especially when news was only a few finger-clicks away on his phone screen. He typically hated anything purporting to be "news"—it was often *not* new, and it was often not news*worthy*. These days, most news channels had devolved into 24/7 political spats, or at least the not-so-subtle brainwashing of whatever side it was they tended to align with.

He flicked open the News app on his phone and read down the list of headlines. He subscribed to most of the three-letter news agencies, including some overseas options like BBC World News. When he came across an article that seemed overtly politically motivated, he tried to find an "opposing" article about the same subject—an article written by an agency that typically supported the politicians on the other side of the aisle.

Jake shook his head. It blew his mind that America was so committed to the idea that there were only two distinct trains of thought. It was one side or the other—nothing in-between, nothing outside of those two.

He'd spent a career in the military, fighting against evil all over the world and close to home, only to find out that that "evil" was mostly just a construct that had been created and passed down a chain to the grunts like him. Sure, there were threats: China had been growing more self-involved these past few years, and North Korea was as belligerent as always. Russia was standoffish, as anti-America as they came. Europe and Africa were still locked in their ages-long love-hate relationship, and South America was full of drugs. But the vast majority of the "conflicts" these sites reported on were nothing but misunderstandings—disagreements that were the unfortunate byproduct of two bloodthirsty idiots trying to outmaneuver each other.

He'd spent too many years of his life—five as an intelligence officer in the Army, and four at West Point before that—playing soldier. He'd learned the hard way that "terrorism" was often just a word used to sling hate to the other side of the fence. He'd played the role of counterterrorist plenty of times, only to discover that, to the opposing party, *he* was actually the terrorist.

It had been a difficult pill to swallow at first, but he had developed a crucial skill that had guided the rest of his career and earned him plenty of respect and accolades: he had determined to develop his own personal sense of right and wrong, and to follow that guide above all else.

He did his best to temper his conscience with a healthy dose of reality by at least following along with current events. It had allowed him to develop, over time and with a lot of experience, a great sense of what *really* mattered, how to fight against those who wanted to take that away, and how to stay alive while doing it.

He flicked down the list of news articles, finally finding the news he *really* cared about.

Bruins Trounce Penguins 3–0.

He sighed. Even though he lived close to the nation's most entitled—and worthy—sports city, Boston, he'd been a Pittsburgh Penguins fan since he was a kid. A fan of Mario Lemieux, or *Le Magnifique*, Jake had latched onto the NHL star as a personal hero when he had started playing hockey at four years old. Lemieux at the time was a new player for the Penguins, and he had quickly staked his claim as one of the greats. A larger frame, with the skillset to drive defensemen and goalies crazy, Lemieux was the type of player Jake himself wanted to become.

And Jake had, for the most part, done just that. Enrolling in the United States Military Academy at West Point in 1999, he had played for all four years as one of the largest and most powerful forwards the school had ever fielded. He'd nearly earned a place in the record books until a knee injury benched him for the latter half of his senior year, simultaneously blowing his chances of going pro.

He looked up from his phone, letting his eyes adjust to the now-bright light of the open front door of the coffee shop. A man—tall, thin, but moving confidently in his direction—had just entered.

Jake squinted, forcing his eyes to finish their job slightly faster. He closed his phone and tensed, the involuntary habit of his training kicking in. The man wasn't a threat, but it didn't matter—Jake had long ago made a commitment to himself never to be caught off guard.

"Jacob Parker?" the man asked, sidling up to Jake's table.

Jake was already on his feet. He sucked in a breath, then extended his hand. "That's me. You my 9 o'clock?"

The man smiled at him, then replied. "I'm pretty sure my secretary set it up as an 0900."

Jake cocked his head slightly. "I've been out of the Army for quite a while, sir."

The man nodded, then held his palms up. "Sorry, I know. Just an old joke. Not a particularly good one, either."

Jake allowed himself to relax just a little. He motioned down to the chair opposite.

The man sat.

"Mr… Briggs, I presume?" Jake asked.

"I am, yes. Used to be Captain Briggs, but those days are long gone. Like yours."

"And you're the… Director? Of ICE?"

"I am."

"You know I haven't been on active duty since 2008, and my service record isn't really anything to sniff about."

Briggs maintained his smile with the practice of a professional politician. "I know, Parker. I'm not here because of your *military* service record."

Jake's head lifted a bit, his wide chin jutting out and forward. "I'm not… in *that* line of work anymore either."

"Parker—please, hear me out. I know you're not a detective anymore. You left the force after…" He stopped himself.

Jake tried not to let his face betray any emotion, but he assumed the cards were already on the table.

"I know you're not active anymore," Briggs continued. "But that doesn't mean you're not damn good. The best, even."

Jake shook his head. "I get it. Really, I do. You've got a case that's 'just so different' than all the others, and someone—some *asshole*—decided it would be funny to recommend *me* as your guy. Your golden boy, a perfect track record with Boston PD."

Briggs took a breath, looked around the small coffee shop. It was a favorite of Jake's, just a small two-room thing with slanted floors and decaying walls. The tables were mashed together in a way that he would normally hate, but it was somehow charming. The place was on the main street, only two blocks away from his apartment. When he felt the need to get out and get some sunshine, he often grabbed an overpriced cup of coffee here and walked around downtown Hudson.

"I'll be straight, Parker. I'm looking for a guy I can trust to figure this situation out. It isn't like anything I've ever seen."

"And you—the director of one of the largest US government organizations outside of the military itself—need *me*? Don't you have a whole room full of interns for this type of thing?"

"I do. Multiple rooms. But that's not the point. You're a pro, Parker. You know it, I know it, *everyone* I asked knows it. It's close to here—no more than a few hours' drive—and believe it or not, I don't have tentacles *everywhere*. A few hours is about as close as I can get. So I start doing some research, figuring out who's around, and guess what?"

"My name pops up."

"Your name pops up. Jake—you're the guy. I need someone who thinks outside the box. Someone who doesn't necessarily think the establishment's way of doing things is the *only* way of doing things."

If Jake were keeping score, checking all the boxes for "things to say to woo me into agreeing with them," he would have had to admit to himself that this man, Briggs, was saying all the right things. However, he'd been trained—both by the United States Army and the exceptional, rigorous courses offered through the Boston Police Department—to ask questions.

"You and I both know that's a bullshit way of getting on someone's good side."

Briggs grinned. "Fair."

"Anyone who's got half a brain knows that you can yell 'the system is broken' in a bar and find fifty guys willing to die for your cause."

"I don't think you're willing to die for my cause."

"What *is* your cause, Briggs?"

"I want to solve a case. My entire department wants to solve this case. It's about American lives."

"It always is."

Briggs looked like he was about to get up and leave for a second, but he shifted his gaze downward and recovered, then looked back up at Jake. "It *always* is, Parker," he said under his breath. "Stop bullshitting with me. You don't want to help, that's fine. I've got a long list of candidates, and not a lot of time. But you haven't even heard what the case is."

"I don't 'take cases' anymore."

"I know. That's mainly why I sought you out. But you took the meeting, right? Don't you at least want to hear what it is?"

Jake waited. He had to admit he was a bit miffed that he'd been told this meeting was intended to "pick his brain" about his thoughts on the local New England political scene. But he also had to admit that he understood the man's desire for secrecy. Whatever was plaguing Director Briggs, he knew how to keep things under wraps.

"Okay," Jake said. "What's up? Why fly all the way out here to meet with me? I'm not a detective anymore; you knew that already. But you want my help for something. What is it?"

Briggs leaned forward. Smiled. Shifted in his tiny chair and looked directly into Jake's eyes.

And then he explained.

CHAPTER 7

"Nine days ago, we got word that a family up north had been detained. Separated," Briggs began.

"Why?"

"Why were they detained, or why were they separated?"

"Yes."

Briggs looked at Jake for a moment, no doubt trying to place Jake's nonchalant disregard for Briggs' authority. The truth was, to Jake, this man wasn't in a position of authority. Jake had been assigned no "boss" for the past three years, and he liked it that way.

"They were *separated* because our current system requires it. It's the only way to protect the individuals involved. They were *detained* because they'd entered the United States illegally. A cop found them, Border Patrol decided they needed a bit more time to figure out why they were here in the United States, so then they became our problem."

"Are they really a problem?" Jake asked.

"They became our *charge*. To find out what they're doing here, illegally."

"Could they have just accidentally crossed the border?"

"In truth, yes," Briggs said. "And that's most likely what happened. But that doesn't mean it wasn't illegal. I don't like that it's this way, but the system is set up a certain way for a reason. These individuals could have entered accidentally, or they could have done it for malicious reasons."

"But they weren't just individuals, were they? They were a family?" Jake already knew the truth, but it felt better to ask the question aloud.

Briggs seemed like he wasn't going to answer at first. Then he nodded. "Yes."

"And now they're bouncing around the ICE system," Jake said.

"They're not 'bouncing around,' Parker," Briggs countered. "But yes, they're now the custody of Immigration. Two parents, two children."

"Separated."

Briggs nodded.

"Right. Why?"

"Why were they separated?" Briggs looked incredulous.

"*Why* are you here?" Parker replied. "What do you want me to do about it?"

"The man, Paul Stermer, and his wife, Elizabeth, were brought to an ICE facility where they were examined by a Doctor Edemza, but a day after being printed and checked in they complained of stomach pain. A staffer there checked them out and noticed they had high blood pressure and there were early signs of blood pooling just below the surface of the skin. Otherwise completely healthy people."

"So they're sick?"

"They were," Briggs nodded. "They were quarantined as best we could manage, but—"

"They *were*?"

Briggs nodded. "Two days ago, they passed away, but then we found another case, very similar to theirs, in another facility. We're not sure how the people are connected, but it seems both may have been exposed to something contagious before they entered the United States. We're watching for more cases before we bring in the CDC, and we'd like to know what exactly we're dealing with, but I need someone out on the front lines, trying to put together the individual threads."

"Where are the Stermers now?" Jake couldn't help but feel more interested in the unsolved case. It was part of his identity—he solved problems, and he was good at it.

"Their bodies are being kept in a state facility in upstate New York, awaiting a proper autopsy."

"And the kids?"

"The kids are being taken care of."

Jake didn't feel like opening that can of worms; he actually wasn't sure he wanted to know what "being taken care of" meant to Immigration and Customs Enforcement. He felt for the children—innocent kids who'd just lost their parents and probably had no idea what was going to happen to them. He couldn't imagine what it would feel like to be a child, separated from their parents in a foreign country, pushed through a system that had been designed by people who had the lucky privilege to never experience the inner workings of it.

"I'm not a doctor."

"I know what you are, Parker. You're a detective."

"I *was* a detective."

"Parker," Briggs said, his voice falling into a tone that implied seriousness. Jake couldn't help but find himself compelled to pay attention. "Enough bullshit. I've got a lot of places to be, all at the same time. I'm here, in person, because I need *you*."

Jake swallowed. "You think… you think someone was behind this? That they *planted* this disease on the family and the other person who has it?"

"Just on the parents. And yes, that's what I believe. It's why I need a *detective* on this, not just a few scientists from the CDC. If it's criminal, and they're still out there…"

"Then they may have already planted it on more people," Jake concluded. He looked up at the cracking ceiling tiles of the small coffee shop. "That's why you're here in person. This isn't about reuniting a split family, or something your employees can handle.

This is *political*. You can't have something like this getting out. The contagion, of course, but really the *truth* that someone did this on purpose."

"Well, I wouldn't put it exactly like that. But yes, this is important to national security."

"And your job."

Briggs looked like he was going to rear back and punch him, but he recovered. "No, Parker. I don't give a shit about my *job*. As far as money is concerned, I have enough of it. I don't do this job for the paycheck. Fact of the matter is the job is just a job, but the reason behind it is what attracted me to it. The chance to fix something plaguing this nation. The system isn't perfect—we all know that—but it can be better, and I'm trying to get it there. If something like this gets out—that there is a virus that's potentially harmful to the citizens of the United States, and that it originated in one of *our* facilities…"

Jake finished the man's sentence. "Then you've got a pretty big problem."

"A pretty big problem, indeed."

Jake waited a few seconds, and Briggs gave him the space to think. Finally, he looked back up and into Briggs' eyes. "Okay," he said. "I get it. So, you want me to poke around a bit, figure out what's going on and what happened to those people, and make sure it doesn't happen again."

"Yeah, that's about right."

"And I'm not working for a department, so I'm not going to have to abide by their rules—that what you're thinking, too?"

Briggs' head fell sideways a bit. "Well, yes. But really, it's about simplicity. I don't have any bureaucratic hoops to jump through this way. No one to convince other than you. And the money—"

"I'm not worried about money."

"I know you're not. That's another reason I want you."

"How so?"

"Because the money doesn't matter, but that doesn't mean I want someone running around lighting it on fire. You don't strike me as the lavish, expensive private detective sort of guy."

Jake cocked an eyebrow.

"Exactly. So, you tell us what you want, what you need. You get a card; it's taken care of. That's it."

"That's it?"

"Well, as for reimbursables, sure. For salary…" Briggs slid a piece of paper across the table.

Jake almost laughed at the cliché until he saw the amount written on it.

"This is the salary for the project," Briggs said. "You finish it in a week, you get to keep it."

Jake's jaw dropped. "This… this is government money. Tax money."

"Yes," Briggs replied. "And it's the sort of thing hard-working Americans would want taken care of as swiftly and quietly as possible, wouldn't you agree?"

"Fair point, but like I said, I don't need money. This is a lot of it."

"Give it back, then. But I've got to pay it out to someone. That's how this government stuff works. Our bean counters don't really like 'pro bono' stuff."

Jake sniffed, still scoffing at the amount on the paper in front of him. Finally, he grabbed it, slid it over to his side of the table, then pushed it down into his jeans pocket. He looked back up at Briggs, then extended his hand.

Briggs shook it, smiling.

"I'll start today," Jake said. "But I'm going to need some help. I'm not medically trained, or anywhere near smart enough to be looking at virus outbreaks. I'll need support."

"I figured as much. Like I said, you've got a blank check. Get it done, no matter what it costs. Don't be reckless, but figure out how to stop this thing before it *becomes* a thing."

Jake nodded as he stood up, Briggs following his motions. The two men shook hands once again. Jake's nearly six-foot-three-inch frame usually towered over people, but he and Briggs were perfectly eye-to-eye now.

"Thanks, Parker. I've got your email address. I'll send over anything else you need, including my personal cell. Don't hesitate to reach out with anything you need."

"I'll be in touch."

CHAPTER 8

The Next Day

Albany, New York

Jake Parker walked into the "facility" skeptical and hoping he wasn't wasting his time. After meeting with Briggs in the Hudson coffee shop, he'd driven from Massachusetts to a small hotel in Albany, New York. He'd taken the better part of a day to get here, then spent the evening and this morning preparing, packing a small backpack full of clothes and ensuring his weapon was cleaned, oiled and extra magazines were packed into his shoulder bag. The SIG Sauer GSR had been one of his favorites at the department, used by the guys in SWAT. Many of his fellow officers opted for the familiarity and ease-of-use of the Glock models on offer, but Jake had always had an affinity for the heavy duty .45. During his time as a detective, he'd never left the house without arming himself first, but he'd dropped the habit within a year of his resignation.

Briggs had emailed some information, explaining where his teams at ICE were with the investigation. Jake knew Briggs had the resources to handle it on his own, but the more he thought about it, the more he realized how smart it was for Briggs to bring in a third-party investigator, someone who wouldn't be bound by the constraints of the organization.

He liked Derek Briggs. A military man who'd chosen a second career doing something he believed would make a difference, he seemed to have a similar background to himself—military career, then public sector, trying to make a small difference in the world.

All of it added up to the kind of man Jake used to see himself becoming—someone who cared about his career and wanted to make sure he was doing it for the right reasons. There was a time in his life when Jake believed in his country and his career, and he would have jumped at the opportunity to become something like what Briggs was now. No matter Jake's thoughts about ICE or any other government body, Briggs genuinely seemed to be trying, even though the period of his life when Jake had wanted to be like him was long over.

The ICE facility in Albany he was now walking into was actually nothing but a nondescript building split into two shared spaces inside—one side for a United States Postal Service administration office and the other for Immigration.

Briggs had mentioned in the email that they wanted Parker's take on a man who worked for ICE and was involved in the medical examination of the Stermers eight days ago.

Saiid Edemza, M.D., was waiting somewhere inside.

There was a black button panel affixed to the wall near the glass door, a camera mounted to the space above the entrance, pointed down. Jake pressed the call button on the panel, then waited. A second later, he heard a zipping sound and then a click as the door opened. He walked inside and found himself in one of the saddest lobbies he'd ever stood in. Fluorescent lighting glared down at him, and a stained carpet stared back up. It looked like a failed dentist's office. Drop ceiling, off-white walls, no pictures or decorations or even fake plants.

A lone man sat behind a Formica corner-shaped desk and raised an eyebrow when he entered. "Help you?"

Jake wasn't sure if he'd just missed the first half of the man's question, but he immediately knew he didn't want to stand around and talk to him any longer than necessary.

"Jake Parker. I'm here to see a doctor—Saiid Edemza?"

The man nodded, then pointed down the hall. "Third door on the left."

Jake thanked him and continued on. There were a few people standing near an office door, and all of them looked as sad as the facility. *Is it the lighting?* Each of them seemed tired, the coffees they held in styrofoam cups doing little for the bags under their eyes. One of them looked up at him as he walked past, but none of them said anything. Two others shuffled down the hall farther away, disappearing around the corner.

An extension cord snaked out of an open door on his right, running the length of the wall to the T-intersection with the other hallway.

Jake sighed. *Good enough for government work, I guess.*

The third door on his left was unlocked, and he turned the knob and stepped inside. Two faces greeted him, a man's and a woman's. Both were officers. The woman was wearing the blues and badge of the local department. The man's badge matched, and hung from his belt, almost hidden beneath a loose-fitting overcoat. He extended a pudgy hand toward Jake as he entered.

"Detective," he said.

"Not anymore."

"Name's Rutgers. This is Sergeant Mabry." He motioned to the woman, but she was busy reading something from a chart in her hand. "You want to talk to him?"

"Who?" Jake asked. "Edemza?"

Rutgers nodded.

Jake looked around the room. A single folding table, two chairs, a filing cabinet in the corner, and more of the same stained carpet below his feet. *Is it stained or is that some kind of terrible design?* One wall was made of glass, and through it, in an adjacent room, he could see a Middle Eastern man sitting in a chair in the center of the room. There was no table in front of him.

"What is this, some sort of interrogation?"

Jake looked at both officers, then back at Edemza. Edemza couldn't see them, he knew, but the man stared straight at the glass panel.

"It's unlocked?"

Rutgers nodded.

Jake left the room and turned right, then opened the door to the interrogation room. Edemza's eyes widened, then squinted.

"Hey," Jake said. "I'm Jake Parker."

CHAPTER 9

"You're with them?" Edemza asked.

"I, uh… no. Not really. Independent. Trying to figure out what happened here."

"Aren't we all."

Edemza spoke with a slight Middle Eastern accent, clipping consonants and lifting a few vowels, but his English was otherwise perfect.

Jake had read Briggs' team's brief on the doctor. Edemza was well-credentialed, a graduate of nearby Syracuse, then Johns Hopkins, and he'd done a stint as a general physician before landing the role with Immigration and Customs Enforcement, working in the Immigration Health Services Division, where he'd been for the past five years. He was good at his job, and he traveled a lot. Unmarried, no children, Edemza had been assigned to just about every corner of the United States in the years he'd been working for them. Most of his work was in general assessment—ensuring that immigrants and detainees were healthy and carried no contagious diseases.

He'd interacted with the Stermers only once, for a period of about one hour total, eight days ago, two days after the Stermers had entered the United States.

Jake decided to start there. He found a folding chair in the corner of the room, unfolded it, and sat down across from Edemza. He wanted to keep the man's face in full view of the cops in the opposite room.

"Tell me about the Stermers."

Edemza shrugged. "They were healthy, at least I thought."

"The entire family?"

Edemza frowned. "There were only two—Mr. and Mrs. Stermer."

"I see," Jake said. "Go on."

"We ran the usual tests, and—"

"What are the usual tests?"

"People are brought in, fingerprinted and added to the system. When they're ready and we have an opening, patients are all screened—basic heart rate, blood pressure, visual examination."

"Physical?"

Edemza shook his head. "No, not unless we believe there to be something going on that warrants it. I have heard that there were signs of blood pooling in their system, and both had high blood pressure, but I assure you those symptoms were not present at the time of my examination."

"I see," Jake said again. "So, you saw nothing out of the ordinary? What about blood work? Wouldn't that have caught something?"

"We don't test blood, generally. We saw nothing to suggest it would be necessary."

"Why not? It's not too expensive?"

"It's not, but—contrary to what you may have heard—we do try to honor the humanity of the detainees we see. A blood test can seem rather invasive. Not to mention it can lead to potential legal trouble if we run tests on someone who has insurance back in the country they're coming from.

"Besides that," Edemza continued, "it's difficult to manage. Where to put the samples, how to keep them long enough for testing, et cetera. I suppose if we had, we may have caught it, but—"

"Caught what? The virus?"

Edemza frowned, then nodded. "Yes, I guess. I am not sure it is viral, or I believe I *would* have noticed something physical. Lesions, reddish skin, something of that nature. But yes, a blood test may have picked up on it. Perhaps not."

"Right," Jake said. He paused, thinking about what to ask next. He had almost zero medical training so felt his line of questioning quickly running out of steam. But that didn't mean he couldn't learn something from the doctor.

Suddenly he realized why Edemza was here. This was an *interrogation*, after all. He shifted in his chair, deciding to start fresh.

"Edemza," he said. "Let's start over. For the record. Sound good?"

Edemza shrugged.

"Okay, Edemza—Saiid. Male, 49 years old, doctor and general physician, correct? Unmarried, Middle Eastern descent. You're Iranian?"

"Yes. All of that is true."

"And you've worked for Immigration and Customs Enforcement for how long?"

"Just over five years."

Jake didn't have a notepad to scribble any answers or leads, but he assumed that's why the other two officers were waiting behind the glass. With any luck, this would all be recorded anyway, saving them all time.

"And you happened to be in the area when the Stermers were detained?"

He nodded. "I was. Here, actually, in Albany. They sent me up to Clinton, where they were being held. I examined them and was heading back here about an hour later."

"And you... did nothing but perform the examination?"

He nodded. "Just the examination. Routine. They have a single doctor—he's called Gerald—on-site as well, but he was unavailable that night, so I filled in. He is the doctor who then found the strange anomalies in their system and called for the quarantine."

"I see," Jake said.

"They think I am a suspect," Edemza said. He swallowed. "They think I did this."

Jake didn't respond. Edemza was looking over his head, through the glass, trying to see the officers behind it. Then he turned back to Jake.

"I don't even know *what* it is, what killed them. I am still trying to piece together the timeline myself. They were in the United States for two days before I examined them, at which point they were perfectly healthy. Dr. Gerald examined them after they began to complain of stomach pains, and they perished shortly after that. When I asked to follow up with them, I was told their bodies are still in quarantine, awaiting an autopsy; they told me it was unsafe, then they had me come here. You know I'm staying here, right?"

Jake didn't know that. There must have been a room set up somewhere in the building. The doors into the building were electronically sealed; it was possible Edemza was being held here, in a sort of corporate prison. He shuddered, feeling sorry for the doctor. His mind raced with the legality of it. *Can they do that? Keep him here against his will?* And then, *Is it even against his will?*

"Listen," he said. "I'm trying to figure this out, too. I was just brought in a couple of days ago, so I'm making my way through it from the beginning. But I'm good at this stuff."

Edemza swallowed, not taking his eyes off Jake. Jake could sense that he was scared.

"I'm *good*, Edemza. I'll figure it out. I promise. If you had nothing to do with it, you'll be fine."

He paused, then stood and prepared to leave.

"And if you *did* have something to do with it…"

He didn't finish the sentence.

CHAPTER 10

Two calls.

Those were the words running through Jake's mind as he left the ICE facility and headed to his car. The drive back to his hotel would take twenty minutes. He figured it was just enough time to make the two calls.

Long ago, a mentor and friend he'd served with—the detective who had brought Jake under his wing when he'd joined up—had told Jake something he'd carried with him for years.

"Never work alone," Jorge had told him. "When you take a case, and you don't already have a partner assigned to you, make two calls: find someone you trust, and get them on your side early."

Jake remembered nodding along as his mentor gave him the tip.

"And the second call?" Jake had asked.

"Find someone smarter than you to be your asset. Someone uninvolved in the case, and get them involved."

Jake had mulled over this as he'd interviewed Edemza. The doctor wasn't acting guilty. Yet Jake knew all too well that *not seeming* guilty didn't always mean one was *not* guilty. Edemza, like plenty of other criminals he'd met, could just be a good actor.

But there was more to this case that Briggs had brought him in on. Edemza had stated clearly that he wasn't sure what had killed the couple. He had never seen any symptoms, nor had he seen the bodies after they had perished. Jake wanted to speak with the other doctor, Dr. Gerald—he would email the man later that evening.

So far, he had to trust Edemza—if he didn't know what it was that had killed these people, then there was no way Jake could know, either. He needed outside support.

His first call was to an old friend, Beau Shaw—his ex-partner—a man he knew would be interested in the case, simply because he knew how good a detective he was.

But there was another reason—one they would no doubt talk about soon. He wanted to handle that conversation in person, where he could read his friend's face.

He held up the phone and waited until the man answered.

"Hey," Jake said, when Shaw picked up the phone.

"Jake Parker, calling me?" his friend answered. "What fresh hell is this?"

Jake laughed. He rarely called anyone—his own parents had passed away years ago, and he didn't have any extended family close enough to maintain a regular relationship with. "I know it's strange. But you'll be happy to know I'm not calling just because I miss you."

It was his friend's turn to laugh. "Well, shit. And here I was thinking you'd gotten soft on me, brother."

"Sorry to disappoint. Hey, listen. I'm working a case, and I need—"

"You're working a case? What the hell? Where?"

"It's a contracted thing. Not for the department. Actually, a government contract."

Shaw whistled. "Damn, man. That's a contract for sure. What sort of work?"

"Well," Jake said, "I'd rather explain it in person. You working the next few days?"

"I am, but I've only got a couple in-persons coming up. I can wiggle a bit. What do you need?"

"I'm in Albany. It's a bit of a drive, so I can probably get you on a plane. Can we meet up tomorrow? I'll explain everything then."

"Albany? Come on, that's barely two hours. No problem—send me the details and I'll make it happen. How long we talking? A week?"

"Probably," Jake replied. "At least. But we can touchpoint as often as needed, so old man Mills doesn't chew you out." Mills was Jake's old coworker, and now Shaw's boss at the Boston Police Department. He'd "almost retired" about fifteen times, and Jake thought he had to be pushing seventy. He was certainly pushing forced retirement.

"Don't worry about Mills. He owes me one. Anyway, man, I'm glad to help out. Send over whatever you got, and I'll take a look."

Jake thanked him. "Hey, Shaw. One more thing."

"What's up?"

"I need a 'second call.' Someone to help as an asset. You think you can dig up some old files and see if there's anyone qualified in the database?"

"Sure thing. What you looking for?"

"Well, it's medical-related. Infectious disease stuff. Someone at the CDC might work if we've got that? Money's not an issue, so get someone good."

Shaw paused. "Okay, sure. I'll check it out and let you know."

Jake thanked him again and hung up.

Two calls.

There was, of course, no limit to how many assets a detective could have—some collected them like trading cards. But Jake had always preferred the simplicity of keeping things close, sharing information with only those he knew and trusted and whose credentials checked out. It was during the roguish early years of his career, when he preferred to go it alone, that his mentor had told him about his 'two calls' rules.

He turned the car onto Western Ave—146—and headed southeast toward town. A sign for the Western Turnpike Golf Course caught his eye, but he could only see a single flag and hole from this angle. He tried to remember the last time he'd played golf. It had been years, and he'd never been good at it. But he enjoyed the activity, the solace of it. If there was time, he told himself, he'd have to check out the course here and see if he could persuade Briggs to throw in a round or two through his per diem.

Before he'd even finished the thought, his mind was quickly thrown back into the present, focused on the task at hand. As much as Jake hated to admit it, he had missed this. He had missed the work.

He hoped Shaw would be able to find someone.

CHAPTER 11

The Next Day

There was still snow on the sides of the road, packed into roundish blobs of hardened ice and covered in streaks of dirt. Beau Shaw gave himself plenty of room at each stoplight as he navigated through the streets of Albany. He doubted there was still any ice left on the roads, but it never hurt to be careful.

As an active-duty officer for the Boston Police Department, Shaw had seen plenty of gruesome accidents resulting from sheer negligence. People ran red lights in the middle of the day, completely sober. Adding icy roads to the mix was a recipe for disaster.

Shaw hadn't always been so focused on safety, but after his wife had passed away from cancer, eight years prior, he'd become a different man. He understood life—and death—better, and while he knew nothing could bring her back, the least he could do for her was protect his own life with the care and attention that she'd given hers.

He turned left at the green arrow, then pulled into the lot immediately on his right. The hotel's name and front entrance were lit up in a yellow glow, but the front of the building was dark. The few windows with lights on inside were covered by curtains, allowing only a dim orange outline to peek out the sides.

One of those rooms, he knew, would be Jake Parker's.

His friend had a few quirks—all harmless, and all weird. One was his desire to book rooms only on the side of hotels that overlooked whichever was the busiest road approaching it. Another quirk was Jake's desire to leave the room's lights on at all times.

He was supposed to meet Jake in the tiny bar just off the lobby of the hotel, and he knew Jake was likely already there, preparing for their face-to-face meeting with a stout or porter, or whatever was the darkest beer on tap.

That was another one of Jake's quirks, but it was one Beau himself tended to oblige: both men loved beer—the more obscure, the better—and whenever the weather dropped below fifty degrees, they both tended toward the darker varieties.

Shaw got out of the car, closed the door, then walked over to the opposite one and opened it, retrieving his leather shoulder bag and small carry-on suitcase. He didn't expect to stay here for more than a couple of days as it was only a two-and-a-half hour drive back to Boston. He could always drive home, grab a new set of clothes, and drive back, checking in with his department as needed. His new boss, Mills, had hardly batted an eye when Shaw had told him he'd be gone for a few days; but when he'd mentioned Jake's name, he knew Mills would have let him stay in Albany a year if need be.

Jake Parker's name was near-legend to the officers and detectives back at the department. The kid had been an ace cop and then a true detective—the type of man who wanted justice over law, one who went by the book for as long as it was appropriate, then never batted an eye when it was prudent to make his own way. It was like a superpower—Jake Parker knew right from wrong, and even when it looked an awful lot like the guy was chasing something no one else could see, Jake would eventually hold up the prize.

He could figure out a complex problem by tackling it from multiple angles at once, rather than the typical way of working it from one angle, then the next, and so on. Jake seemed to be able to hold a thousand contradictory ideas in his head all at the same time, to recall an individual thread of knowledge necessary to cracking a case seemingly on a whim.

He always had a reason for bending the rules, but the reasons all stood up to scrutiny after the result was revealed.

He had almost always come out on top, and he'd been on track to set a department record for cases solved. His arrest record was through the roof, and to date not a single one of them had been appealed or found in need of further requisite action.

Shaw had heard stories about Jake's time before Boston PD, working for a branch of Army intelligence in global anti-terrorism, a task force similar to the very one he ended up on at the local level. Jake had been a hard-driving, unrelenting force for good, bringing down international terrorism cells before they'd even had a chance to get off the ground.

It had all been very miraculous, very promising, and Shaw had been honored to call the man "partner."

That's when things began to change.

They had served together as detectives for a couple of years, but Jake had been recruited to a special anti-terrorism task force, which had him traveling more often and becoming somewhat of a recluse when he was around. Shaw understood—it was one of the many pressures of the job—but it had caused a bit of a rift in their relationship.

When Shaw's wife had passed away, Jake had been there in person, but his mind hadn't been. When pressed, Jake had claimed to be working on a case that still had him completely tied up.

Shaw had dropped the matter, and their relationship slowly began to crystallize into a professional, courteous one. Their banter had become trading case tips and working the odd job together, and their calls had become less frequent.

Finally, it all fell apart.

During a terrorist attack a few years back, Jake's wife had been killed in collateral damage from an explosion after a Boston PD raid of a local café. The department's anti-terrorism task force had been trying to identify a possible terrorist target, and information had been confused, leading to a botched operation. The details had plagued even Shaw, who hadn't been involved with the case in any way, but it was the nonchalant way the department had handled the situation—eventually leading to a state hearing and investigation into the department's darker sides—that had finally caused Jake to hang up his badge.

Ever since, the two had remained distant. To Jake, calling the man his best friend wasn't a great reach: he was really Jake's *only* friend, and since Jake had become rather antisocial, he had no interest in replacing some of the friendships he'd let lapse.

Shaw knew all too well that one never "moved on" with their life after a loss like that—they simply moved forward. Jake would carry this with him forever, so it was the least Shaw could do to make sure his friend knew he was there to help with the burden. He would do whatever it took to help Jake with the case.

He walked to the front door of the small hotel, then entered. From the lobby he could see Jake's large frame, hunched over a beer, looking directly at him.

Shaw smiled. The beer was dark as night.

CHAPTER 12

The two men embraced. Shaw thought he felt Jake holding on for an extra few seconds. He wanted Jake to say something, to tell him how things had been and that he missed him. But Jake had remained silent during the embrace, and Shaw himself hadn't spoken up, either.

The pair released and smiled, then turned their attention to the bar. Jake pulled over a stool, then slid along a beer, which Shaw caught with his right hand. He lifted it to his lips, then saw that Jake was waiting with his own in his hand.

"Right, sorry," he said, clinking his pint glass with Jake's. "My bad. Cheers."

"Cheers," Jake said. "First round's on me."

"*All* rounds are on you, brother," Shaw replied. "You dragged me all the way up here."

Jake feigned shock. "What? You said it wasn't much of a drive. Man, I'm going to have to ask for a higher per diem."

Shaw sensed that his friend wanted to move immediately into business. He sighed. *Plenty of time to catch up later,* he hoped.

"So, you have a per diem. That means you're not doing this pro bono?"

"Nope," Jake said. "Working for ICE."

"ICE?"

"Immigration and Customs Enforcement," Jake answered.

Shaw frowned. "Interesting. They want—no offense, either—they want *you?*"

Jake shrugged. "Yeah, I guess. And they're willing to pay dearly for me. I guess something about getting a third-party investigator involved who's not currently tied to any other orgs is an important play."

Shaw mulled this over for a second. "ICE, huh. You didn't say it was ICE."

It was Jake's turn to act surprised. "What? Have some history with them?"

Shaw shifted in his seat, then took another sip of his beer, trying to act casual. "No, I don't. Look, man, it's—it's not a real *thing*, it's just…" He looked down.

"It's because you're black."

Shaw hadn't expected him to just come out and say it. But it was true, and it was his reason for hesitation. He nodded. "That… and, I mean, you know my history. My *family's* history."

Beau Shaw was the product of immigrants—his father and mother had left Côte d'Ivoire years before he was born, but they'd struggled to make a way for themselves in the United States. As if getting a start in a new country wasn't enough, they had both been pressed to their breaking points to achieve their citizenship status, a multi-year, multi-state process.

Those in charge of the customs and immigration process at the time hadn't helped—on the contrary, they had made every step of the way for Shaw's parents miserable, and nearly impossible. Shaw had told Parker that during one especially harrowing incident, his mother had been separated from his father and was nearly deported back to Côte d'Ivoire based on a government worker's claim of a "missing file." Shaw's father had used their last remaining dollars to find a copy shop that allowed him to fax a doctor from his hometown and have it sent to the United States.

Beau had been born shortly after that as a *true* citizen of the United States, and his parents had tried their best to shield him from the struggles they had faced early on. He'd grown into a fine young man, eventually becoming a police officer and detective, and as he grew into an adult, he had taken on his parents' struggles as his own.

He had never had the opportunity to show them what their America had become, one he had had a small part in shaping—both of them had passed away a year before he and his wife were married. Shaw had told Parker once that his life's mission was to create something he truly believed in. To do his part—no matter how small—to make his country a better place.

It was getting better, but there were some streets in Boston he still hated walking down alone—even wearing blue, even during daylight hours.

For Shaw, it wasn't about "being black" as much as it was about "being from *somewhere else*." The America he wanted to live in wasn't segmented into classes of people from America and from elsewhere. He wanted a country that truly took pride in having a melting pot of civilizations and skin colors and religions, all working together and operating as one.

Until then, it wasn't an America he felt he could have shown his parents.

"Sorry," Jake said. "I didn't—I didn't even think about it. I didn't consider it."

Shaw waved it off. "I'm being dramatic, man. No worries. It's an important case, I'm sure, and you know much I believe in this stuff. Besides, I wanted to see you anyway. If it means I have to slog through a few meetings with ICE, so be it. *I* ain't an immigrant."

"For what it's worth, I'd love just as much to go punch some of these government thugs in the mouth, but this is actually about something… different."

"It's not about immigration?"

"Well," Jake said, "it is. But in a roundabout way."

Shaw took a drink and raised an eyebrow.

"It's about a family. A *white* family. English. Came here accidentally, through Canada."

Shaw smiled in understanding. "So if word gets out…"

"Right, media will have a heyday with it."

"Can't be having that."

"Can't be having that," Jake repeated. "That's why ICE is all over this. Trying to rein it in before any news or Associated Press gets wind of it."

"How's it work?" Shaw asked.

"Well, the story is they were lost at night, ran through a Border Patrol area—when they were sleeping, I guess. Got picked up near Richford, Vermont, by a cop, who brought them in. ICE got involved shortly thereafter, doing their thing."

"I'm sure 'their thing' wasn't what the family had in mind."

Jake shook his head. "They were split up, actually. Parents went to somewhere close to here."

"Parents?"

"Yeah," Jake said. "And that's not the shitty part. They had kids—boy and girl."

Shaw closed his eyes. "*That's* the shitty part?"

"Well, yeah it is, but it still gets shittier. Both parents, a few days ago, croaked. Some sort of sickness. Viral, we're thinking."

"Please tell me *that's* the shitty part."

Jake took a long, slow sip to finish off his beer. He made a motion to the bartender to grab another round, and then turned back to Shaw. "Wish I could say that. But that's why I'm here—why *you're* here, too."

"Okay, I'm one of your calls, I got that much. I'll bite—what's going on?"

"Well, my contact at ICE, guy named Briggs, says they think they might have been infected *on purpose*."

"The disease?"

"Yeah."

"Before they entered the country?"

"We don't know. That's part of what he wants us to figure out. ICE wants to make sure the contamination, whatever it is, is contained. And Briggs wants to make sure the media doesn't get out in front of this, either. Even a false alarm would be hell to an organization like that."

"Yeah, I bet," Shaw said. He rubbed his shoulder. It was still sore from a department-wide softball game during the summer. *Getting old sucks,* he thought. "So you've got me, and you wanted someone in medical. 'CDC or someone like that,' I think you said?"

"Yeah."

"Well, I didn't have a CDC asset, and I had to call around a bit, but I think I've got someone. We're supposed to do brute-force stuff, right? Get the case rolling, collect the evidence, prepare for handoff?"

"We might not even hand off," Jake said. "Briggs wants a third-party, but he also wants it wrapped up tight. I think we're here for the long haul. Find whoever planted the stuff, make sure there's not more of it, and get it cleaned and below the table before the other orgs come knocking."

Shaw listened and nodded along. It all sounded pretty straight-forward. They were trained professionals, but they wouldn't be producing detective work for any specific department. Their information and what they uncovered would go directly to Briggs and his team, for their perusal and decision-making.

It wasn't exactly common, but it also wasn't unheard of. A large organization needed to perform regular voluntary audits on their systems and practices, and this was no different—Briggs had been wise to choose a team of individuals who could swoop in and get back out without causing a bureaucratic nightmare. In order to prevent a spool of red tape from wrapping the investigation and turning communications into a nightmare, Briggs had given Jake and his team direct access. They wouldn't have a ladder of underlings to get through to reach Briggs.

It wasn't exactly protocol either, but Shaw appreciated the simplicity.

"So," Jake said. "About that second call."

"Yeah," Shaw said, pulling out his phone. He'd just received a text message. *Right on time.* "Looks like she's here."

CHAPTER 13

Jake's attention was pulled toward the front of the hotel as soon as he'd heard Shaw's words. In that same moment, the lobby doors slid open and a woman strode in. She didn't turn, didn't nod or wave at any of the staff. She walked directly toward Jake and Shaw.

She had a petite build, short stature, but she walked with the confidence and purpose of a woman on a mission. The woman's chin was up, and Jake could see her face clearly. She was beautiful, with olive skin and deep, dark eyes. Her hair was black and cut short, curving around the sides of her face, lapping at the tops of her shoulders.

She wore a light overcoat despite the snowy conditions outside but didn't appear to be cold. She walked toward them, already sure they were her target. When she reached the pair, she slung the coat off her back, revealing an attractive, perfect-fitting black blouse and long, slender black slacks. The woman reached out a hand, first shaking Shaw's.

"Eliza Mendoza," she said, calmly and confidently. "Nice to meet you."

She turned to shake Jake's hand just as Shaw spoke. "Not *Doctor* Mendoza?"

She smiled. "Technically yes, but that's my mother's name. Just call me Eliza."

"Eliza," Jake said. "Pleasure to meet you. You're my second call?"

She looked confused. Jake realized that Shaw hadn't briefed her.

"Oh," he said. "It's a… just something I used to say. Shaw was my first call, you're my second." He paused. "Even though he called you."

Idiot, he thought. *Just stop talking.*

Her chin lifted and her mouth pointed up at Jake. "I get it," she said, still smiling. "I'm here to help. Your case, or whatever it is you're doing."

Shaw cleared his throat. "Yeah, uh, it's a case. Jake just filled me in, but we could use another beer. You want one?"

She shook her head. "I don't drink. Beer, I mean."

Jake glanced at Shaw, who was presently trying to hide the fact that he was checking out Mendoza. Shaw caught his eye and looked away.

"They have wine, I believe," he said. "Want a glass?"

"No thanks. It was a long drive," she said. "And I've got some studying to do."

Both men frowned.

"I'm teaching a few classes at Syracuse, mostly microbiology, parasitology, and cellular reproduction. Nothing fancy."

"Right," Shaw said. "Nothing fancy."

"I like to be ahead of the class, make sure I'm all caught up and stuff."

"Of course," Jake said. "So, you want to grab a seat? I can bring you up to speed."

She glanced at her watch. "Sure, I've got a few minutes."

A few minutes? Jake looked at his friend. *Who is this?* She'd come in as if she owned the place and now she was dictating terms for the two of them. Last he checked, Jake thought he was in charge. He rolled his eyes toward the bartender so Eliza Mendoza wouldn't see it.

They sat at the bar for another twenty minutes discussing the case and all that Jake knew about it. Shaw filled in a few of the details about where he thought Eliza could best help, and Eliza, for her part, mostly remained silent, nodding along and taking notes here and there. When the two men had finished explaining where they were with the case, Eliza immediately stood and left, claiming to have more studying and work to catch up on.

They all exchanged phone numbers, and Jake was near the bottom of his third beer when he got a text from Eliza.

Come up when you can. Room 309.

Jake looked up at Shaw, then smiled. "Duty calls, I guess."

"That's Eliza?"

Jake nodded. "She probably has a few more questions about the case. Seems pretty studious to me."

"Studious, or more likely she's into you."

Jake stood. "You've had too much to drink, brother," he said. "It's probably time for me to head up anyway. We've got a big day tomorrow. You good to go?"

Shaw stood up as well. He looked as though he wanted to add something, but held his tongue. He nodded. "I'm good. It's good to see you, Parker."

Jake wanted to say more, to explain how sorry he was that he'd been incognito for the better part of three years. Since Mel…

Instead of saying anything at all, Jake simply nodded. They shook hands and Jake walked toward the elevator.

CHAPTER 14

Jake rode the elevator up. He had already checked in and unpacked his single change of clothes and suit, which he had hung up in the hotel's closet. He rarely wore the thing, but he figured having something nice to wear at any important meetings that might come up was a good call.

He got off on floor three. Room 309 was about halfway down the hall and the door was cracked, the long lock mechanism folded into the space to hold the door open.

Still, he knocked.

"Come in," he heard Eliza's voice answer.

He pushed the door open and stepped inside. The room was cool but not cold. It smelled of lavender and vanilla, and he wondered if it was a perfume or some scent Eliza had pumped into the room. Either way, it sure was inviting.

He walked toward the center of the room and saw that it was a mirror-image layout of his own. A single king bed, a writing and work desk, and a flat-screen on a stand pushed up against the long wall. The floor lamp in the corner was lit, as well as the double lamp near the bed's headboard.

Eliza was sitting cross-legged on the floor, in the space between the bed and desk. She had a well-organized semicircle of manila folders and stacks of loose papers in front of her, and there was a red pen tucked behind one ear. In her right hand was a blue pen.

She glanced up, looking at him from behind a pair of small glasses.

"Hey," he said. "My bad—I didn't realize you were in the middle of something."

She pulled her glasses off and stood. She had changed clothes and was now standing in white silk pajama bottoms and a loose-fitting T-shirt. Whatever design had been on it had long faded. Eliza pushed a strand of hair behind her pen-less ear.

"Not a problem. Thanks for coming up. I just had a few more questions before I got back to my grading."

Jake glanced down at the floor. "That what those are?"

She nodded. "That and some research for the upcoming presentation series I'm giving." She didn't offer more information than that, and he watched as she checked something on her phone, frowning down into its glowing screen.

Jake rocked on his heels slowly. He stuck his hands in his pockets. He and Eliza stood face-to-face for another few seconds. "So," he said. "What, uh, did you need to ask about?"

"Oh, right," she said. "It's about our case. Your friend Shaw brought me in as the 'expert,' right?"

"Well, yeah. I mean we both did. But he found you, I guess."

"Right. Well, in order to do my job as well as possible, I need to have access to the same information you two have."

Jake turned his head to the side. *What's she playing at?* "Okay," he said. "That's easy. Done."

She shook her head. "No, it's not."

"And... why would you think that?"

"Because, Mr. Parker—"

"Jake."

"*Jake*—because of our conversation downstairs. You filled me in on who we're working for on this, and what they're expecting. ICE wants us to figure out what the disease is that's caused the deaths so far so we can prevent further loss of life. And, if possible, whether it was put there with the intent to harm."

"That's correct. Eliza, can you be more specific? I haven't—at least not on purpose—withheld anything from you. And if you thought that we had, why didn't you mention it down at the bar?"

She glanced at the door, and Jake got the hint. He pushed it closed.

"Jake, listen. Your ICE contact, Briggs, and his team believe that the culprit here could be something like measles."

"And?"

"*And* I find that hard to believe."

"May I ask why?"

"You may, but it's not really worth our time discussing it. You can trust me—I have plenty of reasons to believe that this has nothing to do with measles."

"Okay, fine. I'll bite. What *is* it, then?"

"That, I have no idea."

"Eliza, we're talking in circles. You had me come up here because you had something to tell me about this case, or something to ask me, that you clearly didn't want Shaw around for. What is it?"

She paused, then flicked her eyes around the space a few times. For the first moment since he'd met her, Eliza displayed a slight air of vulnerability. "Jake, Shaw told me a bit about how a case like this works. We're the third-party investigative team, and we pretty much have free authority to do whatever we'd like. Question anyone we have probable cause to question, and peek into any files and folders we can."

"That's about right."

"But we can't actually *see* these bodies. We can't perform an autopsy."

Jake caught his breath. *So that's it.* She'd already read the so-called 'rules of engagement' regarding this case, and what ICE's expectations were for it. Due to state- and federal-level constraints, the bodies of the diseased victims were being held *in situ* at Immigration's closest designated morgue. They were considered "locked down," kept in a low-temperature, vault-like anti-contamination chamber with an airlock access point. The bodies of the Stermers would be safe, but there was more information needed before anyone was allowed to safely access the chamber for analysis. Boxes needed to be checked, i's dotted and t's crossed. It was typical government protocol.

Until then, no one was allowed in or out, and the most-recent memorandum stated that a full autopsy "would be scheduled upon later notice," which was government-speak for "no one knows what to do."

"We… can't. But we have access to their medical records, as well as the records and notes of the mortician and their team."

"But if the mortician hasn't actually *performed an autopsy*…"

Jake sighed. "I know, I get it. ICE will decide when the autopsy will happen, and they should allow us to be present for it. Unfortunately, though, it's government. Briggs' team will let me know when they've got the mortuary team in place. We're not allowed to do anything that will interfere with the investigation—"

"Jake, that *is* the investigation!"

"Well, we can always—"

"If I can't *examine* the bodies, I can't provide my professional opinion. One way or another, I need to see those bodies. Up close, in person. They're being kept somewhere that I *know* isn't a huge facility. The bodies will eventually be moved to the dead-person equivalent of Fort Knox. Possibly to Atlanta, at the CDC. Not only is that halfway across the US, it'll be *impenetrable*."

"Eliza, the bodies are contaminated. You understand that, right? Whatever killed them could be—"

"It wasn't measles, Jake," she said. "Or anything related to it."

"How do you know?"

Eliza looked as though she were about to launch into a well-prepared lecture, but she restrained herself. She took a long, deep breath. "How long do you have?"

Jake walked over to the desk and pulled the chair out. "Consider me your student."

CHAPTER 15

Eliza Mendoza was a hard-working, standout professor and she was on her way to a tenured position at New York University. She'd already produced reams of research and as many publications to prove it, and when she found the time between her teaching schedule and furthering education, she had no shortage of short-term job opportunities.

This one, as detective Beau Shaw had explained, was going to be different. He couldn't promise fame or fortune, but—as he'd told her over the phone yesterday—he knew she wasn't interested in those sorts of things.

To be honest, she wouldn't mind a bit more of both. But the promise to her was that solving this case might come with some esteem that she could trade for a better position somewhere, should she want it.

She'd done her due diligence, checked all the boxes, and finally decided that she would accept the case. It would be a new position for her—working as a third-party auditor on a possible international health case—and that came with the freshness and intrigue that piqued her interest.

Now, standing in front of Shaw's old friend and partner, ex-detective Jake Parker, she felt the rush of adrenaline she often felt before a lecture she'd given countless times. She knew the material, and—even more importantly—she knew exactly how to deliver it to get her point across.

"Okay, first—measles is a virus. It's human-to-human only, and it was considered eliminated by the CDC about twenty years ago. Made a small comeback recently, but the CDC has kept it in check."

"We know this already. But Briggs said they believed it could be *related* to measles. Like in the same family or whatever."

"*Second*," she said, as if Jake hadn't even spoken, "it could be one of the most contagious viruses we've ever had the pleasure of dealing with. The speed with which it overtook our Patient Zeros means ICE will be struggling to keep it contained since it will have already been exposed to others before they died. We need an update from Briggs on additional cases—at this point there *has* to be another case or two at least. But if it was anything close to what measles was, we wouldn't have to wait around to find out. We'd *already* have an outbreak on our hands."

"So therefore it's *not* measles?"

She shook her head. "It's not contagious enough. It can't be. We've only got two confirmed deaths. And those two confirms could have the answers we need."

"Testing is still underway. ICE is trying to figure out which employees and civilians might have come into contact with the Stermers, and how to reach them to bring them in for testing."

But she shook her head. "Still, it doesn't add up. In fact, based on what we know so far, I have to agree with Edemza's conclusion. I'm pretty sure it's not *viral* at all."

Jake paused, no doubt trying to piece things together in his mind, then looked back up at her. "Okay, so it's bacterial?"

"Good guess—and maybe. But the truth is, I don't know. I *can't* know. But if I could—"

"Eliza," Jake said, his voice dropping a few decibels. "We *can't*. Look, I know there are rules for a reason, and trust me, I know that sometimes they should be broken. But *these* rules... I mean, it could hurt a lot of people."

Eliza waved the comment aside. "Trust *me*, Jake, we're not going to release the next H1N1 by walking into that mortuary; I guarantee it."

"But Briggs said specifically—"

"Briggs is playing by the rules. That's good. We'll give him plausible deniability, *and* the case. All wrapped up with a bow on top."

Jake raised an eyebrow.

"What?" she asked.

He smiled. "Nothing. It's just… refreshing, I guess. You're really in this. That's good. But we can't afford to lose this early in the game. What if we get caught? What if we—"

"We *won't* get caught. Worst-case scenario is we walk out of there with no more information than we had before. But even then, it gives me a thousand more jumping-off points."

"But Shaw is—"

"Jake," she said, finally feeling the moment of truth coming upon her. "Why do you think I had you come up here, alone?"

Jake stopped, then waited for her to speak again. She knew his type—he didn't like being tested, and he also didn't want to say something and step in it. But he knew where she was going with this line of questioning—she could see it on his face.

He smiled, and she knew she'd finally reached him. As by-the-book as he seemed, she knew there was at least a hint of rebel in the man. After all, Shaw had told her he had been a great detective—you didn't get to be that good without knowing when and how to bend the rules.

She had already thought it all through; now he would have to catch up. She knew he would have played it the same way had their roles been reversed, so it was only a matter of time.

He stood there looking dumb for a few more seconds until his head fell back a little and his eyes narrowed. "I see," he said. "Good call."

"You get it?"

"Yeah. Shaw. He's my partner—*our* partner—but he's also unnecessary to this little excursion. No sense getting him involved."

"He still has a reputation to watch out for," she added, urging him on.

If Shaw was implicated in all of this, in what they were considering, it could mean the end of his career. Jake didn't have a career to worry about—if they got caught, he'd get a slap on the wrist and have a hard time getting another role as a well-paid consultant to the government, at least until the powers-that-be were replaced by shiny new upgrades. But from what Shaw had told her about Jake's background, it wasn't like he needed these jobs anyway.

"Yeah," he said. "I'm with you. What you're talking about is not going to fly with Briggs, or anyone else who reads the debriefing later though."

She shrugged, looking up at him while he processed it, wearing a sly smile that she hoped was attractive, or at least cute.

"And if we get caught, there's *your* career to worry about, too."

Her expression changed to a feigned pout. "I'll just say you forced me into it. That you were reckless, careless. I'm not a trained detective, remember? So I don't know the rules…"

She was joking, playing with him. She hoped she was selling it.

A moment passed, and then, "All right," he said. "Fine. You're on. We go check out these bodies. I'll work on getting Shaw away for a day, but we're in and out. Got it?"

"In and out," she said, the sly grin returning to her face.

CHAPTER 16

The Next Day

Morning came sooner than Jake had hoped. His hotel room faced the front parking lot of the hotel, just as he'd requested, but it also faced east. The blackout curtains covered the majority of the wide window, but the minuscule crack on the right side seemed to have grown by a foot overnight.

The light had spilled into the room with a splitting directness that had caused Jake to sit bolt upright in bed, groggy and breathing heavily. He'd crept out of bed and into the shower, not bothering to turn on any of the lights in the bathroom. The room lights were still on—an old habit of his—and the light from the bedroom was enough to guide him.

Seventeen minutes later, he stood in the lobby of the hotel, waiting for Eliza. He checked his diving watch, noticing that the small nick on the top-right side of it had grown. It had been a gift, and he never went anywhere without it.

He'd also never used any of its features other than the clock.

Now, the watch told him that the woman still had three minutes to be on time, but his mind told him that she was going to be five minutes late, at least. He scoffed quietly, then put his left hand into his pocket and began examining the lobby, trying to find that sacred bastion of early morning hope: coffee.

He had almost finished analyzing the locations of the chairs and tables scattered throughout the neighboring breakfast area when movement to his right caught his eye. The elevator. The door opened, and Eliza walked out.

She wasn't just on time—she was early.

"Morning," she said brightly.

"Hey," he answered. "I was a bit early. Figured I could grab a cup of coffee here or on the way, but I didn't want to make you wait around."

"I had two cups in the room," she said. "I'm good. Went through my upcoming presentation and started researching a bit about measles-related vaccinations."

Jake's jaw fell a little, and he shifted and sniffed, trying to pretend as though he wasn't impressed. *Surely she didn't get up that early?* "Oh, uh, you didn't stay up late last night then?"

"Yes, I did," she said.

And that was the end of it.

Together they walked to Jake's car, parked beneath his floor on the opposite side of the lot. He walked a few steps in front of Eliza, then hurried toward her side of the vehicle when they neared it, stopping when he caught a strange look on her face.

"I'm not your date, Jake," she said, grabbing the handle of his car and opening it. "This is work. I can open my own door."

He considered trying to play it off, but instead opted for a more direct approach. "Right, understood. But…" he waited until she was looking at him. "Are you saying that I'd have to open your door for you if this was a date?"

She laughed, ducking her head as she slid into his passenger seat. "Yes. I am."

He walked around the car and copied her movement, sliding in and then starting the vehicle's engine.

"But also if I *do* find the time to go on a date, I prefer driving."

He couldn't help but smile. He was far from being ready to date again, but it felt strangely good to think about it. He looked over, watching the woman buckle her seatbelt. Could he date again? And if so, could it be with someone like this? She was so different, so unlike…

"Speaking of driving…" she said, interrupting his thoughts. She looked up at him.

"Oh, right." Jake pulled the handbrake down and put the car into gear. He pressed gently on the gas pedal, then guided his Corolla out of the hotel's parking lot and onto the access road.

He thought through the events of the day ahead—he planned to call Shaw in a few minutes, to send him out ostensibly to explore who might have come into contact with the Stermers, to see if there was any information he could glean from those people, and—more importantly—to discover whether or not this thing was contagious.

If Shaw found anyone, he'd be able to get them into the system, to quarantine them and begin putting the pieces together as to how they were related to the person who had possibly planted the disease on the Stermers. Shaw was a brilliant detective. If there was anything to glean from the evidence around the Stermers' deaths, he would find it.

Truthfully though, he'd send Shaw away so that he and Eliza wouldn't inadvertently put his career in danger. What they were planning was against every rule in the book, and even though Jake was no longer a detective, it was difficult for even him to agree to it.

But Eliza was right—they *had* to know more about this virus, this contagion. They *had* to find out what exactly it was, what had caused it, and what it might do if it got out. They had been extremely lucky that the bodies of the two victims had been isolated and kept away from human interaction after their deaths. There was still the chance that the infection had spread to the men and women who had handled their bodies. Briggs' latest update included a note that there were potentially a few more cases ICE was analyzing, but they weren't sure yet if they were actually related or just cases with similar symptoms.

They needed at least a cursory examination of the bodies.

CHAPTER 17

Highway 90, New York

Eliza sat in the passenger seat of the old Corolla. The smell in the nearly two-decades-old vehicle was something between musty and familiar, like the smell of her grandmother's sweater. If this Jake Parker character kept dirty gym clothes and running shoes in the backseat like so many other men she'd known, he'd at least had the decency to attempt to mask the odor with an air freshener.

The seat was comfortable, and she'd nearly fallen asleep twice since they'd left the hotel for the two-hour journey to Clinton, New York, where the Stermers' bodies were being kept. Oneida County was currently working toward replacing their coroner system with a full staff of medical examiners and offices, and though the expensive move was still in progress, Clinton already had a modernized medical examiner's office with a fully functional "clean room."

They'd passed through Utica on their way, and Eliza had tried not to notice that Jake had opted for the longer route that dodged a few tollbooths to save a whopping four dollars. She'd heard from Beau Shaw—and read in a few online articles last night—that Jake Parker had won a court case involving the state of Massachusetts that had netted him four million dollars. The case itself had been a massive public event. She had a vague recollection of it herself, and she wasn't surprised to learn that Jake had become somewhat of a recluse since then.

But Shaw *hadn't* given her many of the details. He'd mentioned, when selling her on the job and the man running it, that Jake's wife had died in an explosion, and that the investigation into the events had led to a lawsuit against Boston PD. The news articles had added that the case had ended with Jake's self-proclaimed retirement.

"We've got time to chat, if you want," Eliza said.

Jake eyed her from the driver's seat. "'Chat?' You don't really seem like the type of person who enjoys chatting."

"What's that supposed to mean?"

"I guess, I don't know, you're just kind of intense."

"Intense?"

"Like, serious. Good at your job."

Eliza scoffed. "And being good at my job means I don't like to chat?"

Jake sighed. "Okay, never mind. Let's chat. What do you want to 'chat' about?"

"Tell me about your wife."

"Pass."

"Jake, I'm just trying to get to know—"

"Read the papers; it's all online. The entire state knew everything about her, about us. I'm not interested in digging up old bones, so you can just drop that one, okay?"

She took a breath. His reaction was harsh, but she guessed it also wasn't unwarranted. There were open wounds here, wounds that would take *much* longer to heal. She made a note to tread carefully.

"Okay," she said. "Sorry. How about college? You went to West Point, right?"

He nodded.

"Hockey?"

Jake shifted in his seat.

Okay, she thought. *He's warming up.*

"Yeah," he said. "I was a center. Good, too. Until I busted my knee, just like all the great sports movies. 'Young Hotshot's Dream Dies on the Ice.'"

She laughed. "Ouch, that's rough. But you still got to be a hotshot. As a detective."

He shrugged again, watching the road as he changed lanes. "I guess. I was good, sure. But, you know, it's not like TV shows and movies. Being a detective is pretty much just learning the rulebook and paying attention to stuff. It's not hard to do, really."

"You had a record for cases shut."

"I did."

She waited, but he didn't offer any more information. She was still feeling him out, and her initial impression of the man yesterday was that he was the James Dean, *Rebel Without a Cause* type, somewhat emotionally compromised, torn between official, state-sanctioned justice and the justice that comes from within.

But it looked like she'd been wrong. Jake Parker now seemed more like the type of guy who played by all the right rules, checked all the right boxes, and yet had the world turn on him. He'd taken it personally, opting to shun it all and pretend it hadn't happened.

"What are you thinking about?" Jake asked.

She glanced over. He was smiling, a half-grin that gave his eyes a mischievous, delightful brightness. "Nothing," she said. "Just trying to figure out who I'm working with. Slotting you into the yearbook."

"The yearbook?"

"Yeah," she explained. "It's something I've always done. Helps me figure out how to deal with people. How to work with them better. I imagine the people as pictures in a yearbook. Each page is a different personality, then on each page, each slot is like a gradation of that personality."

"And which page am I on?" Jake asked.

"No idea. Maybe somewhere between 'hotshot hockey player with broken dreams' and 'hotshot detective the world chewed up and spit out'?"

"Wow," Jake said. "You've got whole pages that specific?"

She laughed out loud at this. "Okay, fine. Probably just the page called 'hotshots.'"

He seemed to appreciate this assessment, though she knew there were still questions on his face. She waited a few seconds, but he didn't ask them.

"Anyway," she continued, "I'm still figuring it out. It's nothing, really. Just helps me present myself in a way that's accommodating. Makes it easier to work with people, I've found."

Jake frowned. "You change who you are, depending on who you're with?"

"No," she said. "That's not it. It's more like… recognizing that sometimes the way I come across—as a woman who's very smart, very good-looking—can act like a deterrent. Make it harder to get things done."

She expected Jake to take the bait, to engage in the usual "not me, I'm above that" line.

Instead, his smile widened to a full-width grin. "So, you think you're *very* smart and *very* good-looking, huh?"

She rolled her eyes.

CHAPTER 18

Jake's Corolla slid past Big Sal's Pizzeria and Restaurant and over the last stretch of asphalt and into the parking lot. The tiny, one-story county sheriff's office and mortuary facility was tucked behind two split rows of trees. The building looked like a post office, bricked and painted the official "government facility beige," complete with a faded red horizontal line over the tops of the windows, but the grounds were surprisingly attractive and well-kept.

He aimed his car toward the front door, finding all of the spaces empty. It was still mid-morning, but it was Sunday so there were no cars in the lot. He figured anyone working would be parked in the rear of the building.

So far, he hadn't seen anything in terms of security, but he also knew that the medical examiner's office shouldn't be completely devoid of life, even in the middle of the night. In order for the on-site physicians to do their jobs, the facility would have to have full-time maintenance crews and support staff, and at least two of them would need to be here at all times.

Jake hoped that by showing up on a Sunday, the typical government employee schedule—strict 9-to-5, Monday through Friday—would be in effect. That theory seemed to be proved to be true—he couldn't see any life inside the building. No lights, no movement.

"How do we get in?" he asked.

"You're a detective," Eliza said. "Don't you know how to pick locks?"

He made a face. "You have a very misguided understanding of what it means to be a detective. And I'm *not* a detective. Not anymore."

He unbuckled his seatbelt and opened his door, stepping out. He stretched as Eliza copied his motion from the opposite side of the car.

"Seriously though—how do we get in?"

"Jake," she said, walking toward the front door. "It's not a prison. It's a medical office."

She reached the building's entrance and tugged on the door. It opened easily.

Yeah, but how do we sneak around inside and examine these dead guys?

He followed her inside, where he saw a low, yellowed Formica desk that cordoned off the back right corner of the room. No one sat behind it.

Eliza walked down the hall until she came to an open door. He watched as she peered inside, then turned back to him. She shrugged, then shook her head.

"No one's here?" he asked. "Why? Isn't this a secure facility?"

"Jake," she said, "it's a 'secure facility,' in the same way the post office in Podunk, Georgia, is a secure facility. They probably have one, maybe two, people working at any given time. One of them's probably in the bathroom."

"So we wait until they're done?"

Her eyes narrowed. "*No*, Jake, that's not at all what I'm implying. Come on," she said, turning back around and now hustling toward the end of the hallway, where she turned left.

Jake's internal klaxon was sounding, and he had to remind himself that this wasn't a normal case. He wasn't "on the job" in the sense that he was working directly for a city government. He wasn't really working for *anyone*. Briggs had tapped him not because he was a great cop, but because of the plausible deniability he'd be able to invoke if things went south.

Still, it felt like breaking and entering, even if the door was unlocked and no one had been there to protest.

He took a deep breath, held it, and followed Eliza to the left.

He turned the corner and nearly bumped into her.

"They've got a full airlock and filtration system," she said. She was working the handle on the airlock door, testing it. "It's unlocked. We'll want to suit up, and they've got a handful of rubbers hanging from those hooks inside."

"You call them 'rubbers'?" Jake asked, eyeing the white suits and head coverings that hung just inside the first of the doorways.

"Sure," she said. "Level A hazmat suits, Teflon and Tyvek rubber. What do you call them?"

He grunted a half-laugh and came up closer to her. "Eliza, this is a serious offense. If someone catches us—and they *will*; they've got to have cameras in here—we're toast."

"No," she said, "if they catch us and figure out who we are and then figure out to tell Briggs before we get back out, *then* we're toast. We're here to solve a case, right? And that case is lying inside these doors, refrigerated, waiting for who knows how many suits to crawl over themselves before anyone examines them."

"In. Out. Okay?"

"If you're afraid of some government grunts telling us we broke the rules, then you can kindly wait outside."

Jake's head rolled back slightly. He was starting to understand a bit more about who he was now working with; who Shaw had found to help them out.

He didn't know what it was, but he didn't really want to argue with her. Something about her attitude, her entire demeanor, made him want to run in behind her and do whatever it was she told him to do. There was no doubt in his mind of her intelligence and experience, as well as her determination.

But he was also starting to believe her. He was starting to trust her.

CHAPTER 19

It took the pair another fifteen minutes to get suited up and for Eliza to explain to Jake exactly how to move in the suit and operate its radio and breathing apparatus, and then they were ready to enter the room. To Jake's knowledge, no one else had returned to the facility. The halls were silent as they prepared to enter the airlock.

Jake felt like an astronaut about to embark on a spacewalk, the rubber suit around his body pressing in. He moved as naturally as possible, but still the giant one-piece outfit was awkward. Eliza, for her part, seemed totally comfortable. The smaller suit she'd chosen even seemed to bend and curve in the right areas, and he caught himself looking when she turned away and started toward the inner doors.

What's wrong with me, checking out a woman in a hazmat suit?

She pressed a button on the wall and the inner doors slid open. Jake felt the escaping air change the pressure around him. "We don't need long," she said. "No pictures, no samples, just a visual examination. Won't take five minutes."

He swallowed, feeling the anxiety begin to creep over his arms and hands. He'd always felt it, a tingling of excitement and fear just before walking into an uncomfortable situation. It was like being onstage—there were always butterflies, but you just learned to push through them. He'd gotten especially good at pushing through it since Mel had passed away, but he'd also come to learn that anxiety was a lot like a viral infection—it liked to grow in strength, to test its limits. He had worked hard to keep it under control. More than that, he'd spent his military career drilling, training, following orders. Control was ingrained in him, but it didn't make dealing with anxiety easy.

He stepped into the inner room. It was a morgue, complete with a row of square doors against the far wall, behind which he knew were the corpses of deceased persons waiting to be examined. Each door was numbered and had a tiny handle underneath the placard symbols.

In front of the row of doors sat three cold metal examination tables. Sterile, utilitarian, purpose-built. These tables weren't meant for hospitality; the subjects laying on them wouldn't be interested in comfort or bedside manner.

He shuddered, then took a few more steps into the room. It already felt cold, even through the suit's protective layer.

"It's probably around 40 degrees," Eliza said. "It doesn't have to be freezing to stave off decay, and bodies are easier to work with if they're not frozen solid."

Jake gulped. "Right. Of course. Can't work with body bricks."

She turned and gave him a quizzical look. "Are you afraid of dead people, Jake?"

"No. Of course not. I just… don't really *like* them."

"Yeah," she said. "I prefer them in their 'alive' state as well, frankly. But like we said—in and out."

He nodded and followed her to the end of the row of doors. There were lights hanging from the ceiling, the kind of ultra-bright movable lights you might find in a dentist's office—one over each table. But they were turned off, and the light in the room was coming from above. Fluorescent strips tucked away behind diffusers, flush with the rest of the drop ceiling. They were dimmed, but provided enough light for Jake and Eliza to see their way through the room.

Eliza walked over to a computer along the opposite wall and saw a three-ring binder next to it. She opened it and flipped to the last page as if she'd been here a thousand times and knew exactly what she was doing.

"How do you know what to look for?" Jake asked. He'd been in a morgue before, but never a 'clean' room that required hazmat suits, and he'd never been in one without the mortician or coroner present.

"Well, it's just deductive reasoning, detective," Eliza said, turning and winking at him. She flipped through a few more pages and ran an index finger down the page protector sheet. "Here," she said. "Mr. and Mrs. Paul Stermer. Ages 44 and 47, respectively. Drawers 6 and 7. Special note about hazardous materials, etcetera."

She whirled around and started toward the far side of the room.

"Wait," Jake said. "Eliza, whatever is inside those drawers could be extremely infectious, and we're just going to... open them?"

"We have to know, Jake," she said. "They're going to do this, too—just when they get around to it. You heard it from Briggs; no one in or out until they figure out what's going on. They'll work to mitigate any outbreak potentials before they return to the bodies to examine them. That could be a few days, could be a week."

"And what if we let it out?"

She smiled. "Jake, come on. We're in a *clean room*. Closed off by an airlock chamber, with hazmat suits. And—I know you don't want to believe this—I'm *really smart*, and I'm *really good* at my job. I'm not going to let anything out of this room we're not supposed to let out."

He met Eliza's gaze.

Finally, he spoke. "Fine. Okay, just hurry."

She nodded and her smile turned into a look of smugness, but Jake couldn't help but think it was rather cute. She'd played him, knowing that he was interested in the truth far more than he was a rule-follower interested in following orders. He'd almost made a lifelong commitment to the Army; it was the obeying of orders, point-blank, no-questions-asked that had given him pause.

Now, he was breaking into a morgue, examining a known risk, with a woman he was strangely attracted to, no matter how hard he tried to remain neutral.

He shook away the feeling, choosing instead to focus on all the rules they were currently breaking.

CHAPTER 20

She'd never performed an autopsy, but Eliza didn't feel like that was something she needed to tell Jake—he didn't seem like he needed any more reason to back out. During her undergraduate studies, she'd had the opportunity to do an onsite with a mortician, but she'd opted instead to take the time to study for finals. Either way, watching someone cut a body open wasn't exactly what she would call "proper training." Still, she didn't want Jake to know that as a professional parasitologist she was much more in her element with a microscope than she was with a scalpel.

She stood to one side of the drawer while Jake stood on the other. She'd chosen Mr. Stermer first, hoping that by choosing the larger of the two bodies she'd have more space to work with.

"Open it up," she said.

Jake pulled the drawer's handle, and the shelf slid out easily. The corpse on the shelf was naked, but a thin blue paper blanket had been draped over him. The paper was stained in some places, spots darkened against the rest of the sheet. Not blood, but something liquid. The dead man's feet poked out the bottom of the sheet, and Eliza immediately noticed the pale white flesh in stark contrast against tiny blackish lines—capillaries under the man's skin.

"Weird," she whispered.

"What?"

She didn't respond. When the shelf was fully extended, she examined the man's head. More of the tiny, blackened veins spiderwebbed over his face and neck. Furthermore, the man seemed bloated. She'd seen bodies in a similar state of decay, but those had exclusively been exposed to large amounts of water, or even submerged for some amount of time after death.

As far as she knew, these people had *not* been submerged before or after death.

She pulled the blanket down about six inches to reveal the dead man's shoulders and chest. More of the blackish veins appeared before her eyes, and the external carotid artery on the man's neck had signs of stress. It seemed as though the sternocleidomastoid muscle just beneath the flesh of the man's neck had distended; the neck itself seeming swollen and ready to burst.

"It's like it's under pressure," she said to herself. "Like there's something that caused swelling before he died, and it didn't let up *after.*"

Jake didn't speak, but she saw his hazmat-covered hands gripping the sides of the shelf. She had a feeling he was holding on with a white-knuckled grip, the sort of grip used by a man who was standing by the bed of a woman in labor. Not afraid, but not entirely sure what to expect.

I'm with you, Jake, she thought. *I have no idea what to expect, either.*

She looked up at Jake. "Grab a scalpel."

"Huh?"

"A scalpel," she repeated. "You know—a shiny metal knife, used for cutting people open?"

He was shaking his head. "No. No. Absolutely not. We're not cutting him—"

"Jake, this is important. See the distended musculature in the neck? The blackened veins? His jugular looks like it's about to pop—from the *inside.*"

"So what?"

"So it's not normal, Jake. I want to know what's causing it."

"He's dead. Dead people get all bloaty. Besides, if we poke it with a sharp object, won't it pop all over us?"

She couldn't help herself. She laughed. "'Bloaty?' 'Pop all over us?' My God, you *are* a cop. Christ, Jake, this is an *examination*. Let's *examine*."

Jake delayed for a few seconds, but finally walked toward the row of tables against the opposite wall, where she'd found the computer and binder. While he looked around, she turned back to the dead man in front of her.

"What are you hiding, my friend?" she asked. "What secrets do you—" She stopped. Frowned. Blinked a few times, then looked back down.

What the hell?

She shook her head, trying to focus again on the pale flesh in front of her.

"Got one," Jake called from across the room. She heard his footsteps returning to her, but she kept her eyes focused downward.

From somewhere far off, she thought she heard the sound of a door closing.

"Did you hear that?" Jake said, his voice tense. "We need to get—"

She held up her hand and opened her palm. Jake placed the scalpel in it.

"Eliza, seriously, we need to start…" Jake's voice trailed off, then she heard him smack his hand against the metal door of the next morgue shelf. He leaned against it, leaned down. Looked at the body in front of them. "Eliza, I think something moved…"

She felt her legs go weak. *There's no way we both saw it,* she thought. *No chance of it.*

She gripped the scalpel tightly in her left hand, forcing it to calm, pushing away the shaking feeling. She lowered it, holding it directly above the man's collarbone.

There.

Again, just the slightest of pulses.

Like a heartbeat.

She shook her head.

"You saw it, right?" Jake asked. "You saw it move, like—*there!*"

She slammed the scalpel down and into the man's dead flesh, forcing herself to act without thinking about what she was doing. She pulled the instrument toward herself, drawing a thin, dark horizontal line just below the corpse's collarbone.

The scalpel caught on something near the end of the line, and she tugged at it until it fell through the skin freely once again. She extracted the utensil and held it straight up, waiting. Then, with a shaking right hand, she placed a finger above the new wound and applied a small bit of pressure. The laceration split open a half-inch, and…

"What in *God's name is*—" Jake's voice was a whisper.

She dropped the scalpel and backed away from the shelf.

The opening in Mr. Stermer's chest began to writhe, to pulsate, as tiny, spaghetti-width strands of *something* appeared from the slit.

She put a hand over her mouth.

"Eliza, what the *f*—"

"I don't know," she said, her voice no longer calm and collected. "I have no idea."

The things were *alive*. Moving, writhing, fighting and dancing and twisting themselves around one another until their tentacle-like ends were poking out of the hole in the dead man's chest. The miniature, reddish-white strands spilled outward and onto his skin, just a few millimeters out of the hole, as if testing the environment. *Exploring.*

Each was like a tiny hair, with a thicker base and unraveled strands of red webbing at the ends, and together the entire mess of them looked like a fine spray of red dust particles had banded together to form a knitted whole.

Another door slammed, and Eliza heard footsteps again.

They were getting closer.

"Jake," she whispered. "Get a test tube, or a bag, or something to put it in."

Jake didn't respond.

"*Jake*," she said again. "Get something to put it in. They're almost here."

CHAPTER 21

"Hey! What the hell are you —"

Jake heard the sound of a man's voice crackling through the speakers in his hazmat helmet. It was tinny and thin, but it didn't mask the man's annoyance.

"Eliza, *now*! Let's go."

Jake tugged on Eliza's arm and her hand nudged the scalpel off the table, the metal instrument clanging to the floor.

The footsteps had stopped outside the airlock and Jake knew the man was waiting for them. There was nowhere else to go, no other way out of this chamber. He had been correct in assuming there was a camera watching them, hidden somewhere in this room.

Jake felt his mind wanting to panic, then the training and experience kicked in. *I was a cop,* he thought. *I was a soldier. I can get us through this.*

They were in small-town America in upstate New York, and they'd just been caught investigating a body that was involved with a case they were legally a part of. The fact that Briggs had expressly forbidden anyone from performing an autopsy of any kind on the Stermers' bodies until certain regulatory paperwork had been processed was beside the point.

"You two," the voice said again. "Can you hear me in there?"

Eliza was standing next to Jake now, at the doorway that led to the airlock. She was holding the glass tube he had given her, but he couldn't see inside it. She was gripping it tightly, covering it from view.

Jake was still stunned by the findings from inside the chamber, but he forced himself to speak. "Yeah," Jake said, putting some annoyance into his voice. "And you're disturbing us. Give us a minute to get these suits off and I'll explain."

"Explain? You're trespassing on state property, snooping around—"

"Hold on," he said.

Jake tapped the button to open the sealed door, then he stepped over the threshold and waited for Eliza to follow before closing the door once again. Immediately, the fans inside the airlock began cycling the air, pushing cold, fast air over his suit while the vent circulated it out and into a hidden purifier.

"We're not trespassing. We're government officials. Contractors. Working on the Stermer case."

He hoped that by invoking the Stermers' name, this staffer would give them a break. He didn't want to get Briggs involved this early. He'd be pissed that Jake had broken protocol, and might even remove them from the investigation.

"How do you know about them? Who are you?"

Jake pulled off his helmet and found that the man's voice was also being piped into the airlock through a pair of recessed speakers on the ceiling. The man was standing by the outer door, pressing a button on a wall-mounted intercom whenever he spoke.

He wasn't sure if there was an active microphone in the room he could talk through, so he waited. Eliza was pulling off her own suit, and when she finished, she tossed it through a swinging trashcan-style receptacle on the wall marked "contaminated." Jake noticed that she had kept the test tube in the hand farthest from the man, and when she was away from the receptacle, she deftly slid it into her pants pocket. Jake nodded at her, then pressed the button on the other door. It swung open and he was standing face-to-face with a member of the medical examiner's staff.

Jake stuck out a hand, grinning the most innocent grin he could muster. "Jacob Parker," he said. "West Point, for a while. Boston PD, for a while. Private sector now. This is Eliza Mendoza, the parasitologist who has been hired to look into the Stermers' case. I'm sorry if your manager didn't tell you we might be coming."

The man opened his mouth to speak, but Jake was already sidestepping him and walking toward the front office near the entrance to the building.

"Hey. Hold on," the man said, chasing after Jake.

Jake stopped abruptly by the front desk and the staffer nearly slammed into his back. "Oh, hey. Sorry about that." Jake turned, holding a notepad and pen. "Here, we gotta go, like, quick. But this is the number of Director Briggs, of Immigration Control, if you've got any follow-up questions."

The man's eyes widened in surprise.

Good, Jake thought. *That name rings a bell for you.*

Eliza walked up behind the man and stood next to Jake. She didn't say anything, but she'd adopted a similar goofy grin.

"Sorry we went ahead when we couldn't find you in reception," Jake said. "But we're in a *huge* hurry, as I'm sure you can imagine. Gotta head this thing off at the pass, if you know what I mean. Nice place, by the way. I've been in a coroner's office more than once in my career, but *this* place is impressive."

The man frowned. "Uh… thanks." He looked down at the sticky note Jake had handed him.

"Again, feel free to give Briggs a ring. I know no one was here guarding the Stermers, and we didn't have time to wait, so hopefully he'll understand."

Jake was already turning to leave the building by the time the man regained his composure. He pushed the door open and held it for Eliza, then waved at the man as the door pressed closed. He heard Eliza laughing quietly as she passed him.

He waited until they were in the car, seatbelts buckled and the vehicle in reverse. He slid the car out of the parking space and began driving out of the lot and back to the highway.

"That was *amazing*," she said, laughing loudly. "What... How did you *do* that? I mean, that guy was falling all over himself."

Jake shrugged. "Redirection. We invoked the wrath of the Director of ICE, pointed out that the Stermers were back there totally unguarded, *and* didn't give him time to speak. Best of all, none of what I said was a lie."

She nodded. "Impressive."

He laughed, feeling the pressure inside him recede as they pulled away from the examiner's office. "Like I said. No lies."

"No lies."

He checked his blind spots and began to merge back onto the highway, then looked over at her. She was staring at him. Like she wanted to tell him something.

"What?" he asked.

She looked away. "Nothing. Just... thanks. That was perfect. You had my back in there. I made you do it, and you had my back."

Jake shrugged again. "It's nothing. You're my partner. I always have my partner's back."

CHAPTER 22

Jake checked in with Shaw to confirm they'd meet up again tomorrow. Jake had lied and explained that they wanted to pull some samples from Eliza's lab in Syracuse and they would just stay at Eliza's house for the night. Jake didn't mention their trespassing adventure to Shaw.

Jake had heard Shaw snigger under his breath, but his ex-partner didn't press him on it. Jake could have easily turned the tables and questioned Shaw's previous twenty-four hours, like a micromanaging boss, but he didn't. He knew Shaw was capable; he didn't need to be babysat.

Still, it seemed odd that Shaw hadn't turned up anything useful—or anything at all. He wanted to know Shaw's movements, his questionings, the steps he'd taken, as if Jake were Shaw's supervisor. Technically he was, since Jake had brought him onto this case. But Jake didn't feel right about it. Shaw was a good cop. He'd have turned over information if he'd found any.

Though Jake couldn't tell Shaw, the real reason for the stop in Syracuse was that Eliza had enough equipment and testing chemicals at her home to study the strange tube-like organism she'd extracted from Paul Stermer's body. And if she needed anything else, her laboratory at the university would be ten minutes away.

As they headed to Syracuse, Jake couldn't get his mind off the events of the day; and as the adrenaline released during their stint at the medical examiner's office started to ease off, he began to feel very tired. Eliza had offered to drive, but he told her he'd be able to make it to her house. He might crash later, but for the moment the drive helped him calm down and start to process what they'd found.

Eliza Mendoza's home was small with a well-kept exterior. Her two-bedroom, two-bathroom single-story house, set off the street and near the university, had a sprinkling of trees in the backyard and a single massive oak in the front. She led him inside, and Jake immediately got the feeling that he was walking into the home of a hoarder.

While he kept his own home lean and sparse, Eliza's was filled—floor to ceiling in some areas—with books. Textbooks, nonfiction, even a few piles of novels. Boxes sat in one corner, filled with some unidentifiable reams of paper.

In the center of the living room, on a couch that barely had room for a single person, sat another three boxes. One of these was empty, its contents spilled out onto a glass-topped coffee table.

"Sorry," she said. "I can tidy up a bit, just give me a minute."

"A minute or a week?"

She shot him an evil glance, but he saw she was smiling. "I work a lot. My house is pretty much my storage unit. I spend more time at my office. Which, I might add, is *spotless*."

"Ha," Jake said. "I'll believe it when I see it."

She made a comment about going to go "freshen up," a mysterious statement Jake assumed women used when they simply needed to hit the restroom and were too embarrassed to admit it. He nodded as she left the room. He started to move to sit down, but wasn't sure where to go or what was appropriate. He hadn't been in another woman's home alone since he and Mel had been dating. Instead, he stood by the living room in the hallway, looking around and waiting.

Eliza returned in two minutes, wearing a t-shirt and shorts. He tried to force his eyes to remain on her face rather than on her long, slender legs. "Oh," she said. "I thought you'd… I guess there's nowhere to sit, huh?"

He shrugged. "No big deal."

She shook her head and then smirked at him. "Listen, Jake. This is a *job*, remember? No reason to get all fidgety and weird."

"*Fidgety and weird?*" Jake asked. "I'm appalled. I'm taking this investigation seriously, it's just that usually when I investigate, there's room to do so."

"I said I'd tidy up," Eliza responded, moving toward the living room. But instead of picking up any of the junk lying around, she simply made her way through the maze toward what he assumed to be the kitchen and dining room. "But I'll do it later. Come on, I've got tea."

Jake hated tea, but he followed her into the tiny dining room. A small circular table, much like the one he had back in his apartment, sat in the center of the space. A decent-sized kitchen with matching black appliances was to his left, an open doorway that led into a utility and laundry room to his right.

"Have a seat," she said. "Want to try this tea? I got it from a cute Ethiopian store in Boston. A mix of herbal remedies that's good for inflammation."

Jake raised an eyebrow. "You know, my inflammation's doing fine right now, and the fancy tea would probably be wasted on me. I'm more of a black coffee guy."

She eyed him, looking up and down, then huffed into the kitchen. "Of course you are, Parker."

He waited in the rickety wooden chair for another two minutes, watching her pour a half-pot of filtered water from the refrigerator into a kettle and place it on the front burner of her stove. Then she prepped the tea in a metal ball and set it to the side.

She took care in her work, meticulously moving around the kitchen. Then, as if suddenly remembering that Jake was there,

Eliza pulled out a black, single-cup coffee machine from deep within a cabinet, plugged it in, and dumped a cup of water straight out the tap into the lid. She dug around a drawer and retrieved a plastic coffee pod, which she then shoved into the top of the machine and smashed it down.

Jake watched all of this with interest. Apparently this woman took pride in her tea ritual but didn't think too highly of coffee. *Or coffee drinkers.*

Finally, as both liquid elixirs were heating up, she came back into the dining room. She grabbed the chair across from Jake and reached into her pocket. She placed onto the table the glass vial containing the disgusting little worms she'd pulled from Stermer's corpse.

Jake shuddered as she set it down. The things were still there, writhing, more slowly now, crawling over one another and examining their newly lit surroundings by making minuscule rotations with their "heads," or whatever the reddish feathery parts on one side of them were. "You're going to get that out *here*? I thought we'd have to do that sort of thing at your lab, at the school or something, to keep things safe and contained. Maybe like in one of those boxes that you access by reaching through the holes, into thick gloves for your hands."

"An anaerobic glove box, right." She shook her head. "No, I was thinking about it on the way. I know what it is already."

Jake cocked an eyebrow.

"It's a parasite," she said. No emotion, as if she were simply discussing a class assignment.

"And?"

"*And* that means that if it *is* contagious, it's something that will have to be spread through *touch*."

"As in, as long as we don't touch it, we're fine?" Jake asked.

She nodded. "Yeah. Basically. Well, kind of. I mean, it's extremely rare for a parasitic infection to be transmitted through anything *but* some sort of contact. This is a living organism, right?

So we'd have to somehow come into contact with it physically for it to jump to us as a host. And since right now it's far from microscopic, I find that—at least in its current state—rather impossible."

Jake knew that *something* had happened, but he didn't want to press too hard. There was still too much of this he didn't understand. "But it got into the Stermers somehow."

"Yes, again, my guess is it would have been much smaller when it was ingested, but judging by how large it is now, probably not microscopic. It was transferred to them somehow, entered their bodies. Point is, *now* what we're looking at is the adult form of whatever it is—and, most likely, it's too large to contract its disease unless you flat-out eat it or have sex with it."

Jake shot her a glance.

"Sorry," she said. "It's true. But, like I said, unlikely. And what's more, these little guys are dying—they need a host to stay alive and multiply, and without one of those…"

"Okay, so we're safe to handle it?"

She leaned her head sideways. "No, I'm not saying that, since we still don't exactly know what it is. But we are safe to *observe* it, maybe even pull a bit out and examine it under some glass."

"Right," Jake said, letting out a deep breath. He was feeling more and more uncomfortable by the minute. He'd almost forgotten how this felt, the early stages of a case. As a detective, he thrived for the moment *after* this—the moment he had his first breakthrough, when his work building and putting together the pieces of the puzzles earned him some small insight. "So what can we do? Even with a microscope, we won't really know what it is, right? Don't we have to send it somewhere?" He wanted that breakthrough, but he also knew this was far from a normal case. There were clues that he wasn't going to be able to find alone.

She laughed. "Yeah, Jake. When you and your cop buddies needed stuff analyzed, like blood and fecal matter, and whatever else it was you scraped off the floor of the crime scene, you'd send it away, right? To be 'analyzed'?"

He nodded.

"Well, people like me are the ones who do the analyzing. We look at this stuff all day, every day, and poke it with needles and drop goo on it to see how it reacts. That's basically it. Enough positive tests against known parameters and we make a judgement call and send the results back to you."

"I'd always meant to thank you guys for that," Jake said. He offered a sheepish grin as well.

"Much appreciated. Anyway, I *do* have a microscope here that'll work, and the stain and some tests we can run. It might not be conclusive of anything specific, but it'll at least give me a direction to start searching."

"Okay, great," Jake said. "What do you need from me?"

She started to stand up, and she leaned over and patted him on the shoulder. "You're the cop, remember? I'm the parasitologist."

He arched an eyebrow.

"So if I need to arrest something or shoot something, I'll call you in. Otherwise, just sit there and look pretty."

CHAPTER 23

The Richter Optica UX1 was the gift Eliza never thought she'd wanted. Her parents had given her the microscope when she'd been accepted into graduate school, and she remembered laughing at the idea that she'd turned into a true, real-life nerd. *Who asks for—and gets—a microscope as a present?* she'd thought at the time. Sure, as a girl, she'd spent hours down by the creek at her house catching and examining bugs, butterflies, and anything she could fit into her jars, but she'd never imagined herself moving into an actual career doing that sort of thing.

But, like most things in life, she'd come to learn that opportunities presented themselves at every turn. It was up to the opportunist to accept them and turn them into success. She'd been presented with opportunities plenty of times, and it was her constant longing for knowledge—the desire to understand the world on a micro level—that she'd followed most often.

That longing had turned into success after success, until she found herself on the doorstep of a career in parasitology, both teaching and studying the exact same sorts of things she'd loved doing as a kid.

She'd walked through that doorway with her head held high, knowing that she'd chosen a career path as much as it had chosen her. She was now a "professional nerd," and she loved it—personal microscope and all.

She plopped the heavy black case onto the dining-room table. Usually she kept the instrument in her second bedroom, which she had converted into a study and small laboratory, there was no room for a second person in there.

She had to admit she was enjoying the company right now. Having Jake around was akin to having an undergraduate assistant in their first week of study—interested but confused, and eager to please but at a loss as to how exactly to help.

She slid the case over to Jake. "Here, open this. Take it out and set it up."

"Set it up?"

"Remember chemistry class in high school? Same thing. Take out of box, set carefully on table, look into eyeholes."

Jake laughed and began working the clasps on the outside of the case. "Are they really called eyeholes?"

"No."

Eliza retrieved a smaller box from the edge of the table that contained slides and stain, as well as two pairs of exam gloves. She began preparing the slide glass and cover slips, and reached for the tube still sitting at the center of the table.

"Just like that?" Jake asked. "Is there any more prep work or anything? Like, shouldn't we make sure that when we pop the top on those things, they won't just jump out and start attacking us?"

Eliza grinned. "You carrying a gun right now, officer?"

Jake looked at her but didn't respond.

"Like I said, if I need you to shoot something, I'll let you know."

He didn't seem satisfied, but Eliza was already busy preparing her sample.

Wearing the gloves, she opened the top of the vial and reached in with a pair of tweezers. She pinched around a tiny, wriggling worm, about an inch in length, but it was wrapped tightly around another strand of parasites. She shook it a bit until they fell apart, and then she pulled out a smaller specimen, this one only about a quarter-inch.

As dangerous as she knew the specimen was, the inner nerd in her was thrilled by getting hands-on with it.

"Okay," Jake said. "Here you go." He pushed the microscope over toward her.

"There's an iPad in the box, too," she said. "Turn it on. It should be unlocked and ready to connect with the microscope." She didn't bother watching to see if he did it correctly, as she was too fascinated by the parasite beneath the lens.

Jake whistled. "Wow. Fancy. We didn't have *these* in high school."

"'Digital remote viewing.' It's basically just a way for microscope companies to stay relevant."

"Microscope companies are relevant?" Jake asked, sarcasm thick in his voice.

She ignored him, speaking aloud as she worked. "So, there are three types of parasites. You've got the protozoa, which are usually single-celled organisms, the kind of stuff that causes diseases like malaria. They're carried by a vector—a mosquito, for example. Then there are what are called ectoparasites, like ticks and fleas. They live *on* their hosts, instead of *inside* them. Usually those jerks carry *another* parasite inside of them, which causes diseases in the host. This is essentially what happened with the Bubonic Plague—diseased fleas carried the bacterium into human hosts through their bite. Finally, there are helminths, which are like these little guys. Worms." She turned on the microscope's lamp with one hand and placed the helminth on the slide, pressing the cover over it. "Sorry, little guy. You aren't going to recover from this one."

She saw Jake watching the iPad screen, and she played with the scope's magnification, moving it down from its max setting to 400x.

She placed her eyes into the eyepieces and blinked a few times, then adjusted the zoom and focus a bit more until the slide beneath the device was in perfect focus.

"Whoa," she heard Jake whisper.

It was truly impressive—a fully functioning organism, no larger than a tiny piece of capellini pasta, with multiple working components that had only moments ago been actually *alive*. She felt the gentle shake and warmth of satisfaction through her body as she fell into her work.

"Okay," she began. "I'm seeing the columnar epithelium inside the cuticle. Segmented. Polychaete, I'm assuming. That chitinous stuff up there? That's why it's called *chaetae*."

Jake grunted, and she looked up. He shrugged. "Sure, whatever you say, doc."

She fell back into her rhythm. "*Very* interesting. Seems to be a bristle worm, but…"

"But what?"

"But those are almost exclusively found in marine environments. Oceanic specifically."

"It's an ocean worm?"

"It seems to be," she answered. "The vast majority—so far, about 98.89%—of these polychaetes are found in saltwater rather than freshwater, but it's kind of like the biological equivalent of the Johari Window: we don't know how many species there are that we don't know about."

"Right," Jake said. "Because we haven't found them yet." He paused, still examining the iPad screen. "And I can see how these things can go pretty much unnoticed. Could be a lot more species of them out there."

"Precisely," Eliza said. "But we *do* have some basic familial characteristics to match them up against. That narrows the playing field a lot. For example, generally, we know some forms of these polychaetes can survive in extremely cold, extremely deep and dark recesses of the ocean. Some were found in the Challenger Deep and the Marianas Trench. And we also know that some can survive in oceanic vents, literal underwater volcanoes—so they can thrive in extremely *hot* environments. But *these* survived and multiplied in a completely different environment—that of a freshwater-heavy,

98.6-degree human. It at least gives us an idea as to what they're capable of living in. And…"

She stopped, looking through the scope again. She blinked more, trying to push aside the small vitreous globules that were floating across her eyes. She readjusted the diopter knob once again, but the strange phenomenon was still there.

"What is it?" Jake asked.

She ignored him, staring intently down at the tiny specimen. She grabbed the tweezers with her right hand, then poked the cover on the glass to move the polychaete around.

Through the microscope, she saw that the side of the worm was slit open, a tiny tear along the tube-like body of the parasite.

But inside, through the folds of the chitinous body, she saw *more* of them. All microscopic compared to the larger body they were tucked inside, and all moving slowly, dancing in a nervous, smooth rhythm.

"Eliza," Jake said. "Fill me in. What's—"

"Jake," she answered, cutting him off as she increased the magnification. "I think I know what these things are."

As she stared down at them, she thought through the possibilities. She rarely missed a detail in this sort of work, and she rarely misclassified something. But this was something she'd never actually seen in person. Something she hadn't thought possible outside of some very specific environments.

And yet the evidence was staring her in the face, magnified close to 1,000 times.

What the hell have we gotten ourselves into?

CHAPTER 24

Jake was watching Eliza work, seeing the same image she was looking at through the microscope on the iPad screen in front of him. Eliza pushed up from the table abruptly and walked out of the dining room. He heard her rummaging around in the living room, in or around one of the boxes, and then she returned a moment later with the oldest, crappiest laptop he had ever seen.

He gawked at it as she dropped it onto the table. "Is that a *real* computer? Like, it actually works?"

She seemed preoccupied, but she nodded. "Yeah. Old work computer I was able to snag for basic internet stuff. Hardly does anything else. They told me its name was *Toshibasaurus*."

"Yeah, I can see why," Jake said.

Eliza quickly changed the subject back to the matter at hand. "This thing—this animal—I know it. I think I do, anyway."

Jake didn't ask the obvious question, knowing she would get to it when she found whatever it was she was looking for. She started hammering away on the keys of the age-old Toshiba. The seventeen-inch-wide screen was absolutely massive, and it seemed almost comical next to the sleek iPad and the high-tech microscope. Jake remembered back to his police days; he and his coworkers used to complain about their equipment, but this was something else.

"Okay," she said. "I think this is it." She turned around the laptop and faced it toward him. "Family *Siboglinidae*, Genus *Osedax*."

Jake stared blankly at her.

"They're a relatively new species, or at least they've only been on the radar for a brief amount of time—I think the first ones were found off the coast of California in 2002 or something. They *are* polychaetes, and the ones we've found so far exist underwater. Saltwater, specifically."

Jake took in the information. He had a lot of questions, and he could feel his detective's mind begin to spin, to prepare for the barrage of data he was about to throw it. "But the Stermers weren't underwater—certainly not in the ocean."

"Right," Eliza said.

"So how did they get infected with these little guys? Did one just crawl onto their skin, or did they somehow swallow it?"

Eliza was shaking her head. "They may have ingested them, but I doubt it. If they're like other parasitic worms, they grow too quickly. They're probably microscopic only when they're born—that's what we're seeing here, in the image. See those little ones? They're the males. All *inside* the female. From what I know about the genus, these males—babies, essentially—live inside this main tube here. Then, when she's ready to reproduce, the female can produce literally hundreds of oocytes at once, already fertilized. Even though we don't know a lot about them, it turns out they're everywhere in the ocean. Monterey Bay found at least a dozen independent species of them just in their backyard."

Jake nodded, trying his best to follow along.

"Like most parasitic worms, they grow, but they're always relatively small, so it wouldn't be out of the question for the Stermers to have somehow gotten into contact with them."

"Okay," Jake said. "Sounds like this is what we're dealing with. Good, we know *what* now. But, again, *how?* These things live at the bottom of the ocean floor, right? So how did two people find them in upstate New York?"

Eliza thought about this for a moment, and Jake watched her, noticing how her brow furrowed over her dark skin. Her hair was beginning to lose its form, a few strands dancing around the rim of her face as she contemplated. "That's… that's what's really weird about all of this. They shouldn't be anywhere outside of a laboratory or the ocean. And they certainly shouldn't be reproducing and growing inside human hosts. I've never seen anything like it."

Jake's mind was racing. These parasites were never meant to jump into human hosts, but that was never outside the realm of possibility. He remembered the COVID-19 pandemic, how the novel coronavirus strain had "jumped" from animals to humans, where it began to spread like wildfire as it morphed and adapted to better increase its reach.

Could that be what was happening here?

"It's not a virus," Eliza said, as if answering his question. "Actually, it doesn't *need* a host to reproduce, to grow. Some parasites are like animals—they can survive and exist without a biological host keeping them alive. We know that because there are plenty of these species living around the world on the ocean floor already. But—also like any other creature—we do know they need a food source to stay alive."

"And I have a feeling you've already got an idea about that."

She smiled, seeming to realize that she wasn't alone in her thoughts. He enjoyed working with her; she was far easier to talk to than he'd originally given her credit for.

"I might," she said. "That's why I grabbed my laptop. These parasites were given the name *Osedax* because of their eating habits. It's a Latin word, actually. It means *bone-eating*."

"Um, what?"

"Bone-eating."

"They *eat bones*?" He pressed the bridge of his nose with two fingers. *Could this get any weirder?*

"That's what they were doing when they were first discovered, and just about every other time they've been observed. There was a whale fall off the coast of California—a dead whale that sank not far offshore—and these creatures were living on the carcass. But they weren't eating the *flesh*, like most of the other marine life. They were working on the *bones* themselves."

"That's disgusting."

"They're a parasite, Jake. A true opportunistic animal, really—they secrete a bacterium that bores into bones and consumes the lipids and proteins, then releases nutrients that the worms can use for sustenance. It's remarkable, really."

He scoffed. "You know, *remarkable* would never be the word I'd use to describe this thing. It sounds... like a horror story."

"To the Stermers, it was," Eliza said. "Remember their bodies? They were literally being consumed from the inside-out. They were bloated, almost ready to burst with how many of the parasites were inside them. I'm not sure how long the Osedax can survive on the remains of whatever carcass they're attached to, but we know it's way past when the host is compromised."

When the host is compromised. Jake shuddered. *Yeah, those hosts were* definitely *compromised.*

During his time in the military, and then at Boston PD, Jake had seen plenty of horrifying deaths—it came with the job. He'd seen the mangled victims of car accidents, gunshot, suicides, poisonings; just about every possible way humans had found to kill or die.

But he'd never seen a parasitic worm eat someone to death from the inside.

CHAPTER 25

The roads this time of night were bare, which surprised Jake. He'd expected a college town like Syracuse to be busier all hours of the day, especially before midnight. But it was summertime, and he figured many of the students had moved away until classes started back up in a couple of months.

He'd left Eliza's place in Southwood on a mission to find food. Their discussion of the parasite had devolved into the realization that neither of them had eaten in hours, so Jake had offered to pick up some takeout. He asked what she wanted, only to hear the all-too-common "it doesn't matter" his late wife used to give him. He'd balked, explained his wife was a picky eater and they'd found over the years that it was far easier for Mel to make decisions regarding food. But Eliza was just as stubborn—she'd told him that she was the least picky eater on the planet, and that anything that wasn't raw was okay with her. That said, they'd both agreed that—due to the organism sitting beneath the microscope—seafood was off the table.

He'd decided on Mexican—tacos were always welcome, where he was from. Eliza had Mexican heritage, but if she didn't like what he came back with he could always remind her of being the "least picky eater on the planet."

He'd found a taco shop near one of the university's student housing developments that was open twenty-four hours, and he'd asked for a few of their special menu options. The food was hot on the front seat next to him and he was on his way back to her place off the Seneca Turnpike when his phone rang.

"Hey," he said, picking it up.

"Jake—it's Eliza."

"Yeah, what's up? I'll be back in about five minutes."

"I… I'm not sure, but I think someone's here."

He gripped the steering wheel tighter with a single hand as he held the phone with his other. "Okay, what do you mean?"

"There's a car parked a few houses down. Near my neighbor's house across the street. I saw them pull up and park when I was getting a research book out of the living room."

"And they got out?"

He could almost hear her nodding. "Yeah, I saw them through the curtains. Two of them. They got out, then started walking toward the house."

"Your house."

"Yes, Jake. I lost sight of them when I came back to get my phone. It could be nothing, but—"

"No, you did the right thing." He shifted the phone to his other ear, glancing around the car. He didn't have anything useful with him—he hadn't had a badge or handcuffs in his possession for some time. "I'm about five minutes away, but I can cut it to four. Eliza, listen to me: lock the front door. I saw the little alarm system blinking in the utility room. Is that for all the entrances?"

"Yes, and the windows."

He knew he wouldn't find it here, but his eyes searched the car's floor and seats for his weapon. He'd left it in his computer bag in Eliza's dining room. He considered telling her about it, but quickly changed his mind. There wasn't going to be much an untrained civilian could do against two attackers, if it came to that. Instead, he clenched the wheel tighter and smashed on the gas, racing around two slow-moving trucks in the right lane.

"Is the alarm working?"

"Yes—I mean, I think so. I've never tested it."

"Okay, that's fine. Lock the front door, and—"

He heard a crash through the phone. *Shit.*

"Eliza—hey, can you hear me?"

No answer.

The phone's tiny speaker erupted in a cacophony of noise. He heard the unmistakable sound of glass breaking, then a man's voice. He tried again, but still Eliza hadn't said anything. Had she put the phone down? What was she doing?

He felt the anxiety swelling in his chest. *Not now, Jake. Not now.* He'd been through hours of therapy sessions after Mel's death, teaching him how to push this exact feeling back into his body, to control it. The problem was that no counselor's office was nerve-wracking enough to be a good test location for practicing the method. It was like working in a shooting range every day, training, and then one day finding yourself in an actual firefight. There was simply nothing like the real thing.

"Eliza!"

Still nothing.

He gritted his teeth and pulled the wheel hard to the right, hoping that there weren't any evening-shift patrol cruisers waiting for him down one of the side streets near Eliza's home. That would be just his luck, getting pulled over while trying to race back to her house.

The car rattled a bit and Jake pressed the gas pedal harder still. He was now moving through the neighborhood at breakneck speed, hoping there wasn't anyone out walking or jogging. The GPS said he had two minutes left, but he knew it wouldn't be enough.

If they'd come to kill her, it wouldn't take two minutes to get the job done.

CHAPTER 26

Jake swerved into the driveway, narrowly missing Eliza's neighbor's orange Syracuse University-flagged mailbox. He didn't bother to engage the parking brake, flying out of the car and onto the driveway and leaving the door wide-open.

He didn't have a weapon, but he hoped that surprise would be enough of a distraction. They might well know he was coming, but they didn't know when, or from what door.

Eliza's house had three entrances—front, back, and garage. The garage door was closed, and the back door wasn't a great option, as Eliza would most likely have it locked, so he took a gulp of air and ran toward the front door.

Jake jumped over a few small hedges and onto the concrete porch, but before he reached the front door, he made a last-second change of plan.

One of the intruders had broken Eliza's front window, creating a hole large enough for a man to fit through. The tall, heavy curtains were still hanging in front of it, and they'd remained closed, save for a six-inch-wide slit between them.

That's my route, Jake thought, suddenly jerking to the left and crouching as he increased his speed.

Jake dove through the hole in the window, scraping by one of the larger shards of still-attached glass and tearing his jacket, but he landed into a roll and came up to a standing position in a single, fluid motion.

There were two men in the living room, both with their backs to him. Huge, hulking, the kind of men who had spent so long either in the armed forces or the local gym that their necks had ceased to exist. Both were facing Eliza, who was lying in a heap on the floor. She shifted, but she seemed to be injured.

No. Jake felt the anger rising inside him.

Jake roared as he launched himself toward the closest man. The other man had apparently heard his entrance and was slowly turning to look, but by the time he realized what was happening, Jake had attacked.

The first man was thrust forward by Jake's tackle and took a line of doorframe with his forehead. He made a thick-sounding grunt as he impacted the doorway that led into the kitchen, but Jake barreled forward still. The man fell heavily onto the section of linoleum just over the threshold of the kitchen, and Jake turned to see where the other intruder was.

Unfortunately, that man was in the middle of an attack of his own.

Jake's eyes widened as the man raced forward, holding a heavy object—something he'd grabbed off of one of Eliza's numerous shelves—and preparing to swing it.

Jake wasn't going to be able to get out of the way in time. He'd pushed himself into the corner of the room, trapped by the large man to his right and a wall to his left. If he moved for the kitchen, it would put Eliza directly in line with this man's attack.

But my weapon's in the dining room, he thought. If he could just get to it, even if one of them had to take a hit first…

Eliza acted before Jake could make a decision. The man ran toward Jake, but Eliza suddenly sprang out from her fetal position and kicked the man's ankle.

It was a perfectly timed blow, and the large man couldn't help but fall. He flew a few feet through the air and his head crunched into nearly the exact same spot on the doorframe his partner had hit.

But neither hit had been significant enough to damage the men, and Jake knew they'd get a second wind in a short few seconds.

"Eliza," he said. "Back door. Now."

She nodded, then lifted herself up and leaped over the man halfway into her kitchen. Jake followed suit just as he was getting up.

He needed to get to his weapon.

The SIG Sauer GSR had been one of his favorites at the department, used by the guys in SWAT. The fact that he'd left it, loaded and ready in a shoulder bag in this woman's house, meant that he was woefully out of practice. During his time as a detective, he'd never left the house without arming himself first, but he'd dropped the habit within a year of his resignation.

He saw the bag on the chair, right where he'd left it, and he raced over and rummaged through it. He grabbed at it, pulling the weapon free of the holster just as Eliza opened the back door.

Jake swung around and prepared for the long-pull first shot after disengaging the safety.

But the men were gone. He heard shuffling in the other room, and Jake walked back to the doorframe, keeping his body safely tucked back away from the opening in case either man was preparing for a second attack.

He carefully turned his head around the edge of the door and peered into the living room.

The front door was open, and the first man had already exited. The second was preparing to step over the threshold.

"Stop!" Jake yelled. "I'll shoot!"

The man paused for a split second, but he hadn't seen Jake's pistol, and Jake knew he wasn't about to shoot at these guys. They had come unarmed, and he wasn't up to date with the breaking-and-entering laws of New York. Shooting them could be seen as an act of self-defense or, just as likely, an act of a deranged ex-cop with nostalgia for the good old days.

Both men were gone in seconds and Jake watched their dark forms disappear across the street and enter their vehicle.

CHAPTER 27

Jake was breathing quickly, heaving through each breath, trying to calm himself down long enough to think straight. The threat—for now—was gone.

And what *was* that threat? It hadn't been death, or they would have killed Eliza. What had they wanted? And who the hell were they? They had been wearing matching all-black outfits, the kind necessary for secretive, under-the-radar work. The stuff mercenaries wore.

Eliza entered the kitchen and stood behind Jake. He watched the car peel out and slide away, and a few seconds later the stillness of the late-evening air resettled onto the street.

"They wanted to scare me, I think," Eliza said.

"Why?" Jake asked. He turned around and for the first time noticed a long, thin gash on her cheek. "Oh, Christ, Eliza. Are you okay?"

She nodded. "I'm fine. Really. They pushed me down and I scraped it on a box. It's literally a cardboard cut."

Jake was seething. "They *broke into* your house and kicked you, Eliza. That's not—"

"It's not okay, no. But look around. They didn't take anything—or even damage anything. They came for *me*."

"What happened?" Jake asked. "Tell me everything."

"They banged on the door, then broke the window to get in. I was on the phone with you. I couldn't really see their faces—I

didn't even look, really—but they were suddenly in here, and I…
I started to run."

Jake watched her face as she spoke. Her eyes flicked left and
right as she replayed the events in her mind. Her hands moved,
darting a few inches here or there as she recalled where the three
of them were when they'd attacked.

"Anyway, they just ran toward me and grabbed me. I dropped
the phone, and one of them pushed me."

He wanted to pull out a miniature notepad from his back
pocket, find a small pencil and begin chewing on the eraser as
he listened to the story. But he knew this wasn't anything like his
detective work.

"I fell, that's how I got the cut. But then one of them kicked
me. Hard, but maybe not as hard as he could have. I think I've
bruised a rib or two, but that's it. That's all they did. Nothing
really. I don't know why I feel so shaken."

She was crying a bit, tearing up and not caring to wipe the
tears away. Her face was rigid, unreadable.

He wanted to reach out and pull her close, to wrap her up and
tell her it was okay, that he was here. But in the same strand of
thought, he wasn't even sure he believed it.

He felt the anxiety beginning to return. Mel's face was there,
suddenly superimposed on Eliza's. He blinked a few times. *Push
it away, Parker.*

"Jake, you okay?"

He shook his head, more to shake off the cobwebs than to
answer her. "Uh, yeah. Just—that was the first time since…"

Since Mel's death that I've felt the urge to take care of someone.

She nodded, then closed the distance between them. She
reached out and put her hand on his arm. "Jake, we're fine. We're
alive. I guess now we understand that this thing is real, and it's
bigger than us."

He wasn't sure what she was talking about at first—he was having a hard time parsing the language—but then he got it. The reality of where he was, what they were doing, came back to him. He nodded.

"I'm going to make tea. Want coffee?" Eliza asked.

"No, thank you. I'm already jacked up too much."

He walked into the living room and looked around at the disarray. Jake thought about Eliza's account of the event. Was it true; the intruders hadn't come to hurt Eliza, nor to steal anything? Or had they gotten spooked when Jake arrived? It did seem as though they had intended only to scare her since they weren't armed... but to what end? "What do they gain by scaring you? And what are they scaring you away from?"

She popped her head back into the living room. "Jake, be honest. It has something to do with this case. This whole thing—we broke into a government facility and performed an illegal autopsy."

He smiled. "I haven't been off the force for too long. And, as I recall, sending two goons on a B&E is *not* an appropriate response to governmental misconduct. I can't imagine that's how they'd do it, anyway. Two guys in black suits to question us, sure—if this were a big enough deal, I could see that. But they were wearing all-black fatigues. Not government shakedown stuff. To send them here to literally just scare you?" He shook his head. "Seems really last-minute. Slapped together."

"So maybe it *was* slapped together, but that doesn't rule it out, that it was related to the case, right?"

"Right."

"I mean what else *could* it be? Two guys, randomly driving down my street, hoping for some action, so they stop and break in and half-assedly mess with the girl who lives there?"

Jake's smile grew. "'Half-assedly'?"

"It's a word."

"Okay, doctor. Whatever you say." He held up his hands in mock surrender. "But we can't just assume that's what this is until we really have ruled out everything else. I wish I would've gotten the license plate, but it doesn't matter. They didn't want to be caught, so I doubt they'd have registered plates."

"You know what *does* matter?"

"What's that?"

"I'm still *really* hungry."

Jake laughed. "Crap, I totally forgot about the food. It's in my car—I'll go grab it."

He moved to the kitchen to grab the holster for his gun. He slid the pistol inside and carried it with him to the car. He needed a belt before he could actually wear the thing, but he wasn't about to let it out of his sight again.

As he reached the car, the door still open and the dome lights illuminated, he noticed his phone, lying on the passenger seat next to the Mexican food where he must have tossed it when he'd run inside.

He saw the blinking icon on the screen. There were two missed calls.

He came around to the driver's side to close the door as he retrieved the food, but he pulled the phone up and looked at the numbers. The timestamps were two minutes apart, the second about four minutes ago. Both from the same person.

Beau Shaw.

CHAPTER 28

Shaw heard the connection begin on the other end of the phone after three rings.

"Hello?"

"Jake," Shaw said. "What's going on?"

There was a pause. It almost sounded like Jake was shuffling through something, or in a hurry.

"Hey, man. Uh, a lot, actually. Why are you calling?"

Shaw knew Jake wasn't being purposefully abrupt—something was obviously on his mind.

"Just wanted an update, man. This not a good time?"

He heard Jake breathe. Calming himself down.

Damn, Shaw thought, *must be exciting over there.*

"No, sorry. It's fine. We—we just had, uh… an incident."

Shaw waited, knowing more of an explanation was coming. He heard the sound of something rustling, like leaves or a plastic bag. Maybe Jake was bringing in groceries for Eliza. If that was the case, Shaw was surprised that they were already playing house.

"Someone came to the house. Eliza's house. They broke in and attacked her."

Shaw pulled the phone away from his ear. "Wait. What? They *attacked* her?"

"Yeah. Roughed her up a bit. She's fine. I came back from getting a bite to eat for us, and they were in the house. They kicked her but didn't leave any lasting damage. Needless to say, she's a bit shaken up. I have to admit, I am too."

"No shit, man. That's insane. Any idea who they were? How many of them were there? Any identifying features or a plate I can try to trace on the system?"

"No, nothing. I tried to chase them down but they were already at the car. Too dark to see the plate. Car looked like something generic, midsize sedan, dark color."

"Shame. Glad to hear you guys are okay though. I'll put the feelers out and see if there are any thugs on the loose in that area with aggravated assault charges."

"Thanks," Jake said. "I doubt we'll find anything. These guys seemed hell-bent on scaring the crap out of her, but not much more. They didn't break anything or take anything, and they pretty much hightailed it out of there when I got back."

Shaw gripped the phone a bit tighter. He knew this was a legitimate case, but a small part of him had half-expected this whole thing to be nothing more than due diligence for Briggs and ICE. He didn't want to see things begin to escalate out of control. In his world, control was everything—those who had it won.

"I can't help but think this is all related somehow,' Jake continued. "Earlier we…"

Shaw waited for Jake to speak again. Had Jake stumbled over his words? Had he just about let something slip he didn't want to let Shaw know about?

"Never mind, man. We're good, just plugging forward with the case. I think we've already made a bit of progress, but we are still working out the details. When we're done, I'll shoot you and Briggs an email."

"Sure thing," Shaw said. "Mind giving me the ten-second version?"

"I'll do my best," Jake said. "But there's still a lot to be figured out. Suffice to say, Eliza is killing it already; thanks for finding her. Basically, you know we thought this was some sort of infectious disease—it is, technically—but it's not caused by something viral. It's actually parasitic."

"Parasitic?" Shaw asked. "How the hell can we know that?"

There was a tense moment while Shaw waited for Jake's answer. This was the reason for his call; this was what Shaw needed to find out. How did Jake have that information? Shaw knew what Jake had been up to, but he wanted to hear it from his friend's mouth himself.

Jake sighed. "Listen, man, I don't think you're going to like this. It's sort of… out of character for me. But Eliza and I went to examine the bodies."

So it was true, Shaw thought. "Examine the… *Stermers*? Jake, are you losing your mind? You can't do that. Their bodies are protected assets of the state, and Briggs flat-out ordered you to stay away until the medical examiner could—"

Jake cut him off. "I understand. I know the implications, and I know that Briggs is going to be pissed. But we had to figure out what we were dealing with before it got out of hand and turned into something we couldn't control."

"Dammit, Jake," Shaw said. "This is going to be something we can't control if Briggs throws us off the case. If he wanted to, he could press criminal charges, and even—"

"Beau, relax. This is exactly why we didn't invite you. You would be culpable, even liable. You'd lose your license. Eliza and I, we didn't really have anything to lose by checking it out. Except for time—she thought that whatever was inside of them would be deteriorating too quickly to fully examine if we waited any longer. And I'm glad we did."

It was Shaw's turn to sigh, and he took a long, forced breath. He inhaled, held it in for a few seconds, then exhaled. He knew they had gone against Briggs' orders—it was why he had called Jake now. But to hear that Jake had actually found something? That was something Briggs hadn't told him. *Had Briggs even known about that? How much had Jake told him?*

"Jake, Briggs knows."

"He what? How the hell does he know?"

"He has to, at least by now. He's *connected*, Jake. This isn't some local murder investigation. It goes all the way to the top—hell, the guy at the top is the one who *hired* us. He's going to find out our every move, and you've just given him a reason to track you every step of the way. You have to call it in yourself, to apologize."

"That's why you're calling? To get me to apologize to Briggs for doing my job?"

"Jake, it's about doing the job the way they want you to. This isn't the department. Sure, he wants results, but he's under a lot of pressure to get them the right way. Through the proper channels."

"Don't patronize me," Jake said. "Weren't you listening? We figured something out. We have more information now, information we wouldn't have had for another week or so."

Shaw thought back to his call with Briggs. He'd known Jake and Eliza had disobeyed his order, but he hadn't sounded necessarily concerned. "Tell me what it is you found, Jake. Maybe we can make this right with Briggs."

"No, we still need to parse the data and make sure what we are presenting is accurate. Like I said, I'll email you both. I'll tell him why we did what we did, and that it wasn't in direct defiance of his order—I was just doing my job and we knew we couldn't wait for his timeline."

Shaw didn't respond.

"Listen, man. I wasn't trying to go behind your back with this one. I just didn't want you coming into the line of fire if things went south. We needed to act quick, and I'm glad we did. It won't happen again, at least not without filling you in beforehand."

Shaw didn't like what he was hearing, but there was nothing he could do about it now except move on. He still trusted Jake. He knew the man had the right intentions.

But he also needed to make sure those intentions didn't cause the dominoes to fall in the wrong order.

CHAPTER 29

By the time Jake returned from the car with the food, Eliza had covered the dining-room table with books and notepads. She was still starving, but the thrill of what she was discovering every minute seemed to quell the hunger for the time being.

"Whoa," Jake said when he entered the room. "I was gone for five minutes and you've turned the dining room into a carbon copy of your living room."

She glanced up at him quickly, nodded, then set her eyes back down onto the microscope. "Sorry, yeah, had an idea and… well, I just wanted to check something…"

He set the bag of Mexican food on one of the chairs and began unpacking it. "I didn't get any drinks, but I figured we could either have water or whatever you've got in the fridge."

"Sure," she said. "Yeah, I've got some stuff in the fridge. Water is good, too."

Jake shrugged and walked into the kitchen while she scribbled a note on the pad next to her. She was in the zone, barely registering what Jake was telling her. Something about food, drinks, messy kitchen. It didn't matter; she was almost finished.

And if she was right…

Jake returned with a couple cans of soda and a glass of water. "Sorry, wasn't sure if you'd prefer soda. It's pretty late, caffeine and all that."

She finished theorizing and set the pencil down. She reached over, grabbed a can, and popped the tab. Without speaking, she downed half the can and looked at Jake. He handed her a foil-wrapped burrito, still warm.

As soon as it touched her hand, she felt the hunger hit her like a ton of bricks. She was famished. She tore through the foil and took a gigantic bite, not even caring that some of the juice inside was spilling out and down her chin.

She took another bite before swallowing the first one, her eyes closed.

"Good?" Jake asked.

"Oh, my God," she mumbled. "Best thing I've ever eaten."

"Well, I take full credit." Jake laughed, tearing into his own foil-wrapped concoction.

The food was from a place she had been to a few times before; a California-style Mexican restaurant that served build-your-own burritos that were each the size of a human head. The ingredients were always fresh, and she hadn't had a version of a burrito there that she hadn't liked.

"You've got good taste," she said. "I may not have grown up in Mexico, but I know good Mexican food."

"So, what were you working on so intensely while I was gone?" Jake asked. "Seems like it took a massive burrito to break you out of your hibernation."

Her eyes widened as she swallowed a bite of food. "Yes! I can't believe what this thing is. I mean, I almost *don't* believe what it is."

"What do you mean? I thought you decided it was a parasite. Something called an Orthodox, or whatever."

"*Osedax*," she corrected. "Yes, right. It is that. But it's where it came from that has me a bit confused."

"I thought it was from the ocean. One of those things that could live anywhere, right? Deep or shallow water, hot or cold, as long as it had some bones to chew on?"

She nodded a few times, sliding her wrist across her mouth to wipe away some of the salsa. "Well, that's what I thought. I mean, I just assumed it was like all the other species that have been found. Even though it's a relatively new species to us, it's pretty clear when you find something how easily adaptive it will be to new environments."

"Meaning you can make assumptions about where in the world you might find another species?" Jake asked.

"Yes, exactly. Among other things, like how successful it might be at a river delta, for example. Or in freshwater outright. We haven't found very many of these things that live in lakes and streams, but that doesn't mean they *can't*. Also, it gives us what we call a 'path of progression' in an evolutionary sense."

"You can figure out which species are older or younger, and where they came from around the world."

"Precisely, Jake."

Jake took a humongous bite of his own burrito, chewed for a few seconds, then looked back at Eliza and began talking before his mouth was empty again. "Well, I'm all ears. Spit it out. Where is our little friend from?"

"That's just it. I'm going to go over my notes again, and maybe send the findings to someone else just to make sure I'm not crazy, but I don't think this particular species is from *anywhere*."

"How is that possible?" Jake asked. "It has to be from somewhere, right?"

"Well yes, but I mean it's not from somewhere *naturally*. In that it doesn't seem to exist in nature."

"This is a new species of Osedax?"

She nodded. "Yes, and based on the striations I'm seeing on the main tubule, this thing doesn't seem to match the genetic makeup of any of its brothers and sisters, or even cousins. We know that they need to feed on bones, and that they thrive in saltwater environments. But I'm not seeing any that are really close to what this one seems to be."

"Eliza, just say it: what's up? Why is this particular species special?"

"Well, Jake, for one, it seems to be the superhero version of its genus. It's hardier, tougher, and more adaptable than anything like it. We know it not only lived inside of the Stermers, it *thrived* there. It grew, multiplied, and spread like wildfire, simultaneously killing its hosts in the process. And it doesn't really appear to be contagious, at least not after a certain point in its growth cycle."

"So…"

"So, I don't believe this species exists in nature, because I don't believe *nature* created it."

She pulled the soda up to her lips and took another long draw from it. This was the moment of truth, really. Hearing what she was about to say out loud wouldn't make it true, but it definitely made it feel more real to her.

"Jake, I think we are dealing with a parasite that was grown in a laboratory environment. It was based on the Osedax, but its creators built it into something more. Something more potent. They wanted something with the features of this parasite, but they wanted it to be a threat to humans. They wanted something that was more infectious. They wanted something far more deadly."

CHAPTER 30

Jake took in the information as best he could: trying to stay removed from it, trying his best to don his detective's brain rather than his emotional mind.

It wasn't easy. This new information meant that someone out there had put the parasite into contact with the Stermers, and had ultimately killed them. It meant that, depending on this person's agenda, there were possibly more—potentially *way* more—cases out there. Infected or diseased people who were now ticking time bombs.

"Eliza," he said, his voice barely a whisper.

"I know, Jake," she answered. "It's remarkable. I mean, this sort of thing is a once-in-a-lifetime—"

"*Eliza*," he said again. "This isn't remarkable. It's deadly. It's already killed two people. How many more are infected? How fast can it spread?"

She looked away, down at her research, then back up at Jake. The expression on her face had completely changed. "I… I'm sorry. I didn't mean to sound nonchalant. You're right. It's a big deal. It's just that this sort of thing isn't easy to do, you know? It takes…"

Jake saw her drift off, her face seeming to mirror her voice. "What? It takes what?"

"It takes a lot of money, for one," she said. "And time, probably. Unless you get really lucky; but this strain of Osedax is crafted, not lucky. It doesn't look at all like it was an accident. I could go into the details, but—"

Jake held up a hand. "No, it's okay. I trust you. I want to push forward though. If this is what you say it is, what does it mean? What's the infection factor?"

She looked through her notes, then started writing a few more. "Okay, right. Well, unlike an airborne virus, these little guys need to be carried to different hosts if they're going to grow and become dangerous. It's a nasty little thing, too. Starts off microscopic—most likely the stage at which it jumps into its host. There, it grows and reproduces, and eventually more microscopic organisms move to the surface of the host's skin, which is the point it becomes ready to infect all over again. So, it's hard to tell what the factor is—how many people one person can infect, for example—because we're not sure of the vector yet, the mechanism it uses to transmit. But we can still make some educated guesses about it. We call that *R-naught.* It's written as an 'R' with a little zero next to it."

"Right, okay, I've seen that before," Jake said. "It was all over the news when the coronavirus was spreading. An *R-naught* of less than one means this thing is spreading from one person to fewer than one other person."

"Yes, exactly. So, that number is unknown. Right now, as far as we know—based on the *very* little information we have—it's less than one. But I have a feeling that number is going to increase *rapidly* the longer we go. The Stermers weren't isolated the entire time they were held at ICE. They interacted with people, touched stuff, moved around, breathed. We don't know how this parasite spreads, how long the incubation period is, what the exact disease vector is. But I'm pretty confident that it takes more to spread than just being near someone else. Because this parasite gives birth to live children, those little guys will have to somehow move to a new host. It doesn't seem like the parasite would be capable of that on its own. Since we know it was *designed*, we can also *assume* it needs to be specifically administered."

"Okay," Jake said, pinching the bridge of his nose. "We need to figure out what this contagion is capable of. We know it can kill grown, healthy adults. We need to discover what else it can do."

"And how to kill it," Eliza added, making a note beneath her scribbles.

"And what I really want to know," Jake said, "is *who the hell made it?*"

Just then Jake's phone, sitting on the table, began to vibrate.

He felt dread creep into him before he even read the number. *Derek Briggs.*

It was the man's personal cell phone number, the one he'd given Jake a few days before.

"This is Parker," Jake said.

He listened as the man's deep baritone on the other end of the line immediately launched into a tirade. "I was informed that you and your doctor friend broke into a government facility and examined the bodies of—"

"Briggs, listen. We—"

"No, son," Briggs interrupted, his voice rising. "*You* listen to *me*. Your cavalier excursion is leading to a veritable shit ton of paperwork and bullshit that I now have to deal with. I expressly forbade anyone from touching those bodies until we could finalize the—"

"Listen, Briggs, I'm going to have to stop you there. I get it— you're in charge. I'm not trying to step on your toes, but dammit, you hired me to do a job. We are doing that job, and we've got new information that I think you'd like to hear."

He paused, waiting for Briggs to descend into an even more animated verbal dressing-down, but none came.

Jake calmed himself, raised his eyebrows toward Eliza, then continued.

"I really do apologize for not letting you know ahead of time, but we didn't *have* time. The red tape would have been enormous, and by the time we chopped it away, there wouldn't be anything left to examine."

"What are you saying?"

"I'm saying we figured out what this thing is, Briggs. And it's not good."

A long pause. "Okay, what is it?"

"I'm already drafting an email. Five minutes and it's in your inbox. It'll have everything you need to make an educated decision, but—and I can't stress this enough—I don't think we're dealing with something we've seen before."

"Fine, Parker," Briggs said. "I'm still pissed, but I'll get over it. I need information. If you've got it, great."

"We do. But before you read the email, I have to advise you that this thing could be devastating if it's even remotely infectious. It killed the Stermers, and—"

"It's killed more than just the Stermers."

Jake felt his stomach lurch.

"I just got word that we've got three more confirmed incidents. Three more deaths."

God. He grabbed Eliza's pencil and began furiously scrawling on a clean sheet of paper, large enough for her to read.

THREE MORE DEAD, he wrote.

"Okay, shoot," Jake said. "Were they in contact with the Stermers? Upstate New York or Canada?"

There was another pause. "No, unfortunately. That would be too easy."

"Come again?"

"Parker, these are three new cases, in three completely different ICE facilities. All spread out around the United States."

"Dear God."

"Yeah, that's pretty much what I've been saying," Briggs replied. "We're already taking actions to shut down and run with none but the most essential employees and agents, and my team is drawing up a battle plan as we speak."

"Okay, good." Jake wasn't sure what else to say. "I—*we'll*—get this email to you. Give us another couple of minutes; we'll be brief and cut out the bullshit."

"I appreciate that." Briggs cleared his throat, then continued. "Parker, listen to me: there was no way the Stermers could have been in contact with people at this wide a reach. It doesn't make sense. That means that this is far more than just an infection and impending pandemic we're dealing with."

Jake had a feeling he knew what the man was going to say, but he wanted to hear it out loud, to have someone else confirm it.

"We're dealing with an act of terrorism."

CHAPTER 31

The Next Day

"Shit," Jake whispered. "Shit, shit." He pulled the Corolla over into the right lane as they sped down the highway.

"What?" Eliza asked. She leaned over and looked at Jake's phone. He was reading emails while he was driving, a bad habit but one that he felt was necessary at this moment.

"New email from Shaw," Jake said. "Those three incidents Briggs mentioned last night? Those aren't the only ones."

"Are you serious?" Eliza looked out the window, a pained expression on her face. "Jake, this is spiraling. When pandemics begin, data often comes in more slowly than new cases. If that's the case here, we could be dealing with a manufactured outbreak."

Jake nodded. "I know. Someone's infecting people—the Stermers, now others in ICE facilities. To the outside world it would seem like a viral outbreak, something that's not being controlled. That's why we're here, to find who's doing it, why, and how they're getting away with it."

"Here" was currently halfway back to the hotel in Albany, where they would check in with Shaw in person but then immediately head out on the road again, aiming to track down some of the people who had come into contact with the Stermers. Jake's sleep had been fitful, and it wasn't just because he'd been on Eliza's hard, uncomfortable couch.

While Shaw hadn't turned up anything directly useful, he had given them a list of people who might have come into contact with the Stermers. They were hoping to touch base with each of the people on the list before the end of the day.

One such person was the officer who had brought in the family up in Vermont, a man named Robert Craig. Officer Craig had pulled in the family after a routine traffic stop, but had called in US Border Patrol when he had discovered the family had crossed over from Canada.

And the email Jake had just gotten from Shaw told him that Officer Craig was now quarantined in a hospital in Vermont, thought to have contracted whatever disease had gotten the Stermers.

Jake filled in Eliza with the details of the email—as well as Officer Craig, the receptionist in the facility in Clinton was also now showing symptoms. Shaw had cc'd Briggs on the message, so they would have to wait for an update from Briggs on what to do next. Normally, Jake would not have thought twice about Shaw including their boss in the correspondence, but after the previous night's events it gave Jake some pause.

Jake tossed his phone to Eliza. "Mind typing out an email response for me?"

"Not at all," Eliza said. "What are you thinking?"

"Well, this cop up in Vermont might have this parasite, according to Shaw. Elevated heart rate, high blood pressure. They're watching for signs of blood pooling. If that's the case, as much as I hate to admit it, it doesn't make sense for us to drive all the way up there…" He didn't feel like he needed to add the rest of the sentence: *because he might be dead when we get there*.

"Right. You want to question someone else? The doctor?"

"Saiid Edemza," Jake said. "No, not yet. I've already met him, and I doubt he's changed his story much. He was the doctor who admitted them. The doctor who finally called it in, Gerald, saw them as well, but by then they were too far gone. We need to question him when we can, but I think we should try to reach out to these other infected patients first."

"That makes sense," Eliza said. "If we can get to them fast enough, we might be able to ask them about Edemza, as well as the Stermers."

"Exactly. See if they knew anything about the doctor, his methods, habits, that sort of thing. We know he came into contact with the family, but as of yet he's not sick. Latest update from the facility is that he is still in perfect health. That's not necessarily suspicious, until it is."

Eliza smiled. "Is that 'detective talk'? 'It's not suspicious until it is'?"

"You laugh, but it's not too far from the truth. Take Edemza. It's not suspicious right now to not be ill. But if he stays healthy while everyone around him is dropping like flies, well, then we'll know who to talk to."

Eliza fiddled with Jake's phone for a moment. "What should I tell Shaw? Should we still try to meet up with him at the hotel?"

Jake shook his head. "No, I don't think we necessarily need to meet in person. Let him know that we are going to talk with the front-desk receptionist who's now sick, to see if she can tell us anything about Edemza or any other information. Tell him that we're in a hurry, we'd like to get there before she's too far gone."

Jake heard Eliza tapping away on the phone. When she finished, she handed it over to him to read before sending. As he finished and pressed "send," Eliza changed the subject.

"What happened last night?"

Jake raised an eyebrow as he focused on the road.

"Not with the break-in," she said. "I mean after. When we were talking in my living room. You... had a moment."

"Yeah, sorry about that. Just snuck up on me, I guess."

"What did?"

Jake sighed. He watched the yellow lines separating the lanes of the highway stretch out in front of him. They were one of the only cars on the road at the moment, and the drive had been peaceful.

Up to this point.

He hadn't wanted to bring up last night's events. The detective in him wanted to solve the case; he wanted to figure out what those two intruders had been trying to do, and who had sent them.

Eliza told him she had slept fitfully, but she was otherwise okay. He hadn't wanted to reflect on how *he* was doing, however.

"Jake," Eliza said. "You know you can talk to me, right?"

Jake felt a flash of anger surge through him. *If I had a dollar for every time I've heard that line*, he thought. He'd been to therapists, professional psychologists, department-sanctioned counselors. He'd heard different strains of the same chorus from each of them, each of them wanting him to know how willing they were for him to talk to them. *Talking doesn't help*, he thought. *Helping helps.*

He looked at Eliza. She was staring back at him. "You know, I'm not really sure I'm ready to do that just yet."

She nodded, scrunching her face into an expression that seemed to say *I understand how you feel.*

He knew she didn't. She couldn't. He appreciated her willingness to try, but it was almost pitiful—patronizing even—when people did that. Shaw had tried many times and failed, and Shaw had been the person, besides Mel, whom Jacob trusted more than anyone in the world.

He saw in Eliza the kind of person he *could* talk to, potentially. Someday. But not today.

He squeezed the steering will with both hands and focused on the road once again. "Sorry if that's hard to hear," he said. "I know you mean well."

She didn't respond.

CHAPTER 32

They stopped at the hotel for a half-hour for Jake to shower and change clothes, then they left for the hospital in downtown Albany, where a makeshift quarantine suite had been set up for the receptionist who was thought to be sick with the parasite. They'd flown her from Clinton, where she had checked in the Stermers.

The woman, Rosemary Jenkins, was in her mid-fifties and had worked for Immigration for the past fifteen years. She had been a chronic sufferer of indigestion and digestive issues, so when she began to feel pains in her stomach, she assumed it was something related. By the time she'd actually called the doctor, the pains had moved from her stomach to just about every place in her body. She was bedridden and in severe pain, but Jake had been informed that she was awake and willing to try to talk.

When he and Eliza pulled into the hospital and were escorted to her suite, they were given a brief by the doctor in charge. The patient was considered to be in a critical condition, as whatever was causing the problem inside of her seemed to be getting worse by the hour. No amount of medication or antibiotics had helped so far.

The doctor and a few nurses helped Jake and Eliza into hazmat suits, not unlike the ones they had worn while visiting the Stermers. It was surreal for Jake, as he knew that everyone in the room, including Ms. Jenkins herself, could see the writing on the wall. Her prognosis was fatal, but she wanted to do whatever she could to help.

Jake turned to Eliza and nearly bumped into her helmet. "You ready?" he asked.

Even through her suit, he could see her shrug. "I guess," she said. "Ready as I'll ever be."

Jake entered the quarantine room and pulled aside the bedside curtain hanging from hooks along the ceiling. The sheet slid along the curved rod until the bed behind it was revealed.

Ms. Jenkins lay there, her eyes puffy and wide, staring at the newcomers.

"Hello, Ms. Jenkins. My name is Jake Parker, and I'm with—" he caught himself. "I'm working with the folks here at this hospital to try to figure out what's going on."

She smiled, but the smile didn't reach her eyes. Jake could tell she was having trouble breathing, as her chest rose and fell in jagged, forced heaves. He couldn't tell if her skin was beginning to show signs of the parasite—the darkened veins just beneath the surface—or if he was simply looking at someone who had spent most of her adult life in an unhealthy state. "I know you need to rest, so I'd like to only ask you a few questions. Please just answer what you can."

Ms. Jenkins nodded.

"Ms. Jenkins, do you remember the family—the Stermers—that were brought into your facility?"

"Yes," she croaked. "I only met two of them. A man and a woman. They were brought into an examination room."

"And that is where Dr. Edemza saw them?"

She nodded.

"Do you remember coming into contact with them? Touching their arm or shaking their hand or anything of that nature?"

Ms. Jenkins shook her head. "No, nothing like that. My job is processing. We have many people who come through and need to be examined before they are placed somewhere. There weren't many people at that time, so I remember them clearly." She coughed and frowned as a deep pain shot through her body. "My job is to get their fingerprints and names, as well as collect any documentation they may have."

"And did they have any? Documentation, that is." Jake looked at Eliza, but she was staring down at the woman on the hospital bed.

"Just a driver's license for the man, Paul, I believe. They did not have passports—those were left back in Canada."

Jake had heard as much from Shaw and some of the emails from Briggs' team. Since the Stermers had been visiting Canada from London, they had passports that they had left in the hotel in Canada, never intending to cross the border into the United States.

Jake looked down at his watch. *Three minutes left.* The doctor wanted to make sure Ms. Jenkins was kept calm and put under no undue stress. When they had called ahead to the hospital to explain that they believed what Rosemary was suffering from was parasitic, the response had been that without a known cure, they could only make her comfortable in her final hours. Jake wasn't about to make this woman's last hours unnecessarily uncomfortable, so he turned over the questioning to Eliza.

She spoke immediately. "Ms. Jenkins, thank you for speaking with us. Right now, you and only a few other people are known to have contracted this disease. We are trying to determine why Dr. Edemza, the doctor in charge of the examinations that day, has not yet fallen ill. Do you have any idea as to why that may be?"

The woman frowned up at Eliza, and then her eyes softened before she spoke. "I don't know the doctor very well, but he seemed nice enough. Have to admit he was acting a bit strange, though."

Jake glanced around, working to place this new information into the narrative. "How so?"

"Well, for one, he was quiet. Reserved. Seemed like he was keeping to himself as much as he could. Didn't come to the break room for dinner or even to just chat, things like that. Now, understand that I don't know the man from Adam, but still. It seemed weird."

Jake typed a note about this into his phone.

Eliza continued. "Ms. Jenkins, I am a parasitologist by trade, and I have some ideas as to what might be causing this disease.

Unfortunately, I don't know how to cure it, but if you could give me some information about what it feels like… what seems to be happening, on the inside…"

Ms. Jenkins clawed at the edge of the mattress as she swallowed, for the first time squeezing her eyes shut. Jake noticed that her eyelids seemed to be swollen, as if popping out of her head.

Finally, she opened her eyes and looked at each of them in turn. "It's… hell. Pure agony. I thought it was gas at first, and then indigestion. But it feels like whatever is in there is just getting stronger, as if there are a thousand tiny matches being lit inside of me all at the same time."

Jake dropped his head. *This thing doesn't just kill, it tortures.* They needed to find a solution. A cure.

It was too late for Ms. Jenkins, and they all knew it. But it didn't have to be too late for everyone else. And how many others were there? How many people were out there growing this parasite inside of them? How many were unknowingly being exposed to it?

Jake had seen a couple news vans parked out front of the hospital as they'd driven in. Always interested in a story, the ambulance chasers must have somehow gotten word that a quarantine had been set up in the Albany hospital. If they found out that people were dying from an unknown disease, it would be only a matter of hours before the news agencies spun up a terror-inducing story that would alarm the masses.

One of the nurses knocked gently on the glass window behind them. Jake turned and flashed a thumbs-up sign. He knew he had a minute left, but it was a minute they didn't need to waste. He had new information, and while it wasn't much to go on, it was more than nothing.

Eliza was already making her way toward the door, but Jake looked down at Ms. Jenkins one final time and smiled. "Thank you, Ms. Jenkins. I truly am hoping for a miracle, but rest assured I will find out what's going on. I will get to the bottom of this."

If she heard him, he couldn't tell. Her eyes had closed once again and her bloated, swollen face seemed to already be in a state of eternal rest.

Jake let out a deep breath as he followed Eliza through the door and prepared to doff their suits.

CHAPTER 33

Shaw had waited back at the hotel while Eliza and Jake were at the hospital. He'd only finished his own work an hour before, and so they all decided to get together in the hotel bar to discuss their next action steps.

He was in the bar now, just beginning work on a bourbon and Coke—a typical grizzled-detective libation that felt right just about any hour of the day—when Jake and Eliza walked in. Shaw called them over and asked the bartender to bring a glass of wine and another bourbon.

Shaw shook hands with both of them and then they sat. He could read on Jake's face that it had been an impactful day.

"I'm guessing by your face this is worse than we thought," Shaw said.

Jake forced a smile as the bartender swung by with his drink. He took a small sip, winced, then answered. "Seven confirmed cases so far, five deaths. And we assume another two deaths are imminent. Hell, Shaw, we don't even know how to *test* for this thing. Patients simply show up in the hospital complaining of abdominal pains. And the staff at the hospital told us their blood shows an extremely high level of sodium and lipids."

Eliza jumped in. "That's because we now know it's a parasite, something in the same genus as Osedax."

"That disgusting little worm thingy you sent a picture of?" Shaw asked. "And you said someone *designed* it? That they actually created this thing in a lab?"

"That's our working hypothesis and best guess so far," Eliza said. "Without another battery of tests and a barrage of new data, it will be impossible to tell for sure, but I'm pretty confident that's what we're dealing with."

"That doesn't seem terribly contagious to me."

"But it's *one hundred percent deadly*, as far as we can tell."

Shaw shuddered. "How do we know we all haven't been exposed to these creepy-crawlies?"

"Well, for one, we're not dead yet," Jake said. "We're thinking it's something that has to be essentially placed onto—or *into*—each host, individually."

Shaw chewed on an ice cube for a moment. "So it seems that if someone did design this little bastard, they intend to wreak as much havoc on the US population as possible."

Jake looked over at Eliza, then back at Shaw. He took a longer sip of the whiskey. "Well, I'm not so sure that's accurate."

"Do tell."

"Well, our working theory is that whoever released this *doesn't* intend for it to wreak havoc. Not through the transmission at least. They're going for fear, for targeted, specific infections. They want a calculated, controllable spread. For whatever reason, they chose to drop it into an ICE detainment center first."

"Okay," Shaw said. "I can buy that. For now, anyway. We need more information. We need to be testing for this thing way out on the front lines, long before people are symptomatic."

Jake shook his head. "No. We have to remember Briggs' directive: we are not here to try to *fight* this disease. We are not here to *study* it. If this really is an act of terrorism, we're here to prevent more attacks."

Eliza frowned, but Shaw simply sat in silence as his ex-partner spoke. He saw that same flash of intensity inside Jake now, that same drive and brilliance that made him such a damn good detective. He watched in awe, excited to see his friend starting to return to his old self.

Jake continued. "It's up to Immigration—to Briggs and his team—to fight this thing on the ground. It's up to them to get with the CDC and figure out a way to stop it before it spreads. But Briggs needs us somewhere else, fighting the battle on a different front. He needs us to figure out who the hell made it, why they did so, and more than anything else, he needs us to make sure it's not going to happen again."

CHAPTER 34

The Next Day

Jake woke late, still feeling tired but knowing that trying to get back to sleep was a lost cause. He'd showered, shaved, and sat on the edge of the bed watching Albany's local news station fight over misinterpreted headlines about what might be quarantined inside the hospital. Thankfully none of the medical staff had spilled the beans, but Jake knew it was only a matter of time before someone filled them in on the few details they knew.

By the time he reached the lobby and found Eliza, he discovered that she had already worked through two cups of tea and was starting on a third. He made himself a cup of coffee and joined her.

"Find anything useful in your studies this morning?" he asked.

She shook her head, not lifting her eyes from her laptop. "Nope," she said. "Just working on some school stuff now."

"I see." Jake sipped the coffee and watched her work, wondering if she ever stopped.

She stopped typing, then looked up at Jake and smirked. "You're probably wondering if I found anything useful to *our* case. I have not. Not yet, anyway. But I was up late last night studying this strain some more, and yes, I did find it useful."

Jake rolled his eyes. "I wasn't judging you for working on the day job if you're worried about that. Are you always this syntactically correct?" he asked.

"'*Semantically* correct' is probably the phrase you're looking for."

Jake laughed.

"And yes, I am."

She closed the lid of her laptop a minute later and pulled a yellow legal pad from her computer bag. She smacked it onto the table and then fumbled around for a pencil. "I was actually checking to see when the lab would be available at Syracuse," she said. "So not *technically* schoolwork. I just needed to frame it that way when sending the email to make sure it'll get set up properly."

"Right."

"Anyway," she continued, "I'm assuming they'll be open for new trials in a few days, for a small window, which won't be soon enough—we need a full laboratory analysis on the worm, like, yesterday."

"Can we have Briggs call in a favor somewhere?"

"Probably. Yeah. That's something you can email over later."

Jake shifted in his seat, feeling the sensation of forward progress coming over him. It was akin to the feeling he got just before cracking a tough case, the feeling of satisfaction and elation. This was a similar—albeit far more reserved—version of that.

Jake pulled up his emails and flicked through them. He rarely got emails of any importance these days, so it took no time at all for his eyes to land on one from a .gov email address. *Someone from ICE, probably*, he thought. He clicked it and the email opened.

As he read, the feeling of euphoria died. *This can't be true.* He didn't want it to be true.

"What is it, Jake?" Eliza had apparently read the forlorn look on his face.

"I just got an email from a mid-level ICE administrator. I asked Briggs to send along anything they could find on Dr. Saiid Edemza."

Eliza waited.

"And it's good news. We might have found our guy. I think Edemza's the one behind all of this."

"Really? Why do you say that?"

Jake paraphrased from the email. "Well, for starters, he changed his prescription deliveries a couple weeks ago. The drugs he administers, while working for ICE, to any detainees or immigrants—he changed companies."

"What does that even mean?"

"I don't know yet," Jake said. "But it says here that Dr. Edemza had his medication service changed from a company called *Pharland* to one called *AEG*."

"Well, that could be something, right?"

Jake agreed. "Yeah, it could be. I'll look into the company a bit more. But it's this next thing in the email that caught my eye."

"What's that?"

"Well, apparently, our friend Dr. Edemza is showing up in the FTO database."

"The FTO?"

Jake nodded. "A list maintained by the government. FTO means *Foreign Terrorist Organization*."

CHAPTER 35

"This is Briggs."

Derek Briggs was in a hurry. These days, he *always* felt as though he were in a hurry—assistants trying to keep his schedule in check, government meetings to kick the proverbial can down the road, and no shortage of general day-to-day work-related tasks and appointments.

But this week had been especially trying. The constant flow of information and *mis*information—usually a casualty of a never-ending game of telephone—had doubled. It was like a Los Angeles freeway: no car was free and no one on it was getting their way.

He took a deep breath, listening for the voice on the other end of the line. The caller was one of the few people on the planet that had this personal number. His assistant had it changed every quarter, not because of spam or junk phone calls, but because keeping it "fresh" meant he was keeping his circle of informants up to date and on their toes.

"Briggs, this is Shaw."

"What is it?"

"There's been… well, not an incident, sir, but I think there will be."

"An incident?" Briggs asked. "What the hell kind of incident? I'm up to my eyeballs in media requests from across the pond, asking about the Stermers and how they died. There's… talk."

Shaw ignored the comment and pressed on. "Sir, I'm in Albany, checking around for anything other departments might have come across."

Briggs appreciated this man's ingenuity—it was a good idea, trying to use the existing infrastructure to ferret out information that might prove valuable.

"And you found something."

"I did, sir. Something came across the desk. Still not sure it's anything major, but it was passed along through an encrypted network we all use—sort of like the Govscan."

Govscan was the vernacular term for the nationwide database of conversations. A relic of the phone-tapping and privacy-encroachment debacle of two decades ago, Govscan remained in place as a useful second-by-second update tool. It was simply an encrypted website, accessible and shared by most federal-level organizations, updatable by any of them. Part forum and messaging board and part real-time espionage tool, Govscan allowed organizations like ICE to participate in an intelligence-gathering and sharing network. If a group like the IRS somehow came across information they deemed to be worthy of follow-up, they could submit it directly into Govscan, where an algorithmic engine parsed the data and extracted keywords, immediately cross-referencing the entry with other similar entries. Then a separate organization like ICE could get an update if a keyword in the entry matched one of their search terms—something that might help them track down illegal immigrants, for example. Many state police departments had begun building a similar network for police activity. In smaller states, where jurisdictional lines were bound by geography, having a real-time update tool had already proven valuable.

"Okay, what is it?" Briggs asked.

"A note—or a piece of one. In Spanish, and then coded further. We just caught a snippet of it, but it seems there will be 'an event' sometime in the next two days."

"Shaw, that's not much to go on. 'An event.' What does that even mean?"

"Sir, I'm still trying to find someone to get through the code and make sense of the whole thing, but they also mention the word 'Dilley.'"

"Dilley?"

"Yes, sir. Dilley. Does that mean something to you?"

Briggs didn't respond. *Dilley*. The word did, in fact, mean something to him.

Finally, he pulled the phone closer to his mouth. "Do me a favor and fill in the rest of your team—they'll want to know as well."

"What would you like us to do?"

"Well, it depends on what we're dealing with. If you can decode the rest of the message, great. Either way, they're talking about the location of ICE's largest detention facility. It's in a place called Dilley, Texas."

Briggs gripped the phone tighter. He knew Dilley well. Back when he'd first started the job, he had traveled to the main ICE detention facility locations spread around the United States, both as a mission to come across to his constituents as a real, down-to-earth advocate of change, and to get a feel for the actual integrity of his organization's efforts.

To his knowledge, none of his predecessors had visited the facilities, and most of them had never set foot in Dilley. The South Texas town was far too low on the totem pole of importance for those types, so it had been Briggs' number-one priority upon accepting the role: get to Dilley, see the nightmarish conditions of the barbaric system with his own eyes, and then figure out how to change it. Figure out how to fix it.

So far, he had taken decent steps toward that goal, but he often felt as though he were living in a constant state of failure. The state of immigration in the country was beyond appalling, and though he had worked hard to change it, there was little visible effect so far.

Dilley was the predominant example of the current state of ICE affairs, so Briggs had made it his mission to know everything going on in and around their largest center.

"Shaw, figure out how to get the rest of the message. I want to know what it says. Don't worry about Dilley—that's something I can handle from here."

"Yes, sir. Thank you."

Shaw hung up, and Briggs stared down at his phone for a few seconds before placing it back onto his desk.

CHAPTER 36

Jake and Eliza were on their way back to the ICE offices in Albany. Again. To talk to Dr. Saiid Edemza. Again.

Jake had told Eliza about his first encounter with the man. The doctor hadn't seemed to be hiding anything, and Jake was usually pretty good at finding the cracks in an interrogation subject.

But apparently he *had* missed something.

Eliza had spent most of the morning studying up on the parasite, but she'd reached a point where they simply needed more data, and that data wasn't coming in quickly enough.

The biggest surprise so far that day had come in the form of new cases: there was only one.

Briggs had sent an email to Jake informing him that there was only a single new active case. A man who worked as a janitor in the same office as the receptionist had come down with similar symptoms and was now hospitalized. Unfortunately, he was very likely to die by that afternoon, so Jake determined that it wouldn't be worthwhile to make the drive back to Clinton.

They were happy to hear that there was only a single new case, but they also knew that there was still a lack of testing—they weren't sure yet *what* to test for—and that the numbers would likely soon begin to swell.

Even then, Eliza seemed to be having a hard time with the numbers. Jake watched her as he drove, scratching out and rewriting something on her legal pad.

"It doesn't make sense," she finally said. "These numbers don't add up."

"The known active cases?"

"All of them. Active cases, total deaths, total recovered."

"So far, no one's recovered," Jake said. "Meaning we have to assume this thing is deadly."

She nodded. "Definitely. I'm sure it is. But the R-naught? That number seems really low."

Jake considered this. "But I thought we agreed that the testing would increase that number, as in, the more we test, the more active and confirmed cases we find? That would push the number up considerably."

"It would," Eliza said, biting on the end of her pencil. "But we *know* some of these people came into contact with the Stermers before they died, right?"

Jake nodded. There were more cars out today, and he had to slow down to miss an aggressive, overzealous lane-changer who decided he needed to be in Jake's lane *right now*.

"We know that they came into contact with the police officer, Robert Craig, who died last night," Eliza said.

"Yes."

"But *that* officer also was in contact—at least we assume—with other officers, right? Up in Richford. I mean, he called it in to Border Patrol, and then he would have spoken with someone in person when they came to get the Stermers, right? And what about the sheriff from that station? She was there, too, the morning after the Stermers were brought in."

"Yeah, that's true," Jake said. "So far, neither the sheriff nor anyone else from that station's called in sick."

"And the receptionist—she was definitely around other people. Detainees who were brought in, the ICE officers and agents who *brought* them in—some of those people should be infected bad enough now that we'd know it. Or they'd be dead already."

"So maybe this thing *isn't* as infectious after all," Jake said, thinking out loud. "Maybe it's deadly, but it takes a good-sized dosage of it for someone else to get it."

Eliza did the scrunch-face routine again as she stared at the numbers. "Well, I'm definitely making some assumptions with the math here, but it still seems fishy. Even though this is a para-site—and the vector is likely contact-transferal, in that one host has to literally touch another person to pass on the disease—it seems unlikely that whoever designed this purposefully made it less contagious than it would have naturally been."

"Yeah, that doesn't make sense, if, as we have to assume, this is a terrorist threat against America. You have another theory?" Jake asked.

"I don't get it. It *should* be transferable through water, food, or human-to-human contact, but in that case, surely there would be more deaths by now. We're days into this, and it's far from pandemic levels yet."

"What are 'pandemic levels'?" Jake asked. "You mean America isn't freaking out about it yet?"

"Well, that, but we also have no reason to suspect that at this rate of infection there's anything to actually worry about—some people will die, but the vast majority of the population simply will not come into contact with it. It's not like this thing is turning into another coronavirus pandemic. The problem, of course, is that whoever it *does* come into contact with has about a zero percent chance of surviving. Our thinking has been all wrong; the parasite isn't transferred person to person through contact with the skin—it can't be, because it enters the skin almost immediately. It *must* be passed from the surface—some material—to the host."

Jake nodded, remembering all too well how insanely terrified the nation had been during the most recent viral epidemic. While the media had certainly done their part in spreading the panic, the virus itself had been impossible to control. Tens of thousands had perished, and many more had been hospitalized. The real fear of it all had more to do with the speed with which it propagated throughout the population.

That pandemic had been caused by a virus that was highly contagious but not terribly deadly. This one seemed to be the exact opposite: not terribly contagious, but with a hundred percent death rate.

Eliza was right. So far, this "pandemic" Briggs seemed worried about was hardly that, with barely a handful of deaths in as many days. But instead of feeling reassured, Jake felt suspicious. It meant they were missing something.

And missing something in an investigation was never acceptable.

"How else could a parasite be passed on?" he asked.

Eliza thought for a moment. "I mean, outside of physical contact, food, water, I guess it could be consumed orally in something like…" she trailed off, as if realizing something for the first time.

Jake's eyes widened. "Like medication?"

"*Exactly* like medication," she said. "My God. I'm such an idiot. Edemza's a doctor. He's been issuing medications to patients every day for five years. Of course, that's how this thing can be transferred to new hosts."

Jake felt a surge of energy running through him. Edemza's façade seemed to be crumbling. He could feel a breakthrough coming.

"And he just had his supplier switched out," Jake added. "Sounds a bit suspicious, no?"

She smiled back at Jake, just as they pulled into the ICE office complex.

CHAPTER 37

It was the same building Jake had been in before, days ago. It was the same sad building—an ICE criminal detention center—with the same sad lights and stained carpet, and he led Eliza to the same sad anteroom where, behind the wall of glass, he knew Dr. Edemza waited once again.

What was different, however, was that both Eliza and Jake were stopped at the front desk and asked to verify their identity and have their fingerprints recorded. It wasn't exactly a strange request, but Jake mentioned to the young man that he hadn't been asked for that a few days ago.

"New system," the man shrugged. "We thought you were in the database before, but it's been too long since you were active as a police officer." He then looked at Eliza. "And she's not in the system at all."

Jake placed his right fingers in a line on the dark-blue pad of ink and pressed down, then applied them to a sheet of paper the man had produced. It had his name, birthdate, and a few other vitals already typed up and ready. If this kid was anything, he was efficient.

Eliza gave the man her own fingerprints, and within two minutes they were on their way down the hall to see Edemza.

Today there were no police officers—no Rutgers or Mabry—in the antechamber to greet him, so when they finally prepared to enter the room Edemza was in, Jake wasted no time filling Eliza in on how they'd play it with the doctor.

"I'll do the talking," he said, "but I want you in there with me."

"Good cop, bad cop?" she asked.

Jake couldn't tell if she were joking or not, but she wasn't smiling. "Uh, no," he said. "Me, you. *That's* the best strategy in these sorts of things. We're here to get the truth, not trick him."

"Got it."

"And if there's something about the parasite you need to know, tap me on the shoulder or get my attention. Don't just ask it—we need to make sure we're not giving him more information than he's giving us."

"Got it," she repeated.

Jake turned and walked through the threshold into the hallway, then again to enter the room. He knocked twice, then opened the door. It was still unlocked.

"Dr. Edemza," Jake said, his voice bright. "We meet again."

"So it seems," the man said. He was seated in the center of the room, the entire setting a carbon copy of their conversation a few days ago. "I hope you are well."

Jake smiled. "Thank you, I'm fine. This is my colleague, Dr. Eliza Mendoza."

She nodded, flicked her eyes around the room, then did an awkward half-bow that made Jake frown.

"Why don't we all grab a seat," Jake said, motioning for Eliza to sit in one of the folding chairs where Edemza was already seated. "Dr. Edemza, I'm hoping we can pick up where we left off last time. From our previous conversation."

Edemza stretched his hands to his sides, palms up. "The sooner we do, the sooner I may be able to get back to my life."

"Yes," Jake said. "That's correct. I brought Dr. Mendoza because she is an esteemed parasitologist. As you know, we believe this contagion to be parasitic in nature, and—"

"As I know?" Edemza asked.

Jake swallowed. "My apologies. As I *assume* you know, this contagion is parasitic in nature, and we believe that it causes—"

"Mr. Parker," Edemza said, interrupting once again. "Please do not insult my intelligence or yours with mind games. If you wish to convict me of something, I suggest you do it succinctly and overtly, so that I may efficiently provide my rebuttal."

Jake was a bit taken aback. He'd interrogated plenty of subjects during the course of his career, and a good number of them had sought to play the *smarter-than-you* card. Few actually were, and even fewer were innocent. But there was something in Edemza's air that struck Jake as odd. It was the same demeanor he'd picked up on the last time they'd spoken; the man had an elegance and directness that was neither welcoming nor rude. He wasn't cocky or arrogant. There was no pride behind his words, only truth.

"Very well, sir," Jake said. "We believe that you have been administering a parasitic infection to your patients at Immigration."

Edemza's face moved very slowly. First, his eyebrow raised a millimeter, then his chin. Finally, his eyes squeezed closed a quarter-inch. "I see. And how, may I ask, have you come to this conclusion?"

Oh, he's good, Jake thought. *Really good.*

He turned to Eliza, prepared to ask her a question. Then he thought better of it.

No, that's exactly what he wants. He needs to know how we caught him.

And yet, in a small corner of his mind, Jake didn't believe Edemza was the culprit. He didn't see the guilt on the man's face, poorly hidden behind his eyes like with so many other thugs and criminals he'd brought in and questioned. The man seemed genuinely curious.

"Well, I was hoping *you* could tell us the answer to that question," Jake said.

"The question of how *I* have been killing ICE detainees?"

"You know there's more than one?"

"There were four Stermers, correct? Husband, wife, two children? And the two adults are now deceased?"

Well, that's true. Okay, point Edemza.

Jake sniffed. "Right. There are more. *Including* the officer who brought the Stermers in. He died last night, actually. We're waiting for confirmation, but I'm almost positive that this same parasite will be found internally. Starts microscopic, then expands and grows and multiplies until…" Jake made a ball with his hands and then burst it, opening his fingers and spreading them apart.

"That is… quite interesting," Edemza said. "And I assure you, I knew nothing of this thing."

"Did you recently change providers for your medication?" Jake asked.

"Are you implying that whatever this is it's inside the medication I give my patients?"

Ignoring Jake's earlier request, Eliza spoke. "Well, Dr. Edemza, we think it might be the case—"

"You *think*?"

"Sorry, yes. We're still working on the details, which is why we came to you. We're starting to realize that the parasite is not contagious, at least in a traditional sense. It must be transmitted via direct contact between surface and host, or by oral ingestion."

"Because it is not contagious," Edemza said thoughtfully. The room fell silent, and he looked up and over Jake's head. "Well, I apologize. I will not be of any help to you today."

CHAPTER 38

"Come again?"

"I just said I will not be able to help you."

"You don't agree that medication would be a perfect way to transfer the parasite into hosts?" Eliza asked.

"Oh, no, I never said that. I *do* believe it would be a success-ful—if expensive and a bit over-engineered— vehicle for the infection."

"Then why—"

"But *I* did no such thing. You can check the medications yourself. Typical antihistamines, acetaminophen, albuterol. I do not run a pharmacy here. There are very few things I am allowed to treat in the patients I see. General painkillers and refills on the drugs they are carrying with them when they enter the country are typically what I administer. Children have inhalers, adults usually need something to get rid of the constant throbbing headache of moving their entire lives across a well-protected border."

"We get it," Jake said. "So, medicine would work as a vehicle for the parasite, but you are claiming to be innocent."

Edemza leaned forward, his chair creaking, and looked directly into Jake's eyes. "I *am* innocent," he said. "And, I might add, this is exactly the sort of 'America' I wanted to fight against. The kind that assumes everyone who wants to enter this country is a crook. Most of us *know* that is not true, but our systems don't seem to reflect that belief."

He's losing it, Jake thought. *He might crack. We just might get a confession, after all.*

But whilst a confession would be nice, what Jake *really* needed—what every truly solved case needed—was a motive.

"These people come to this country because they need *help*, not persecution. And what do they find when they get here? A prison cell. A wall of bureaucracy a mile high, only because of the color of their skin. Waiting around for no one to save them—there is no one to save them here. This is a dead-end, Mr. Parker."

Jake wanted him to continue, to get to his point and confess, and he didn't want to interrupt the man. He felt Eliza shifting in her chair, knowing she must be feeling the same way.

"These men and women—and their children—they have been through *hell* to get here, because the lie they have been promised is the lie of a better life. *You* are part of this problem now, Mr.—"

"I'm just doing my job, Edemza," Jake said.

"You are doing *someone's* job, but you are simply adding more mess to the pile. Have you ever stopped to consider *why* you do the things you do? Is it because you read them in a book, and you just assumed that those who wrote the book are smarter than you? That they knew the answers already?" He paused. "My job here is to help people. It always has been. Not everyone who comes through these doors is well-intentioned, but to assume the worst, *first*, is a woefully misguided oversight."

Jake took a long, deep breath. He closed his eyes. *This guy might just rant instead,* he thought.

"My point is this: I am being held here against my will. No charges have been prepared against me. Yet I am not free to go. Why is that? Is it because of my *own* skin color? Because I was born in a country that is currently at war with *this* country?"

Jake couldn't help himself. "Maybe it's because we know of your involvement with a terrorist organization."

Edemza suddenly stopped, his mouth falling open, appalled. "I… I cannot believe… *this* is the charge you throw at me now?"

"Do you deny it?"

Jake watched Edemza's face melt into fear, surprise, confusion. And then sadness. He saw the man blink multiple times. His eyes filled with tears.

"How… how can I deny anything? You come at me with charges—accusations—that are so far from the truth you cannot even hear evidence against it. I have done nothing wrong and yet I am accused of betraying the very country that has allowed me to succeed. All for what? For some assumption that I am behind this just because a cousin I have not seen since I was a boy is involved in an organization your country deems to be 'terroristic'?"

Jake felt a lump rising in his throat. He imagined Mel sitting next to him, hearing this man's passion and commitment to his story, his beliefs. He knew Mel would believe him. That had been her superpower—empathy.

Jake had learned some of it from her, but it still wasn't second nature. He wanted this man to be innocent, but he wasn't sure why.

"I am no terrorist, my friends," Edemza continued. His voice had fallen, and Jake imagined it echoed his thoughts. "I did not infect any of my patients."

"Do you have proof of that?" Jake asked. "We want to believe you, but—"

"Proof? Of course, but I fear that it will not be enough, that you will simply disregard my truth for the truth *you* wish to believe."

"Edemza, just help us make a case that you're innocent."

"The medicine," he sighed. "It's all still with my equipment. It has not been touched, as far as I know. You will see that the medications have not been tampered with. If anyone has become ill by my hand, I assure you it was outside my realm of knowledge. But there is no way I could have done such a thing. It is impossible."

"It could have been someone you didn't even know. Someone that wanted to use you—"

"*No*," Edemza stressed. "It is impossible. My pharmaceutical provider changed recently, but, again, your claims are impossible."

Jake filed away the details of the sentence: *My pharmaceutical provider changed recently.* He made a mental note to look further into that fact later as he continued the investigation.

"Why is that?"

"Because of the Stermers. The couple I saw that night, who are now dead because of this parasite. I'm telling you it is impossible that *I* gave it to them, because I did not give them any medication."

"You didn't?" Eliza asked.

Edemza shook his head. "They did not need anything. They were healthy, in good spirits, even. I simply asked them questions and was on my way."

Jake pushed his fingers against his forehead. He wanted to scream. He wanted to push his chair over and break something. He'd come here to get answers. Now he had only more questions.

This isn't how this was supposed to go, he thought. They had real reason to suspect that Edemza was actually involved, and now he'd just blown it all up.

Sure, they needed to verify it first. It would be easy enough to do. Check the inventories and compare them. But then what? Did it prove anything other than what Edemza had already admitted? He had a feeling Edemza's story would check out. He had a feeling the man was telling the truth.

If the medication had been replaced with a pill form of the parasite, the Stermers *hadn't* gotten it from Edemza, unless he was lying. Jake had no reason not to believe him, but the main problem was that it would be nearly impossible to prove.

He couldn't question a corpse.

CHAPTER 39

Shaw was doing his best to keep the two others at the table calm. Jake sat across from him, while Eliza sat to Shaw's left. They were once again in the hotel's bar, a sort of makeshift office where the three could gather and share updates on the case face-to-face. Although it was lunchtime, none of the team ordered food.

Dr. Saiid Edemza was still being held in the ICE criminal investigation offices, to be released as soon as his charges were dropped. When that would be, no one knew. Shaw felt for the man—if he were actually innocent—as he knew he could potentially be locked up for a month or more, awaiting acquittal from ICE prosecutors.

Jake had wanted to debrief over the phone, to keep working, but Shaw had information to give him—plus, he knew Jake would work himself to death if there weren't some built-in breaks throughout the week.

Reluctantly, Jake had agreed. Shaw had distributed cups of coffee all around without them asking.

Eliza had switched to tea, and Jake had reached over and started working on her untouched cup of coffee.

"Hey, Jake, come on man. Take it easy."

Jake looked over the mug at Shaw.

"You okay? You seem like you're stressed."

"*Stressed?*" Jake asked. "You're kidding, right? We're dealing with something *crazy* here, man. Something neither of us has ever seen."

Shaw held his hands up. "Okay, I get it. Sorry. I'm stressed too, I guess. It's weird, for sure. We're cops, not professional disease-studiers."

Eliza raised her hand. "*I'm* a professional disease-studier. And there's a name for it. In this case, it's epidemiologist."

"I thought you were a parasitologist?" Jake asked.

She looked across the table at Shaw's ex-partner. "You going to defend the difference in court?"

"Wow, okay," Jake said. "Guess we're all stressed." He focused once again on Shaw. "Point is, we weren't hired by Briggs to *prevent* this thing from killing more people. Not necessarily. We were hired to find out what it is, which we've done, and then find the asshole who made it."

"Right," Shaw said. "But besides that, it doesn't seem to be killing a lot of people. Is that what you two figured out?"

"Pretty much," Eliza replied. "It's not spreading like a typical parasitic infection. It's slow but it's deadly. Targeted, it seems, since the cases we've seen are of people who aren't really related to one another, besides the Stermers."

"Meaning that whoever's put it out there is planning to put *more* of it out there," Shaw added.

Jake and Eliza looked at him. He felt as though all eyes in the small lobby had suddenly turned to him.

"I told Briggs about the Boston PD comm data system." Jake nodded, and Shaw knew he remembered the software he was referring to—the online database their department used to track and follow developing intelligence, as well as share it with other departments around the state and nation.

"I found something. I think it's useful, but it's hard to tell. It was in Spanish, and then coded for secrecy."

"Sounds useful to me," Jake said. Shaw heard the edge coming into his voice.

"Again, relax. It's probably something, but it's not something *we* can do anything about. Briggs is already acting on it, so we can keep moving forward with our investigation. From what we were able to decode, it seems like there will be some sort of attack or incident in Dilley, Texas. Within the next couple of days, or sooner."

Jake frowned. "What's in Dilley?"

"Normally, nothing. A place no one wants to go. But in this case, it's relevant. There's an ICE facility there. The biggest one in the United States."

Eliza almost spit out her tea. "The *biggest* one in the US? Shaw— that seems like pretty important information, if you ask me."

"Why? What would you have done about it? Like I said, this isn't our mission—Briggs has a team of operatives, ICE and a local SWAT team, I believe, tasked with getting there and figuring out what's going down. As you said, we're not messing with that. *Our* mission is figuring out who created, developed, and spread this thing, and why."

"And where they're hiding," Jake said. "So, there won't be any more *incidents*."

Shaw nodded slowly.

"Any idea what this incident is going to be, specifically? I mean, I assume 'infect lots of people' is somehow involved, but... how?" Eliza asked.

"No idea. The message wasn't an explanation but just a snippet of communication. Just a single line in Spanish and then coded. My assumption, though? This is related to the parasite. It has to be."

"Why do you say that?" Jake asked. "This could just be another dead-end."

Again, Shaw nodded. "Sure, I guess that's within the realms of possibility. But you're a detective, Jake. We follow these kinds of leads. Even if Briggs doesn't find anything related to this case, he'll likely find *something*. And the fact that it was in Spanish? That suggests we've got a Mexican national or some bent-out-of-shape

Mexican-American working for a cartel or another pissed-off group. If they're trying to get a foothold in the US and do some *real* damage, it's an easy way in."

Eliza frowned. "What's an easy way in?"

"Using ICE," Jake said. "If they're in Mexico, like Shaw thinks, and they want to cause a lot of damage relatively quickly, it's pretty reasonable to assume coming in through immigration is an easy access point for them. Especially a facility in Texas."

"Exactly what I'm thinking. But that's my news; and, like I said, Briggs is on it," Shaw said. "What did you guys find out about Edemza?"

"Nothing that'll put him behind bars without more evidence," Jake replied. "The guy seems innocent. Passionate, but innocent. Unless we can dig up proof that he *did* administer medication to the Stermers, I think he's telling the truth."

"Even the terrorist stuff?" Shaw asked. "I could've sworn there would be something there."

Jake just shrugged. "Who knows? Maybe he's got a cousin who's into some bad stuff back home."

"Yeah," Shaw said, "but those databases aren't just some Excel spreadsheet in Washington D.C. that any old intern can access. It takes just short of an executive order to get someone added or taken off the list. The fact that he's on it means he's into some pretty bad shit."

"Yeah, well, I disagree. If you recall, my gut never failed me on this sort of thing. It was part of what made me good enough to make detective so quickly. The guy's innocent, okay?"

Shaw couldn't argue with that. He and everyone else they used to work with had experienced instances where they'd disagreed with Jake's gut, and they'd all been proven wrong. The man's instinct wasn't what made him *good*—it made him the best.

But right now, what bothered Shaw most was that he was feeling like the odd man out. He could tell that Jake and Eliza were feeling pretty comfortable with one another, and he wasn't necessarily upset by it. But the fact that he was consistently playing third wheel, consistently playing catch-up with these two—or being left out in the cold entirely—was starting to irk him.

"I'm glad you're taking this seriously, Jake," Shaw said. "But don't start attacking *me*."

"I wasn't—"

"We're in this together, man, remember? We're on the same team."

"Never said we weren't."

Shaw held up his hands. "I'm trying to do my job, just like you are trying to do yours. But the fact of the matter is you're acting like you used to act. You're taking everything so damn seriously, like the world's out to get you."

Shaw watched Jake seethe across the table from him. Eliza was busy examining her tea, probably trying to pretend she wasn't there. Jake didn't respond, and while Shaw didn't want to lay into the man, he wanted to make sure he got his point across.

"You know what your problem is?" Shaw asked.

Jake cocked an eyebrow. "What's that, Shaw?"

"You're too damn smart for your own good. Sometimes cases are open and shut. Sometimes they are as simple as some stupid message in Spanish telling us what's going to happen next, and you don't want to stop and listen to the truth of it. You don't want to do anything unless it's hard. Unless you can feel like you got some sort of intellectual victory out of it."

Jake sucked on his teeth for a second, then started to stand. "You done?"

"Yeah, brother, I guess I am."

"Fine. I'm going up to my room, to try to parse all of this shit and figure out what we should do next. Let me know if you get any other secret messages."

Jake looked as though he were about to speak again, but Eliza glared at him, shook her head, and motioned toward the lobby.

Shaw sat silent as Jake and Eliza stood up from the table and walked toward the elevators.

CHAPTER 40

It had been a solid five minutes of sitting in Jake's hotel room before Eliza spoke up, allowing him some time to decompress and figure out what exactly was on his mind.

"Want to tell me what that was about?" she asked.

Jake's eyes fell in her direction, but he didn't speak.

"I know you two were partners once, but I figured you'd let bygones be bygones."

"You're going to have to lay it out for me," Jake said. "We were just having a conversation. Talking about the case, trying to figure out what to do—"

Eliza cut him off before he could finish. "Bullshit, Jake. I'm no expert, but that was *past*. Between both of you. Whatever baggage you guys are carrying, it's going to hurt the investigation. You almost just ran off our best asset."

"Who? Shaw? He's a good cop, but—"

Eliza jerked her head up. "Actually, I was talking about you. *You're* the one who almost lost his head. What's the deal? Is it your…?" She immediately felt the sensation of shoving her entire foot into her mouth. She regretted even starting the sentence, so she hoped that by finishing it short it would be enough.

"My… *what*?" Jake asked. "My dead wife? Is *that* what you think I'm worried about right now? Do you think I'm moping around every minute of every day thinking about nothing but my wife?" She could see his hand starting to shake.

"Jake, no. I—"

"Do you think that because my wife was killed by the same department I worked for that I can't do my job now? Do you think that because Shaw was my ex-partner I'm somehow compromised?"

Eliza wasn't sure what to say. She was getting details about Jake's past that she wasn't sure she wanted now. She didn't know any of this. She had only meant to try to bring Jake back down to earth, to get him to calm down and realize that they needed to keep a level head in this situation.

On the other hand, she knew that he of all people understood that. He, a trained and experienced detective—a trained *soldier*— would know when and how to keep a level head, in just about any situation. She'd seen that so far in him, and she admired it. Yet he had somehow lost it in the past half-hour and now she felt they were racing down a path at a speed they wouldn't be able to control.

Jake turned to face Eliza head-on. "You think that just because you've met someone who's lost a loved one that you know me, is that it? You know all the right things to say—you've read them and heard them from other people, so you think those words are what's going to be helpful right now?"

Eliza felt like Jake was waiting for her to interject, to offer some sort of rebuttal. Instead, he continued.

"You think you know me, just like everyone else who runs into me and hears my story. You think that somehow you are special, that you of all people can help me get through this."

"I don't think that at all, Jake," Eliza said.

"Yeah, well, you're acting like it."

Now Eliza was starting to feel ticked off. "Careful, Jake."

"Careful? What the hell is that supposed to—"

She felt the inner turmoil begin to rise up within her, the anxiety and anger coming to a head and starting to spill out. She hated Jake for making her feel like this, but ultimately she knew it wasn't his fault. She wanted to calm down, to take some time to explain herself properly. But Jake had not given her that luxury.

"Listen, Jake. I feel you. I feel *for* you. I can't imagine what it feels like to lose someone. Especially like that. I hate that that happened to you, Jake," she said. "But I learned a long time ago that it does nothing to pity someone. It does nothing to feel sorry for them."

Jake swallowed, looked out the hotel room window, then turned back to her. "I know. I'm sorry."

"The truth is this case means more to me than you can ever know. Just like you've got your demons, your own past? I do, too. Mine doesn't involve death or spouses, but it does involve family."

"What do you mean?" Jake asked.

"When Shaw mentioned that the coded message he found was in Spanish? Jake, look at me. I am *Mexican-American*. I was born here, but my parents weren't. I've struggled with trying to figure out my place in this weird, messed-up world since I was a kid. I didn't become a brilliant doctor *because* of my background, but *in spite* of it. I grew up with privileges a lot of other kids didn't, but the color of my skin and my last name wasn't one of them.

"I knew people who hated me in college because they assumed I was an 'affirmative action kid,' someone who got in because I have a Mexican name instead of because of my brain. And more often than not, those same people seemed to forget that their white, rich parents sat on the university's board or donated a ton of money to the school every year, or whatever."

Jake chewed his lip. "Sorry," he said. "I didn't think about it that way."

"It's fine, really. In the whole scheme of things, my experience wasn't that bad. Most people don't consider this stuff—it's how we got to where we are. I'm proud of who I became, but I know for a fact that the *vast* majority of the kids in this system now, the ones we're trying to help, aren't going to get *remotely* the same opportunities as I did. Because the system's broken. Because where they're from isn't *here*."

He nodded. "So this whole case means a lot more to you than I realized, then."

"Well, yeah. I have the opportunity to really make a difference in people's lives—people who look like me and who are from the same places as my family. They didn't have the leg-up I did, and if I can do anything at all to change it, I want to. It's not going to completely equalize everything on the planet, but if we can figure out what this thing is all about, we might be able to stop it from getting worse."

"So you think this case is about racism, about privilege, and our enemy is someone trying to cause a pandemic in the United States? I'm not sure. It just doesn't seem to add up."

She didn't speak for a few seconds. "It *does* add up."

"How so?"

"Jake, think about it: if you wanted to take out half the US population with some sort of super drug, you make a disease that's incredibly easy to catch, with a long incubation and ramp-up period, and you make it deadly. That's what a virus is perfect for—it not only infects the host, it infects the vector as well. That's why zika, malaria, those types of mosquito-caused diseases are so dangerous; the virus spreads by infecting the carrier and that carrier infects the host. Other viruses aren't as cruel—they need a droplet from one host to land on another, or by some other direct-transmission mechanism."

Jake's eyes narrowed as he considered this. "Right. But *our* disease—a parasite—is passed on differently, specifically in its smallest, microscopic form, by contact or ingestion. And when it grows large enough to start killing the host, it's no longer able to infect another person. At least not until it breaks out and somehow gets its baby parasites into the world."

"Precisely," she said. "All of that is to say we're dealing with something that's extremely *deadly*, but not something extremely *infectious*. The R-naught is far too low, even with just a handful of cases."

Jake shook his head. "Which means whoever put it into the ICE facilities is specifically trying to harm immigrants. The people in that system."

"A relatively closed system."

She saw the recognition on Jake's face as she said it, and his eyes lit up. "By planting this thing in multiple entry points inside a closed system, it has a higher chance of infecting the people within it."

"And not infecting anyone *not* in it—in this case, the rest of the American population."

"Jesus," Jake said. "No wonder Briggs is worried."

"He should be. If whatever's going to happen in Dilley goes ahead, and if it's related to this parasite in any way, it's going to be a catastrophe."

"And it's a political statement as well, now," Jake added.

"A very powerful one, yes."

CHAPTER 41

Jake was still thinking about what Eliza had said, but he felt the urge to shift gears a bit to lighten up the mood. "It's weird to be working a case and yet not have to check in with a boss or three."

She scoffed. "Yeah, tell me about it. I've got a dean breathing down my neck about something called 'student reports'—trust me, you don't want to know—and a lab tech asking for next-semester credentials for an online portal."

Jake smiled. "That sounds... fun. But the good news is that after all of this crap, you'll get to go back to your normal life and hang out with your husband and 2.3 kids and dog."

She frowned at him. "Is that... some sort of slight against my personal life, or a weird way of asking if I've got a significant other?"

"Both?" Jake said.

She stared him down, then broke out into a laugh. "You know for a *fact* no other human can survive long-term occupancy with me," she said. "And if I even had a *hamster*, I would have trained it to defend my domain against those assholes who broke in."

"Or you would have lost it in all that junk."

She stuck her tongue out at him.

"So... *not* married?"

"Not married," she answered. "Never have been, never will..."

"Too much work?"

She shrugged. "Yeah, I guess. I don't know. I guess I've just always believed that I couldn't have *both*, you know? Be super successful, achieve all my dreams, take over the world and all that, *and* be married."

"Well, I mean, if your ultimate victory is world domination, yeah—I think you're going to have to stay single." He cracked a grin. "Besides," he teased, "I can't imagine anyone wanting to marry you."

"Excuse me?"

"Well, think about it—you're like a walking Web-MD. Can you imagine? Anytime I get sick, you'd be ready to go with all the ways it could be deadly: virus, bacterial infection, never-before-seen parasite from the bottom of the ocean…"

"Anytime *you* get sick?" she asked, a sly grin appearing on her face.

Shit. "I mean, anytime *they* got sick. Whoever it might be. But, like I said, I can't imagine there's anyone out there…"

"Got it," she said, turning back to look out of the window. "Note to self: no one likes me. Never get married."

Jake laughed loudly. "That's absolutely *not* what I was implying, by the way. I'm sure there's another super-nerd parasite-studying professor out there. Just for you. Handsome, too."

She glared at him. "Have you ever *seen* any male parasitologists?"

"Uh, no. Can't say I have."

"Right. So why don't you get back to me when you find one worth marrying."

They laughed and then turned their attention back to their phones, checking emails and messages for any updates on their case or their lives outside of work. Since Jake had almost none of the latter, he was finished first.

"Hey, I totally forgot my laptop charger. Mind if I use yours if it's still in your car?"

"Not at all," she said, shifting and locating the purse that was hanging over the back of the chair. She pulled it onto her lap and retrieved the keys. "You have to go grab it, though. I've got a few more emails to type." She slid the keys across the table. "Mostly to ripped, sexy, bachelor parasitologists who are just waiting around for a female colleague to reach out."

Jake smiled down at her as he stood, grabbing the keys.

"I'm positive that Dr. Sexy-sitologist is just an email away."

CHAPTER 42

Eliza's car was parked near the entrance to the hotel, about fifteen feet away. Jake pressed the button on the key fob and the car lit up with a ping.

He strode to the passenger's side of the vehicle and opened the door, seeing the charger through the window as the door swung open. It was folded neatly in the laptop shoulder bag's large back pocket, and he had his hand on it in a few seconds.

As he pulled his hand back, clutching the charger and cable, something struck him as odd.

He couldn't place it, but something nagged at him as he retracted his hand from the bag. He'd learned to not ignore such things, the subtle subconscious cues. As a detective, he had been trained to notice the minor, hidden characteristics of a scene. They were exactly the things that he needed to pay the most attention to.

But there wasn't anything obviously *wrong*. The car was a car, the bag was a bag, and the charger he was holding wasn't about to turn into a scorpion and stick him in the neck.

And yet... something screamed at him. Silently and loudly, all at once.

He used a trick his mentor, Jorge, had once told him. Jake remembered the time and place he'd first heard it. "Blur the lines," Jorge had told him, puffing on a huge, bold cigar he'd purchased during a vacation to Nicaragua. "Blur the lines, and the unseen becomes seen."

It had bought him a few cases in the past, and most likely a few lives, as well.

Now, as he hovered half-in, half-out of Eliza Mendoza's car, he invoked the old detective's memory. *What is it about this car that makes it something to pay attention to?*

He tried the trick: squeezing his eyes into a blurred version of reality, forcing them to lose focus. He played with the amount; he wanted to still see, but he needed to see the bigger picture, to allow his subconscious to take over.

After a few seconds, he gave up. There was nothing here.

Jake stood and decided to ignore his inner detective, for now. There were always false positives: things that seemed suspicious but were simply out of place—accidental or otherwise. Perhaps not everything in life needed to be cross-examined or studied from a thousand different angles.

He held the charger in one hand as he swung the door closed, still looking through the non-tinted glass into the car's front seats. As the door slammed shut, the car shook.

And *there*—something caught his eye.

What the hell?

The voice inside his head was screaming at him to investigate, to follow its lead. Jake couldn't shake the feeling, so he focused on where his eyes had called his attention.

It was a pair of electrical wires hanging from beneath the car's steering column, halfway underneath the dash. It was the ignition cable and ground wire, and he noticed the two standard wire connectors—white and strikingly obvious against the car's dark interior.

His mind raced. This car was new—no more than a few years old—so it was unlikely the tiny clips that were supposed to hold these wires inside of the dashboard had already dried out and deteriorated. These cables should still have been mounted up and away, out of sight.

And he was quite positive that Eliza hadn't hot-wired her vehicle recently.

That left few possibilities, and the one that seemed most likely was the worst of all.

He walked around to the front of the vehicle and approached the driver's side door, looking down through the window. He knew Eliza's car had been locked, but that didn't mean someone couldn't have found a way to break in without leaving much of a mark. Still, in case someone *had* broken in and left fingerprints on the handle, he pulled his shirt out and placed his hand under it, then gently pulled the handle up with just the tips of his fingers underneath it.

The handle clicked and the car door fell open a crack.

Jake looked inside, kneeling down onto the asphalt of the parking lot. He saw the two wires and their connectors, suddenly wondering why the two wires had been connected *here* rather than farther up the steering column, or farther back, where they would be more out of sight.

And then he saw it.

Two of the electrical wires spilling out of the standard connectors were the traditional green and yellow wires. These ran back up and through the firewall to the battery and starter. Put the key in the ignition, turn it, and the circuit is closed.

But he noticed something else. Two different wires, both black and both nearly invisible against the dark interior, ran along the inside of the car and down toward the carpet. There, they turned and ran up the side of the seat on the floor, and then just over the rubber weatherstripping.

Jake traced the cable with his eyes as he pulled his head closer to the ground. He had a hunch as to what he would find, but he needed to know for sure.

He pulled his head to the side and glanced up at the underside of the vehicle, still following the lines of the two electrical wires as they disappeared into the black abyss of the car's undercarriage.

But unlike the rest of the blackened and oil-stained undercarriage components, there was something that stood out and caught his eye immediately.

Something that definitely *wasn't* a vehicle component.

He heard footsteps, and saw Eliza's feet moving toward him quickly from the front of the hotel.

"Jake?" he heard her yell. "Jake, are you still out here?"

Jake pulled himself back and turned his head toward the side of the building to echo his voice. "Eliza!" he shouted. "Stop! Don't move."

He saw her feet land onto the asphalt and come to a halt, fifteen or twenty feet away from the car. "What is it?" she called out.

Jake's mind raced. He needed to call this in; he needed to get the Albany Police Department here, and have their dispatch get the SWAT team ready, as well as the BDU—Bomb Disposal Unit.

But he wasn't a cop. He no longer had a radio. He no longer had a badge. Nothing that would allow him to get things moving any more quickly than a civilian.

"Eliza," he said, speaking loudly so she could hear, "I need you to call 911. Do it now, tell them where we are and tell them there's a bomb. Okay?"

"*A bomb?*"

"Yes. I can't tell you more right now. Just call it in and then get across the street. In that coffee shop. And call Shaw."

Jake didn't wait to see if Eliza had followed his instructions. He pulled his head back down and examined the bomb. Standard amateur work, like he'd seen before—a pipe bomb, likely filled with a fertilizer-and-fuel payload, just waiting for a spark of ignition. And judging by its size, there was enough mixture inside to take out the entire vehicle and a chunk of the hotel as well, not to mention the other vehicles parked nearby and whatever damage the debris would cause.

He looked up, realizing that his own room was a couple of floors straight up: directly above where the blast would have been.

While the bomb's build itself seemed amateur, using materials found at any hardware store and likely slapped together, Jake also recognized the craftsmanship of the wiring itself. Each of the ignition and ground wires had been severed and shunted together cleanly, using small, white, standard connectors. And the cabling matched the carpeting and rugs in the vehicle. They'd even taken the time to push the wires up against the corner of the rug and carpet on the floor of the inside of her car. They would have been almost impossible to spot had he not caught sight of the two white connectors in his peripheral vision.

Jake pulled back and stood up. If he hadn't caught it, whoever had planted the bomb would have gotten away with murder.

Eliza's murder.

He couldn't imagine why someone would want her dead, and he also hadn't forgotten about the two intruders from before.

Someone out there wanted to make sure Eliza was off this case. But who? And why?

CHAPTER 43

Jake hadn't watched Eliza run across the street to the coffee shop in the small shopping center, but he assumed that she'd entered and disappeared into the mass of people inside. He had left his phone in his room, but there was no way he was going back for it with a live bomb sitting out here in the parking lot. He wanted to warn Shaw inside the hotel, but he couldn't leave the bomb unattended. Instead, he walked to the opposite side of the parking lot and waited for the police to arrive, watching the car the entire time.

Surprisingly, they arrived only two minutes later, much more quickly than the average response time. He waved the officer down and the two exchanged introductions.

Jake gave the officer some details about the investigation without revealing too much, then waited for the officer's backup and SWAT to arrive. When they did, two officers entered the hotel and began evacuating all of the patrons and employees out the back exits. The evacuation took place over the course of the next hour, and Jake was asked questions for an additional half-hour after that. Finally, after nearly two hours of standing in the sun on the hot asphalt of the parking lot, Jake was able to retrieve his laptop and phone from his room.

He returned and walked around the building toward the highway and crossed the street.

He needed to make sure Eliza was okay. He hadn't heard from her at all, and he hoped she was still waiting for him inside.

He entered the coffee shop and was greeted by a friendly but frantic-looking young woman. Her face spoke volumes—clearly she wanted to get out of this place and run away. Every minute, more police cars were entering the parking lot across the street.

"You from across the street?" she asked.

He nodded.

"They—they said… I mean, someone came in and said… that we would be fine here, but it looks like they're evacuating the entire hotel."

Jake tried to calm her down with a careful smile. "They were right" he said, his voice low so others couldn't hear. "You're going to be fine. There's just a tiny little bomb under a car." He shrugged. "No idea why it's there, but it's not big enough to do any damage way over here. The police didn't want to terrify the entire block, so they want everyone to just stay put and stay calm."

The young woman gulped and in a slightly faltering voice asked if he wanted anything to drink. He declined. He couldn't see Eliza, but the place was packed, filled mostly with people from the hotel who were watching as the SWAT team and BDU worked on the vehicle.

As he walked through the establishment, out of the corner of his eye he saw a news truck pull into the shopping center parking lot. He shook his head. *Damn ambulance chasers,* he thought. *Making a buck off other people's misery.*

He took another glance around, finally realizing that Eliza wasn't here. *Strange.* He had told her to wait across the street, and he knew she had gone toward the shop. There would have been no doubt as to which coffee shop he was talking about—this was the only one in sight. Was there a back exit? And if there was, why would she take it? And if she had left their scheduled meeting spot, why?

He walked toward the back of the building and found a hallway with two restrooms, as well as a door that led to a tiny kitchen.

He waited for a minute by the restrooms, but soon both doors opened and two people—neither of them Eliza—walked out.

He pushed the door to the kitchen open and found the exit to his left. No one was in the kitchen at the moment, so he simply walked through and opened the back door, finding himself on a short stoop looking out over a back-alley parking lot, large dumpsters to his right and left.

But still no Eliza.

His mind had been racing since he had seen the bomb—even before, really—and he didn't want to have to worry about Eliza on top of all of that. She was a grown woman, capable of taking care of herself. Yet she had been through hell these past couple of days.

And now she would have realized that someone wanted to kill her. This was beyond breaking into her home to scare her.

She would be terrified to say the least, but why then would she run somewhere else? Perhaps she had decided to move to one of the buildings farther away?

His phone dinged and he felt it vibrate in his pocket. He pulled it out, glancing at the screen. Jake felt a wave of relief come over him when he saw that the text message was from Eliza.

But when he read her message, all the anxiety and confusion returned.

Shaw.

There was nothing else, no other message. Nothing to give him any clue as to where Eliza might have gone.

What was worse, the word only made the entire situation more difficult to understand.

What *about* Shaw? Was she with Shaw? If so, why not just tell him that she'd met up with him? Why not give him their location? He hadn't considered Shaw the entire time he'd been dealing with the car bomb, and now Jake realized he may have been involved in this whole mess.

He shook his head. No, it was all too strange. The car bomb in the parking lot. Eliza gone. A message about his ex-partner.

He pulled the phone up to call Eliza, but after half a ring, the line went straight to voicemail.

Shit, he thought.

He felt things spiraling out of control; he felt the prod of anxiety becoming a dull roar beneath the surface of his mind. He needed to stop and slow down, figure out how to get a handle on it before it was too late. Before he cracked.

He forced himself to breathe. *You've been through worse, Parker,* he told himself. *You've seen much worse and you've come out the other side fine.*

The statement was true, as was the sentiment, yet there was a difference between the police work he'd done before and now. Back then as a detective, while he sometimes missed the nonstop action of a Boston PD cop, he did appreciate the ability he had to distance himself from his cases. Often, in a murder investigation, the murder was over and done long before he was brought to the case. Unless they were trying to track down some sort of twisted psychopathic serial killer, the murder was often accidental or a single premeditated homicide, with little danger that the killer would strike again.

Those cases gave him the ability to think through situations and put together the pieces without them changing in the middle of the game. But now, here, he was *part* of the case. Eliza had been targeted, which meant that *he* had been targeted. When he had chased off those two intruders in her home, he and Eliza had chalked it up to just someone wanting to scare her away from this investigation. But the stakes had just been raised.

He tried Eliza again, but once more it went straight to voice-mail. This time he left a message for her, telling her to call him as soon as possible. And yet, as he did it, he had a strange feeling return. The subtle cue that he'd grown to respect. It was telling him something. Something about the text message.

Was Beau Shaw connected to what had happened? Was he somehow responsible for the bomb? For the intruders? Had Shaw *abducted* Eliza for some reason?

The implications made Jake want to vomit. This was the man he'd called his best friend and partner for years. They hadn't been estranged for long, either, so he found it hard to believe Shaw had completely changed in so little time. Or did it mean that he'd never *truly* known his friend? Not well enough, anyway. *Was he even capable of such a thing?* If so, what game was he playing? What could he want with Eliza now? And if he wanted her dead…

Those thoughts were on Jake's mind as he traversed the length of the alley, hoping to switch back around and get to his own vehicle. He hoped the police officers still in the parking lot would let him leave without more questions.

He lifted his phone and pressed on his friend's face, immediately initiating a call. As he'd expected, it went straight to voicemail. No ringing.

Shaw had purposefully shut off his phone—it would be too much of a coincidence to assume that the phone had simply run out of juice and died.

Jake wanted to scream in frustration. All he had so far were questions—he didn't need more of them. He couldn't answer the questions *he* was struggling with—he certainly didn't need more variables that only further complicated things.

He pulled his phone up again and ran a quick search. He found the number he wanted and then tapped on the screen to initiate the call.

It connected in two rings. "Albany Police Department, how may I help you?"

CHAPTER 44

After Jake had called in Eliza's disappearance and explained who he was, the operator asked him to drop by. The captain was in and could help him—Jake was considered a minor celebrity to police departments in the region, as he'd been run through the wringer during the lawsuit, when Jake's lawyer had simply wanted reparations from Mel's death and uncovered negligence in his own department. Jake had agreed, and fifteen minutes later, he was inside the office of Albany's Finest.

The interior of the Albany Police Department's Central Branch office looked almost identical in every way to what Jake had imagined. A smaller version of Boston. One single holding cell, desks spread across an open room, an offset interrogation chamber down a hallway, two large offices at the far end of the room opposite the entrance. It wasn't a large station, but it did a lot of business. The place was full when he arrived, and some of the officers on duty seemed to recognize him as he entered. They would—his face had been plastered across newspaper headlines for almost a year during the trial.

Jake was inside one of the main office rooms now. He sat across a large desk from the station's captain while the man, comfortably overweight in his mid-fifties, tapped away at a computer.

"I remember your case," the captain said. "Only a couple of years ago, right?"

"Yeah, almost two years ago." Jake shifted in his seat. He wondered if every police department in the United States was forced to purchase from the same catalog. The same chairs, the same faux mahogany desk, the same picture frames holding nearly the same portraits of each of the officers' families. "It's a different sort of case when you're the one everyone's investigating," Jake said.

"I can imagine," the captain said. "Couldn't believe it when I heard it. Seems awful. Sorry you had to go through all of it."

The investigation into his wife's death had led to endless back-and-forth briefings and preparatory meetings with attorneys from the city of Boston, his own precinct, and his personal representation. While the situation had never devolved into an all-out brawl, Jake remembered his time spent in lawyers' offices the same way he remembered the feeling of bile, just before he had to vomit.

Worse, the local news would not let up during the case either, even chasing him down as he left his home and returned later that day. They'd stalked him, waited for him, hoping to get a snippet of the story, so that they could try to weave their own fictional tapestry from a single strand of truth.

While his wife's death had been his worst nightmare, the prevailing investigation and the trial against the Boston Police Department's Counterterrorism Unit was a close second.

"I really appreciate you taking the time to check into this for me," Jake said, the speed of his words reflecting his desire to push things along quickly. "I know you've got all kinds of other things to deal with."

"You talking about that bomb in the parking lot?" the captain asked, chuckling. "No way in hell I would get to be anywhere *near* that case."

Jake eyed him curiously.

"Oh, I mean I *would*, but those cases don't come across my desk. They don't ever ask *me* to come out. You know how it is, son. Running a department is basically just herding cats for a paycheck. All the young guns get the good stuff, and I just sit here and file papers."

Jake watched the man's face as he typed away, the half-smile on his face disappearing after a few seconds. "Well, I appreciate your help now. I just need to know where to go next. I'm not sure who I can trust right now, so any help you can give me is going to be a huge step in the right direction."

"I have a feeling that's true," the captain said, watching Jake from the corner of his eye as he messed with the program on his screen. He turned his monitor so Jake could see. "Okay, I think I've got what you're looking for. Database says there were 14,372 text messages sent through the regional cellular array for your carrier in that particular two-minute span. I narrowed the area from New York to just Albany, and then to the smallest region I could get."

"That should be enough, right?" Jake asked. "From what I remember, we just need to get close so we can run the search and not have it take all day."

The captain nodded, his jowls shaking vigorously. "Yes, yes—although things have improved a bit after some recent updates. The search won't take long at all. No more waiting around half a day for it to spit out a 'yes' or 'no.' In fact…" The captain tapped another few keys and pressed "enter," and the computer displayed a single result. "Looks like that's you. '*Shaw*.' Sent at 3:25 in the afternoon. Sound about right?"

"Yeah, that's it for sure," Jake said. He had received the text from Eliza's phone, which was a Syracuse area code—315. But the number displayed on the origination receipt he was looking at now seemed to be one of the two from the Boston area—857. *Odd.* "Can you get the area code and phone number out of that longer string? It's hard to really know for sure with the delivery package receipt jumbled up with it."

"Of course," the captain said. "Here, looks like Boston. 857."

"Yeah, that's what I was afraid of."

"Oh?"

"Well, if it were *actually* from Eliza Mendoza's phone, it would have been a 315 number. But it's Boston, which means the number's been spoofed somewhere along the line."

The captain nodded. "Yeah, we've been seeing that a bit more lately. It's not cheap to do it the right way like this one—one number all the way to the origination point—but some spammers apparently make enough money sending junk text messages that it's worth it to just buy a spoofer relay system."

"Right," Jake said. "I don't think it's a spammer. Can we figure out who owns that phone number?" He had a feeling he knew exactly whose number it was, and there was a way to verify it sitting in his own pocket.

But he wanted to have a third-party validate it as well.

"Maybe, but we'll have to call the cellular company for that. I can at least get it started?"

Jake waved it off, pulling his own phone out. "No, that's fine, thanks. I'm pretty sure I know whose phone actually sent it. Why he would go and do all of this—set it up like this—I have no idea."

"Seems to be a real roundabout way to play a trick on someone," the captain said, eyeing Jake suspiciously. "Though, you probably aren't just in the middle of some random prank battle at the moment."

Jake shook his head. "No. Unfortunately not. I wish it were that simple, but I have a feeling this is just a way of baiting me into a bigger trap. I'm not sure why, and I'm not really sure how, but I've got that hunch."

Jake looked down at his phone, confirming his worst fears.

The captain was busy working on something on the computer, and when he finished he looked back at Jake. "Only other thing I have access to right here is some triangulation data. These are longitude and latitude coordinates, from the three closest cell towers from wherever the message was sent. It's not perfect, but it's probably as close as we're going to get to figuring out where it originated."

Jake watched as the man copied and pasted the coordinates into a map app on his machine, then pointed at the screen.

"The dots are—obviously—the locations of the towers. That message was sent from somewhere within this triangle, give or take about a mile in any direction. Wish there was more I could do, son. I hate that it's such a big area, but—"

"No worries." Jake stared at the map and the three dots that delineated the boundary of the originating message's cell towers.

He didn't need the captain's help any longer. He knew who had sent the message, and now he knew exactly where the message had been sent from: Jake recognized this area of downtown Boston immediately, and he knew whose apartment lay almost dead-center between these three dots.

"Thanks," Jake said as he rose from the chair, extending his hand. The captain stood and shook it with a firm, tight grip. "You've been more than helpful. I'll keep you posted, but I have a feeling I won't need to. This thing might get out of hand and in that case, *everyone's* going to hear about it."

The captain smiled. "I'm assuming you figured out where you need to go next?"

Jake nodded as he turned toward the door. "I do. Boston, and I can get there in a little over two hours. Time to go to my ex-partner's apartment, and figure out just what the hell he's up to."

CHAPTER 45

There were two major routes connecting Albany and Boston, and Jake had decided on the shorter of the two. Not only was it shorter, but Jake knew from experience that this particular highway was less patrolled than the northern route. Still, the drive was going to cost him another couple of hours.

That was important because he didn't feel like going slow. Today, of all days, was the first time he had ever looked at the speed limit as nothing more than a guideline. Early on in his career as a beat cop, he had pulled people over for going about five miles per hour over the limit. In the Army, the MPs on base would often pull folks over for going one or two miles per hour over, but most of them were jerks anyway.

He flew east on I-90, through Worcester and Auburndale and a thousand tiny towns in-between. The land grew to become more like his hometown of Hudson, looking like his favorite spot near the lake by Brister Freeman's old home. This was New England at its finest, and he was barreling through without even bothering to notice it.

He took the exit for 93, working his way toward the leather district and Essex Street. Shaw still lived in the same apartment he and his wife had shared since they were first married. Because they had never planned to have children, the place was appropriately sized for one or two people. Jake had been there dozens of times, and had always marveled at the industrial-yet-cozy brick-walled building.

As he pulled his car to the right to exit, he noticed someone behind him with their brights on. Strange, as it was only early evening, and there was still enough sunlight to see clearly.

Jake shook his head and continued to merge onto the ramp.

Suddenly, another car came out of nowhere, pulling over into his lane directly in front of him. They had crossed the boundary line separating the highway from the ramp and narrowly missed taking off a chunk of Jake's car.

"What the hell, man?" Jake yelled, swerving to the right to avoid an impact.

But the car in front of him matched his movements. The dark blue sedan, large and boat-like as it drifted side-to-side, kept in front of Jake. Every subtle move Jake would make, the car in front would match. He pressed on his brakes, yet the car simply slowed as well.

He felt a bump from behind, and he looked into the rearview mirror to see the first car that had flashed its lights at him, a matching hue of dark blue, had just rear-ended him.

Jake understood what was happening.

He darted to the left, his left tires bouncing off the asphalt and over the grassy median. At the same time, he sped up, slamming his foot down on the accelerator. Half-on, half-off the road, he tried to get around the car in the lead. The road ahead was empty, but there was a red light about a hundred yards ahead. The highway rose to his left, forming a bridge and a blind spot beneath it. Anyone coming from that direction wouldn't be able to stop in time.

Jake gritted his teeth. Toyota Corollas weren't known for their maneuverability in street races, but Jake hadn't been given a choice. He pulled up on the handbrake and pulled the wheel to the right a quarter-turn, glancing out the passenger side window as the two blue cars drew closer. It was going to be narrow, but if he was going to get away he needed to make a sharp turn in front of these guys and try to put some distance between them.

He hoped the handbrake was functional enough to at least give him a bit of control over the drift he was about to put himself in.

It wasn't.

The Corolla skidded sideways and began to spin out of control, just as the car closest to him tapped the back right corner of his vehicle. The impact caused Jake's head to smack against his window, and for a moment he let go of the steering wheel.

No longer being controlled, the car seemed to right itself and, thanking his lucky stars, Jack applied the brake, then the gas in turn. The tiny car shot forward again, hitting a curb but now facing a long straightaway. The back tire seemed to be limping a bit, but at least Jake was pointed in the right direction.

The two cars behind him had gotten tangled up as one of them hit Jake, and he made sure to focus on his speed, to get as far away as possible. He could see out the mirror that they were beginning to right themselves and resume their chase.

He barely recognized the street he was on, but he knew it was close to Shaw's place. He didn't have time to pull up his phone and get his bearings anyway, so he decided to just drive and try to lose his followers that way. He made a quick left turn, then a sharp right immediately after, and continued, parallel to the previous road he had been on.

He was heading toward the Seaport District and he knew that eventually he would run out of road.

By then, he had no idea what to do. Shaw was normally the one person he knew he could call in a situation like this, and yet he was the one person he trusted least at the moment.

Perhaps Briggs could help? He knew the man was connected, and could certainly pull some police cruisers away from their patrol and send them in his direction. But how long would that take? Was there even time to make the call?

As if answering his question, he caught sight of one of the sedans, once again picking up his lead.

Jake smacked the steering wheel with a palm. "Shit."

He couldn't remember his training for situations like this, aside from the typical "aim for tapping the back-quarter of the vehicle to spin it out of control," and "the best way to end a car chase is to never let them start in the first place." He knew he had spent some time behind the wheel in a mock car-chase scenario, but he wasn't recalling any useful tips at the moment.

Maneuverability had gotten more difficult now, as the buildings were taller and closer together. There were also people walking up and down the street, some stopping to determine the reason for the loud, speeding vehicles.

Just ahead, he saw another red light, and a large, lumbering moving van pushing into the intersection. Next to the van was a line of cars and trucks, spaced close enough together that continuing straight was not going to be an option.

Maybe there's time, he thought. *If I can just get…*

Jake narrowed his eyes and focused on the road, eyeing the corner of the intersection to make sure there were no people standing and waiting to walk across. It looked open, so he made the snap decision before his logical and rational mind talked him out of it.

He jerked the wheel to the right and hopped the curb, cutting the corner of the intersection and speeding forward, landing back on the street after a right turn, just in front of the accelerating white van.

The van honked, but Jake was already moving into the left lane, planning to continue putting as much space between him and the other two vehicles in chase. So far, the plan had worked.

He looked back over his right shoulder, seeing that the two cars had been forced to slam on their brakes after the white van had passed. He looked at the face of the man driving one of the blue vehicles, focusing on it just before the van pulled into his blind spot and blocked his view.

But the look he got was long enough. He recognized the face immediately.

It was one of the same men who had broken into Eliza's house and attacked her. Something told Jake they were no longer playing games, no longer trying to scare her or both of them.

Any of their reckless actions could have sent Jake and his car careening into a building, or a street light, or caused serious damage to other pedestrians.

Whoever these men were, they were no longer messing around.

They wanted him dead.

CHAPTER 46

"How far would you go for something you believe in?"

Shaw started to say something more, but Eliza heard footsteps outside. *Running.*

Within seconds, they were at the door. Eliza screamed as she heard it begin to open. Someone was coming in.

Her yell startled Shaw, who dropped the syringe to the floor in surprise. He cursed, then crouched to pick it up.

He had been standing directly over her just a moment ago. She was duct-taped to a chair in his apartment's living room. They had arrived at some point in the past few hours when it was still daylight, having begun the drive from Albany shortly after Eliza had entered the coffee shop.

Shaw had been waiting for her there, smiling and waving as she'd entered the building. She had looked over her shoulder to see Jake waiting in the parking lot across the street, and had just pulled out her phone to send him a text when Shaw appeared over her shoulder. Surprised by his sudden appearance, she had slid the phone back into her pocket, the text half-written.

"I need to show you something," Shaw had told her. She'd felt a bit thrown by his abrupt manner, but had nevertheless followed him out the back door and into the alley behind the coffee shop, where his car was parked. "You still have that phone? Mine wasn't working earlier."

Assuming Shaw just needed to text Jake or make a phone call, Eliza had handed her phone over to him. He'd then snatched it from her hand and placed it in his own pocket.

"Shaw," she'd said, "what's up?"

Rather than answering, he'd placed a cloth over her mouth. Before she realized what was happening, she was unconscious.

She'd woken up strapped to this chair in his living room. She didn't know where she was at first, but looking around, she saw the signs. Pictures of Shaw and his late wife on the mantle, more near the front door on an entry table, and a large portrait of the two of them hanging near the fireplace.

The apartment was nice, well-appointed and decorated. Not something she would have expected for a man who had lived alone for the past several years.

That said, she wouldn't have expected to be strapped to a chair inside that same man's house, either.

At first she had been terrified. This man she was working with, one she barely knew—a police officer no less—had abducted her and taken her to his home. What did he want with her? Why go through all the trouble?

She had tried asking him, tried playing to whatever reason he had left, but he had been silent the entire time, simply pacing and looking out his window. He seemed to be on edge, scared even. She hadn't seen him like this before—typically he was cool and collected, the epitome of a career police officer who was used to working a night shift in a big city.

Eventually, Shaw had left the room only to return a moment later, holding a syringe. Eliza's eyes had widened as she realized that he was about to inject her with something. *No,* she'd thought. *This isn't how it's supposed to end.*

She had struggled then, trying to rip the duct tape free from her arms and legs, but to no avail. She had wanted to scream. If he planned to kill her, to inject her with whatever this thing was, he might just do it quicker if she screamed.

Instead, he had seemed to be struggling with the decision. It had taken him thirty seconds before he decided to use the syringe.

Surprisingly, however, Shaw hadn't turned the needle toward her. She had watched in horror as he'd held the syringe up in front of him, his thumb resting on the top.

He had pulled up the sleeve of his shirt, revealing the lighter flesh of his left arm.

"What are you doing?" she'd asked him. "Where did you even get that?"

"Sorry about the chloroform," he'd said, ignoring her question. "I didn't want to hurt you, but I couldn't take the risk that you would signal someone while we were in the car. It's crude, but it had to be done."

"Why?" she'd asked. "Why did you have to *kidnap* me?"

He had looked out the front window, not bothering to move the drapes out of the way.

"Shaw, come on. You don't have to do this. We can get you—"

"*Help*?" Shaw had suddenly yelled. "Is that what you can get me? Is that what you think I need? I'm not deranged, Mendoza. I'm more lucid than I ever have been before. I know exactly what I'm doing, what I should've done a long time ago."

"Then *tell* me what you're doing. Why did you bring me here?"

"It's too… There's too much collateral…"

"Collateral damage?" she'd asked. "Is that what you're talking about? You were in on this from the beginning, but I got too close?"

Shaw had swallowed.

"Shaw, listen, I—"

"No!" he'd shouted. "This whole thing—this mess—it was going to save *thousands* of lives, Eliza. Over the years, *tens* of thousands. But you—you and Jake, but mostly *you*—you were too good. You can't be there when he—"

"When *who*?"

Shaw hadn't answered her question. "This is all going too fast, now. I have to do it myself. If I can't make it obvious what this is all for, I've lost. My parents…" He'd trailed off.

Eliza could see he was working through something, trying to parse through some complex equation in his mind.

"Shaw," she'd said, lowering her voice. "Shaw, please. Just tell me why you're doing this. Why you're trying to play both sides."

Without answering, Shaw had plunged the tip of the needle deep into his flesh, wincing in pain. He hadn't aimed for a vein. Whatever it was he was putting into his body, apparently accuracy wasn't needed.

"Shaw, seriously. What the hell are you—"

"It wasn't supposed to be you," he'd said. "You got here and I knew you were going to be too good. I wasn't sure when I first looked you up. I knew you were focused on your career, figured you wouldn't have the time to put into this. I figured you'd half-ass it, you know? Maybe even give it a shot. But then you got lucky."

"What are you talking about?"

"You weren't supposed to find them, you weren't supposed to examine the Stermers. When I found out that you did, I knew there wouldn't be enough time before…"

"Before *what*?" Eliza had asked, becoming more and more agitated. *What the hell is happening?* The fear had worn away into anger. She just wanted to understand now. She wanted answers—she *needed* them.

Who is this man? Eliza felt betrayed, but also as though she had now been pulled into a completely different set of problems, now fighting against some psychopath trying to kill himself.

He had looked down at her, met her eyes. "I'm sorry it had to be this way," he'd said. "It was all supposed to be so much simpler, so much easier. Jake and you weren't supposed to…" He had looked out his window once again. "There's no time left. I'm sorry. The world will know, now. I got my hands on an early test of the parasite. Kept a vial, just in case. In case I needed to prove that I died for something. I died for *this*, and even if I can't infect anyone else, they'll know I gave everything for it."

She saw that he was crying now, tears falling freely from both of his eyes. His voice was still steady, unwavering, but she saw unsteadiness in his eyes.

"What would you do?" he asked her. "How far would you go for what you believe in?"

That was the moment Jake Parker came through the door.

CHAPTER 47

The first thing Jake saw when he burst through Shaw's open door was Eliza. Sitting—strapped down—in a chair, screaming. The second thing he saw was a syringe near her feet.

And then, after stepping a few feet into the apartment, the third thing Jake noticed was the sound of footsteps, heavy, running through the back of the apartment.

"Shaw," Eliza said. "He's still here."

Jake nodded and took off. He burst through the living room, rounded the corner near the tiny kitchen, and saw Shaw sliding the back door shut. It was a first-floor apartment and Shaw had a patio and small fence separating his home from a densely wooded neighborhood park.

He met Jake's eyes. There was recognition there, but something else as well. *Apathy? Concern?* Was the man feeling sorry for himself? Wanting to say sorry to Jake?

It didn't matter now. Shaw had abducted Eliza. Taped her to a chair. *Injected her with...*

It was almost unbelievable—his *partner*, a man he had trusted for years, had done this. Jake wasn't sure what "it" was, but there wasn't time to dawdle and think about it. Shaw had taken Eliza, and had betrayed both of them. Whatever had happened was over and done with, and now there was only one goal: *get Shaw.*

Jake pulled the SIG Sauer GSR from behind his back, where he'd stuffed it after leaving his car. He had grabbed it nonchalantly, by second nature, as if he were back on the force. He hadn't considered *why* he was grabbing his gun—he certainly had not been considering shooting Shaw.

And now?

Was he really going to chase down a man he had once called his best friend, a partner and detective he had trusted with his life? A man he had shared his darkest secrets with. A man whom he knew understood him and what he had been through better than anyone on the planet.

Even as he thought it, Jake knew he was prepared to do it. He would do whatever it took—he always had, and he now knew that he always would.

Right and wrong, Parker, he thought. *Right and wrong.* The world might deem shooting at his ex-partner "wrong," but Jake had long ago stopped listening to those calls. Internally, he knew what *his* "right" was. Beau Shaw was a criminal. He hadn't always been, but now he was. Period.

Abduction, obstruction of justice, all sorts of other minor charges. Jake was running through the textbook definitions of each of them now, letting them scan through his mind as he lifted the pistol and placed his finger over the trigger guard.

"Shaw!" he yelled. "Don't do it. I'll shoot." He paused, nearly choking over the words. "Goddammit, Shaw, I *will* shoot you."

Shaw stared for another second, then in a single, swift motion, he was gone. Over the fence, already running when his feet hit the ground.

Jake pulled the trigger. Two times. The blasts were enough to shock Jake's eardrums into silence. Everything in his mind went blank. The bullets soared quietly, slowly, through the air.

The rounds easily sailed through the glass of the patio door, but the obstruction was enough to send them off-target by a few inches.

Shaw ran to the left just as the rounds sizzled into the hard earth near his feet.

Jake ran forward, but Shaw was still moving to the left. He was out of sight completely in another second, and Jake was fumbling with the door slide when he realized he was too far behind. He'd lost him.

Jake stopped, forgetting the door and turning back to the hallway. He walked through, to where Eliza was still waiting, against her will.

"Are you okay?" he asked.

"You... you shot him?"

He shook his head as he worked with the duct tape. "I missed. He's in the woods now, running toward the harbor. He'll be as good as gone by tonight. Did he inject you with something?"

"No," she said. "He... he injected *himself*."

What the hell? Jake hadn't expected that.

She looked away, and Jake could see she was struggling to fight back the tears.

"What happened?"

She pulled her left wrist free as she answered. "He grabbed me at the coffee shop. Told me to follow him, and... and I did. Jake, why would he even—"

Jake held up a hand. "Stop, don't beat yourself up. No one could have known he was going to snap. I never would have guessed he'd do something like that."

"Then he gagged me—chloroform or something like that—and I... and I ended up here."

Jake squinted, scratching his head. "I don't get it. Why? And why *now*?"

She sniffed back a sob as her right hand popped free. "He did say something about me being 'too good,' or figuring something out too soon. That we weren't supposed to investigate the Stermers' corpses."

"Well, yeah," Jake said. "That was clear to me from the beginning."

"But since we did, we somehow… I don't know. Sped up the timeline or something?"

"I guess," Jake replied. "I'm just still in shock that *he's* behind this."

Eliza nodded. "Me too. Although he seemed hesitant, too. Like he didn't *want* to do any of this. Like it was a burden or something he hated."

"He didn't *have* to kidnap you, Eliza."

"I know. Trust me, I'm not defending him. Just pointing out that this whole mess is far larger than one man's project. No way Shaw could have been everywhere at once—he's got people helping him, spread out around the United States, even."

"Like down in Texas."

"Right," she continued. "And all those places Briggs found new cases. They're working with him, or for him, or something."

Jake took in the information, trying to file it somewhere reasonable. Nothing made sense. The puzzle had gotten *more* complicated, even though he had more information than he had five hours ago. "Did he say anything else?"

Eliza thought for a moment. "Yeah," she said. "It was weird, too. Almost spooky. After he stuck himself with the needle and pushed it in, right before you barged in, he looked at me and just asked me a question: 'How far would you go for what you believe in?'"

Jake couldn't figure out what had gotten Shaw so riled up. Ever since he'd known him, he'd been an even-keeled, calm presence. But… what other trials had the man been through? Betraying everything he knew was so far outside the realms of what Jake thought him capable of, there had to be *something* else. Some reason.

"Was he political?" Eliza asked.

"Political?"

"Yeah—I mean, was he interested in politics, or government, or racial issues?"

"I… I don't really know. I mean, he's a black guy in a country that seems to shoot itself in the foot whenever it tries to help any minority, but… Shaw never really talked about that."

"To you specifically, or to anyone?"

"What do you mean?" Jake asked.

Eliza stood, and Jake watched her stretch and test her muscles. Thank God the man hadn't hurt her, although she was surely shaken. He still hadn't mentioned his own plight in getting here—almost getting run off the road, then being followed.

He remembered the man's face from the intersection. The man recognized Jake, as well. Knew they were on the right track. And if Shaw had been involved with this—if those men were his grunts-for-hire, they'd be…

"Eliza," he said, before she could answer his question. He flicked his eyes right, toward the big front window, noticing a pair of shadows moving across the light. "We need to go. Now."

CHAPTER 48

Jake didn't wait for her response. He tugged her arm and they ran through the apartment, once again passing the kitchen and the hallway toward the patio door, where Jake's two bullet holes had smacked through the double-paned glass.

He slid the patio door open just as he heard a knock on the still-open front door. *Seems a bit polite if Shaw's their enemy,* Jake thought. He remembered when they'd visited Eliza in Syracuse—they hadn't bothered to knock.

Jake pushed Eliza through to the patio and told her to jump over the fence. He then followed suit and slid the door closed behind him, wishing he could somehow lock it from the outside. Anything to slow their would-be attackers down a bit. This had gone well beyond scare tactics and car chases.

He felt the weight of the SIG Sauer. One in the chamber, full mag, minus two shots—seven rounds left, and his extra magazine was still in the car.

He really hoped he wouldn't have to put any more rounds through the weapon, and certainly not all seven. If it came to that, their problems had escalated severely.

Eliza was running toward the woods, but Jake called her back. "No," he said. "Let's circle back around and see if we can get to my car without those assholes seeing us."

She nodded and followed him. They ran to the right behind the apartment building, then snaked around an outdoor picnic table and between two other buildings, toward the parking lot near Shaw's home. Jake hoped the two men were still playing cat-and-mouse and had both entered the house, rather than one posting up in the parking lot to lie in wait for their return.

They reached the parking lot, and Jake glanced around quickly. He didn't see anyone out—bad guy or civilian—but he knew they could be hiding somewhere. As he approached the asphalt lot, he noticed one of the two dark-blue sedans. It was an old Crown Victoria—a good, sturdy vehicle, if a bit old-fashioned.

He didn't see the second one anywhere.

That was good as it meant there was probably only one man in the apartment chasing them, and therefore no one waiting for them in the lot.

But it was bad as well—it meant there was a second vehicle lurking around somewhere, likely waiting for them to leave.

"Come on," Jake said, ducking down and running across the lot toward his car. He'd left it unlocked, and he didn't bother opening Eliza's door for her. They both climbed in, and Jake had the car backed out of the space before they had finished putting their seatbelts on.

Eliza was breathing heavily. He looked at her. Her face was rigid, staring straight ahead as she worked to calm her heart rate and control her breathing. The exertion of their most recent encounter and escape from Shaw's apartment was only adding to the overall feeling of desperation. Even Jake felt it now.

What is this, and what does it mean?

"You asked me a question in there," Jake said as he drove. He aimed for the apartment's back exit, hoping the alley behind the two buildings connected to an accessible street. It would put them at least in position to head north, back toward the highway and away from this area. "You asked if he had ever talked to me specifically about race, or his being a minority."

She nodded, looking over at him.

"No," he said. "I never thought it was an issue he struggled with. I mean, we were pretty much the same level for most of our careers—I moved to detective, but he advanced as well, ending up on the counterterrorism task force."

"You think he didn't struggle with it?"

"'Struggle?' I don't know, Eliza… we talked about it. I didn't feel like it was my place to bring it up, you know? 'Hey, you're a black guy and a police officer… how does it feel?' Not exactly an easy question to ask."

"But maybe he *was* trying to work through some of it—I can't imagine that's an easy position to be in right now in America. Sure, he was a good cop, but still… it would have been something he was probably thinking about a lot. Especially lately."

"What's your point?" Jake asked. He didn't like feeling chastised for not understanding some of the nuanced racial issues, and he certainly didn't like feeling as though he may have severely misunderstood his ex-partner and friend.

"Jake, my point is just that we *know* he's involved with all of this, somehow. And we know that this whole thing is about race, or minorities, or just immigration in general. If it was just some new radical terrorism sect, they'd have blown up a busy shopping mall or government building. If it was fundamentalist—religious—they'd have targeted something that didn't line up with their agenda, like that attack on the gay nightclub in Orlando."

Jake nodded. "Right. But if it's about minorities—just about *all* of the makeup of who's currently in the ICE system—why would Shaw target them? How does that push forward his agenda?"

Eliza shook her head. "I honestly don't know. It seems far-fetched, but there's not really anything else to work with."

Jake pulled the car toward the highway, moving quickly but trying not to drive too fast, to not call attention to them. The highway entrance was two blocks north, and so far Jake hadn't seen either of the two blue sedans around. It wasn't much of a victory, but he was ready to take whatever he could get.

"That's fair. And it checks out, but I'm not convinced it's that simple. It's never that simple."

CHAPTER 49

Derek Briggs pulled the phone out of the golf cart's cupholder and lifted it to his ear. "This is Briggs."

It seemed he hadn't had so many regular calls on a personal line since before he'd joined the Navy. That was exactly why he had ordered his assistant to replace it quarterly.

"Briggs, it's Jake Parker."

Briggs thought the man sounded breathless, excited. He slid the six-iron back into his golf bag and returned to the front seat. He was golfing alone, and there was almost no one else on the course today, so he had time to take the call without worrying about someone behind him trying to play through.

"Parker," he said. "I'm on the course, so I can't talk long. If you've got something on the attack at the Dilley facility, send it through via email and I'll make sure my assistant's on it."

"This isn't about Dilley, Briggs. It's about Shaw."

Briggs' blood ran cold. "What about him?"

"He's involved, somehow. He abducted Eliza Mendoza, and—"

"Jesus Christ. *Shaw* did that?" Briggs knew the surprise in his voice would be heard through the phone line. He'd always prided himself on his ability to remain stoic, a trait that had served him well in the Navy, so it was obvious when the stoicism was replaced by a more audible emotion.

"Yes," Parker said. "And we've been under attack as well, by two guys who were working with him. We're fine, now, but I wanted to see if you could get the authorities involved."

"Sure," Briggs said. "How so?"

"Well, for starters, Shaw's potentially dangerous, though unarmed, and on the loose."

"Got it. I'll have someone log it, but it's going to help to have you call it in, too. I mean, the guy's still *working* for the police department."

"Understood. On it," Jake said.

"What else?"

"Well, uh, it seems he injected something into himself."

At this, Briggs literally pulled the phone away from his ear. "Injected himself? With what?"

"We don't know, but the assumption is that it's the parasite. The same thing he's been spreading around. I guess he freaked, got spooked or something, and decided to speed things up a bit."

Spreading around... Briggs chewed his lip as he listened. "Okay, I understand. He's potentially infected with the same thing that killed our other cases. He's going to be uncomfortable for a couple of days, then very sick. Is that what you're telling me?"

"Yes." There was a pause. "And eventually..."

Briggs nodded, but didn't respond. *Eventually the man would be dead.* "Noted. I'm sorry, Jake. I truly wish things hadn't gone this way. I'm surprised to hear that about Shaw—he seemed levelheaded, not one to go off the deep end like this."

"We agree about that," Parker said. "I'm with Mendoza now, and we're making our way back to our hotel. Might try to get to the airport in Albany before tonight."

"Okay," Briggs said. "Flying to Texas?"

"Yeah, if we can get flights today. We most likely won't make it before whatever's supposed to go down, but we can at least be there to investigate."

Briggs couldn't help but smile. *The kid's driven, that's for damn sure.* He also knew he was feeling helpless, down on his luck, and needed *something* to focus on. For a man like Jake Parker, traveling to the hotspot would be a far better option than hunkering down in a hotel and waiting it out.

"All right," Briggs said. "I've got multiple teams down there now, including the head of my Enforcement and Removal Operations division. We also have boots on the ground for all the major redirection detention centers around the nation. Trying to focus our power on the big targets."

"Seems wise," Parker said. "Keep me posted. We've got a lot to figure out, here. We'll be in touch."

Briggs ended the call, took a breath of fresh golf course air, and placed the phone back into the cupholder. He walked back to the golf bag just as another group of golfers appeared on the tee-off mound behind him.

A lot to figure out, indeed.

CHAPTER 50

"We're going to Texas now?" Eliza asked.

The car shook as Jake pressed the pedal down to the floor, and she could see that they were racing back to Albany at about 90 miles per hour.

Hopefully, any officer who pulls us over will recognize Jake, she thought.

She couldn't help but grab the handle on the car's ceiling above her right hand.

Jake shook his head. "No, no way. Too far, and there's not going to be anything there for us to find except dead bodies. Besides that, I'm not sure we can trust Shaw on the intel. We're going to D.C."

"As in, *Washington*, D.C.?"

"The one and only. If we want to get in front of this thing, we need to confront the devil himself."

"Right, but who's that? We don't even know where Shaw is."

"Not Shaw," Jake said. He turned his head to look at her. "Briggs."

"*Briggs?* You were just on the phone with him. He said we should head to Texas; he'll be expecting us to—"

"And that's exactly why we won't," Jake said. "He won't be expecting us."

"We're just going to show up in D.C., at his front door, and ask him to hang out?"

"Eliza, we've been behind the ball on this the entire time. It's not a feeling I'm used to, and it's certainly not one I like. I don't know who the hell's involved with this parasite shit at this point, but I'm going to start at the top. I'm a detective, remember?"

"So you're going to interrogate the man?" Eliza asked. Derek Briggs was Navy, old-school leadership. She couldn't imagine he'd take too kindly to being cross-examined by the very people he'd hired to solve the case.

Jake shrugged. "I don't know. Haven't thought that far ahead. But I've got a few hours to plan for it. While we're driving, you can get us flights to D.C., soonest they leave from Albany. We'll grab our stuff from the hotel and head right to the airport."

"Fine," she said. "But Jake, what's the *plan*? Let's say Briggs *is* a person of interest now—how does that change the game? If there's really something going down in Dilley, Texas, shouldn't we be there?"

"No," he said, shaking his head. "*We* don't need to be there. But our *proxy* does. Someone Briggs or Shaw can't touch because they won't know about them."

"Who's that?"

"Old friend," Jake said. "He's a retired cop, an old mentor of mine. Retired in San Antonio, but he's got connections everywhere. He can have local law enforcement set up a sort of sting operation in Dilley, figure out if there's anything coming into the facility tonight or tomorrow morning."

"He can do that?"

"I'm not talking about a raid or something crazy, just have a couple highway patrol check in on any box trucks making deliveries. They'll be allowed to search and see what's inside. Really won't be any trouble, and I'm pretty sure we can get them going before tonight."

"I see," Eliza said. "What can I do?"

"You're fine," Jake said, smiling at her. "You've done more than enough already. I think you should just rest and try to—"

"Jake," she said, cutting him off. "I know what you're trying to do. It's sweet. But it's not going to work. I'm in this now, don't you realize that? They tried to scare me away, then Shaw kidnapped me, *and* they chased you down and tried to kill both of us. It's personal now, Jake."

"Still, it's a lot. Especially in the span of a matter of days."

"I'm not backing down, Jake. If we're flying to D.C., I'll get a nap on the plane." She glanced over at Jake to see him still looking at her out of the corner of his eye. "And if you shut up for a minute, maybe a nap in the car, too."

Jake laughed. "Well, who's going to book our flights, then? And I've got a *long* list of stuff for you to do while I chauffeur you around."

"*Chauffeur* me—is that what this is? I'm just some pretty Uber ride? You going to leave me a five-star review?"

Jake shrugged. "If you stay awake, maybe."

She grinned. "What else do you need?"

"Well, for starters, I'm feeling a little out of the loop. It's pretty clear to me based on Shaw's actions and what he said to you that he was trying to keep us *away* from this mess."

"Right," she said, nodding along. "Like keeping us nearby so he could know exactly what we were up to. So we wouldn't stick our noses somewhere he didn't think they belonged."

"Exactly. And he was pretty successful at that, which means we're lacking information. I forgot to ask Briggs, but you can get in touch with his office and get the updated stats on deaths and new cases. I'm sure it's grown, but I also doubt it's a full-on outbreak yet."

"Okay," she said. "On it." She pulled out her cell phone and began tapping out an email to one of the contacts Briggs had given them. "I'll see what the new numbers are, but like we talked about before, I think this is moving a lot slower than a viral outbreak. We know now that the parasite is only transmittable in its smallest form, and that there's an incubation period of a number of days while they grow and mature inside the host, before they're able to reproduce and eventually kill the host."

"All right," Jake said, once again focusing on the highway. "There's one other thing I think we should do. Now that I'm thinking about it, it's something I should've done a few days ago, back before I got you and Shaw involved."

"What's that?"

"I think we need more information about *Briggs* as well. Derek Briggs, decorated Navy veteran and boardroom hero."

"What about him?"

Jake shook his head. "Anything and everything. Current and past relationships, professional and personal. Corporate promises, who he's in bed with—literally and figuratively—I want to know where he sleeps at night and who it's with. Also, if we can find it, I want to know about his childhood friends."

"Sounds like a lot."

"It may be," Jake said. "But in my experience, it's a lot of snooping around when you're snooping someone who's got nothing to hide—everything about them is simply out there, and it creates a mess to wade through. But when they *are* hiding something, that's usually faster to uncover. It may not be easier to dig up, but you can usually tell right away you're dealing with someone who's tried to hide something."

"Okay," she said. "Flights, case update, Briggs. Anything else, boss?"

Jake smiled. "I like having an assistant. It's nice."

Eliza laughed as she finished her email. "Yeah, well, don't get used to it, Parker."

CHAPTER 51

Their flight to Reagan International was just over an hour and a half long, and Jake used the time to run through the information Eliza had pulled together. Eliza, for her part, slept. Jake was amazed at how quickly the woman had been able to fall asleep, not even waiting until they'd taken off to zone out.

Her information was helpful. He had read through the responses to her email. One from a laboratory that ICE owned, and another from an analyst at ICE headquarters. Both corroborated the same information: there were indeed more cases, but neither seemed to think they were dealing with a potential pandemic.

The numbers, the laboratory representative explained, were "intriguing but not scary." Three new deaths since this morning, and what appeared to be a further four new cases. Certainly worth checking into, certainly not a pandemic.

But Jake knew that these people were only working with part of the information. They didn't know *how* the new cases had come to be, only that they were cases worth watching. They didn't know that someone—or multiple someones—had literally planted the parasite in the ICE facilities. They didn't know that the parasite had been designed for a specific, sinister purpose. They didn't know that whoever had done this was planning something bigger—*far* bigger—and that it very likely would lead to a massive epidemic, or at least the fear of one—which itself would cause massive disruption.

He also thought about Shaw's words to Eliza. Had he been trying to tell her something? He had seemed almost hesitant earlier that day, as if he hadn't wanted Jake and Eliza involved. Yet, the man had acted according to some internal compass. He'd made the decision to do what he did.

Shaw had told Eliza that she shouldn't have been there, that she had "figured something out." Something about the Stermers, obviously. Something related to the parasite. Perhaps it was the parasite itself—they were not supposed to know what was causing the sickness and death until it was too late.

Is that it? Jake thought. *Did we ruin the plan?* Perhaps their investigation and autopsy of the Stermers had revealed Shaw's hand too early, and he'd had to adapt, to scramble, to stay ahead of the game.

But then, what *was* the game? What was he planning?

Jake rubbed his eyes, wishing he had an easier time sleeping on planes. The truth was, he couldn't. He was too large and cumbersome for airliners' cramped seats, and he knew he wouldn't be able to get any restful sleep, anyway. There was too much on his mind.

He moved to the other document Eliza had shared with him: a simple text file called *Derek Briggs*. She'd sent it to his phone as soon as they were on the plane, and she was asleep before he'd had the chance to ask her if she'd found anything exciting.

As it turned out, she hadn't.

Derek Briggs was a stand-up, standout guy, the sort of leader real leaders wish they could be. As far as Eliza had been able to discover, he had no skeletons in his closet, no ex-wives airing his dirty laundry, and apparently no girlfriends on the side. He was a man of character.

From what Eliza had found, it seemed the man was being groomed from somewhere higher up in his network for a potential Congressional appointment, and—some hoped—even more. He'd spent a few years in law school as a young man, but most of his career was spent in service to his country. During his deployments, his fellow shipmates all seemed to hold him in high regard, and he'd even won awards as a team leader, voted on by his fellow sailors.

He'd eventually turned to the public nonmilitary sector, taking a job in upper management for ICE, right as it had been formed after 9/11. He'd risen through the ranks, with recommendations from just about everyone he worked with and for, eventually taking over the new organization.

His Wikipedia page, which Parker had scanned in addition to reading the information Eliza had given him, mentioned that Briggs was the child of immigrants himself—his role at ICE, therefore, seemed to be a perfect fit. A man trying to change the system from within.

He was also a philanthropist, interested in supporting research and development in technology and communications infrastructure, and he seemed to put his money where his mouth was—a news article Eliza had linked to mentioned that he'd donated ninety percent of his salary to a program backed by Bill and Melinda Gates to bring sustainable toilets to third-world countries. He was currently also serving on the board of directors for a large philanthropic organization called Atlantic Enterprises Group.

Jake pinched the bridge of his nose. There was a lot to admire about Derek Briggs, and Jake couldn't help but feel inferior when reading about some of his accomplishments. He was only barely reaching middle age and seemed healthy, so Jake also wondered how much more the man would accomplish.

But in everything Jake read, something crept up from the mass of information and seemed to be screaming for Jake's attention. He couldn't tell what it was, or why he felt it. Was it jealousy? Did Briggs have the sort of life Jake had always wanted? Was it something else entirely?

He thought back to what he'd told Eliza—if someone were trying to hide something, it was usually pretty evident right away. Digging into the person's life would generally reveal a lot of information about one specific area—the area they *wanted* the world to focus on.

Jake wondered if there was more at play here with Briggs. The man was certainly connected. He was absolutely capable of hiring a professional branding agency to help him control his online image. But to what end? If he were hiding something, what was it? And why? Most people had skeletons in their closet, but those skeletons weren't always the type that woke up and killed people. If he were hiding something on purpose, it could simply be something that was embarrassing to the man—a failed marriage, a DUI charge, something of that nature.

Jake wanted to consider it more, to let his analytical mind chew on the pieces of the puzzle for a while longer, but the phone on his tray table buzzed. He'd put it on silent when they'd boarded the plane but made sure it was connected to the plane's WIFI.

It was a call from the man he'd reached out to earlier that day—the man helping the case from Texas, his mentor Jorge.

He pulled the phone up to his ear and talked quietly, so as not to wake up Eliza. "Jorge," he said. "Good to hear from you. I'm guessing you got my email?"

"Hey, kid," the older man said. "Great to hear your voice. We need to catch up soon."

"You got it. You say the word, I'm on a flight down there."

"I've got a second master suite sitting empty. In-laws were supposed to use it, but they bailed to Arizona last year." Jorge's voice crackled through the phone line.

Jake smiled and looked out the plane's window at the clouds covering the globe. "Sounds great, I appreciate that."

"And yeah, I got your email. Already started working on it."

"That's great. Thanks, Jorge."

"Yeah, yeah, no problem. Nothing for this old fart to do, anyway." Jorge chuckled, then coughed. "Anyway, I called up the Frio County Sheriff. He is sending two of his patrolmen down there now, actually. And I have a friend of a friend who works there in Dilley, at the South Texas Family Center." Jorge's voice drifted off.

"Is that what it's called?" Jake asked. "The Family Center?"

Jorge's voice returned. It sounded grating, as if he had coughed for a moment while muting the phone. "Yes, that's the name of it. But, Parker, it's closer to a prison than a 'family center.' There are hardly any men there—it was built for women and children, usually coming from Central America."

"I see," Jake said. He knew he could research the center later, but he wanted to get the information Jorge had first. "Thank you for checking with them. Did they say anything else?"

"Yes," Jorge said. "They are expecting a shipment coming sometime this evening. There are a lot of trucks that deliver throughout the month, but tonight is their large delivery."

"Jorge, that's great," Jake said. "That's got to be what we're looking for. I'm on my way to D.C. now, but can you have your team pull a few of those trucks aside and take a peek? I'd love to know what they're delivering."

"I can do you one better. The highway the center is on is state, and there's only one way in. I'm having my boys set up a rally point for the truck drivers—they'll all have to pull over and be searched, 'authority of the Texas State Highways Division.'"

Jake laughed. "That sounds official. I like it."

"The drivers don't care either way—they'll still meet their delivery times and they know they won't be held liable for anything we find."

"Jorge, again, thank you. This is incredible. You've got my number—please let me know as soon as you hear back."

"Of course, Parker. Anything for you, kid. Take care."

Jake ended the call and placed the phone face-down on the tray table once again.

Maybe things are turning up, he thought. *Maybe we're finally getting somewhere.*

CHAPTER 52

The Next Day

In their haste to get to Washington D.C. and surprise Derek Briggs, Jake hadn't entirely thought through his plan on actually getting inside Briggs' building. He was no longer a detective, so his normal flash-the-badge entrance at the doorstep wouldn't work. Besides that, they were planning on visiting Briggs where he worked: in a downtown government building.

Like most government buildings, this one also featured a standard open lobby with metal detectors and two security guards posted behind a desk. When they entered, Jake and Eliza were told to wait aside while the records were checked for their appointment. Since they didn't have one, reception would have to call up and inform Briggs of their arrival.

So much for the element of surprise, Jake thought. In all honesty, he hadn't expected to just walk into Briggs's office and start wagging a finger at the man.

Jake hadn't gotten any more updates from Briggs or his team overnight. When he and Eliza had landed at Reagan International, they'd booked a couple rooms at a nearby hotel and caught a late dinner and even later bedtime. Jake had checked his email a couple of times before bed and once first thing in the morning, finding nothing from ICE. He wanted to know what the latest case records were, to see if the death rate had increased and how many more had been infected since they'd last heard.

More importantly, he'd wanted to find out whether or not Jorge had made progress in Texas, to make sure the sting operation was still on track. Texas was one hour behind them, so there was still time before the day got off to a real start, but Jake couldn't help feeling the nerves as he waited in the downtown office building with Eliza.

For her part, Eliza seemed calm and ready for whatever they might find. He knew she was out of her element—that she would much prefer to be back in her Syracuse home looking through a microscope. Or in a laboratory examining the parasite from a microscopic level rather than studying this case from a macroscopic viewpoint.

Still, Jake felt comfortable around her. They were a good team, and he viewed her as a partner. She was incredibly intelligent and quick-witted, and while they had never trained together, Jake already knew that she was able to keep her cool during tense situations.

Suddenly one of the guards called them over, waving with a hand to approach the desk.

"Any weapons?" the man asked.

Eliza shook her head. Jake double-checked his back and side, where he normally would have shoved the weapon and its holster, even though he knew he had left his SIG Sauer back in Albany at their other hotel. On the force, he'd have had no trouble flying with the weapon, but these days it was different. He didn't have time to go through the rigmarole of getting his SIG through security. If he ended up needing it here, well, that meant they would have much bigger problems to worry about.

"No," Jake said. "You got in touch with him? He'll see us?"

Rather than answering, the guard just waved them through the metal detectors and gave them both guest badges.

"Okay, then," Jake said. "We'll head to the elevator and read signs."

The guard shrugged and turned to the next person in the queue.

When they reached the elevator, Eliza looked at Jake and waited until the doors closed. "So what's the play? What do you need from me?" she asked.

Jake thought about that question for a moment, then answered. "I've done this kind of thing quite a bit, and I have a feeling we'll know pretty quickly if he's trying to get away with murder. Most people tend to overreact the opposite direction when confronted with something like this face-to-face. We'll have to see how genuinely innocent he seems, or whether he's overdoing the 'not guilty' position. We'll start with a debrief and I'll ask him some questions as part of that. You're the parasite's best expert at this point, so I'll need your help explaining what we know about it."

"That makes sense," Eliza said. "This has been complicated enough as it is, and if we can't stop this thing down in Texas, our leads will have pretty much run dry."

"Yeah, that's exactly my worry," Jake said. "But we know almost for a fact that whoever is doing all of this has more planned. It's going to be big, because the preliminary stages of this game are over. We may have forced their hand to act early, but I have no doubt they're going to do something big and bold very soon. If it's in Texas, Jorge's guys will find it."

"That's what I'm thinking, too. Because of the size and necessary vector of this thing, the parasite will need to be in pretty large doses in order to cause a lot more spread than what we've seen so far. It's incredibly inefficient to put a drop of it here and there, infecting one host at a time. They *have* to be transmitting the parasite on those trucks."

Jake nodded and turned around to face the back of the elevator, where a tall, vertical wall of glass allowed him to see down into the lobby of the government building. It was an impressive structure, if a little on the bland side. There was no need for garish visual enhancements, no reason for decoration.

This organization wasn't in the business of creating impressive displays of wealth or providing luxury hotel stays to entice investors; instead, its modus operandi was the implementation of brutally efficient, dehumanized policies. The building was impressive in the same sense industrialized futuristic cities were impressive in movies. Jake felt power here, a sense of self-importance, and an aura of oppressiveness.

The elevator dinged and the door began to slide open. He and Eliza moved toward it to exit, and Jake did his best to push back the growing sense of unease in his gut. *Ignore it,* he told himself. *It's the butterflies again. It means you're on the right track.*

As if reading his mind, Eliza turned and whispered quietly, "Here goes nothing."

CHAPTER 53

"Mr. Parker. Ms. Mendoza."

Briggs' welcome was as brutally efficient and neutral as the building's decor. The director had greeted them upon exiting the elevator, shaking their hands and urging them to follow him to his office.

As Jake walked along, he saw a few people milling about in some open offices, but most of the other doors were closed. The hallway snaked around the corner, but they stopped at a door on the left near the end of the longest side of the building. Jake read the inscription on the wall-mounted plate next to the door.

Derek Briggs
Director

"It's not much," Briggs said as he waved them inside, "but I've never been one for false impressions."

"Not a problem, sir," Jake said. "Thanks for seeing us on such short notice."

Briggs smiled. "It's a pretty important case, so there's no way in hell I wouldn't have time for you two. That said, last we talked I thought you were going to Texas today? And you just arrived from Boston, is that right?"

"Yes," Jake answered quickly, not looking over at Eliza. "Well, it did seem like we would get there too late. And besides, I'm not sure how much good the two of us would be able to do down there. You brought us on to figure out what exactly is happening and who's behind it, not to arrest the low-level bad guys."

Briggs sighed, then walked behind his desk and sat down heavily into his chair. The chair creaked but held his weight as it swished from side to side. He motioned for the two of them to sit as well, which they did. "You're right about that—I've never lacked for scores of people who can do that sort of work. Hell, I've got the police departments of every city we have even a minor presence in on speed dial at this point. They are all waiting around to hear an update from me, to know if their city is going to be the next place affected by this damned parasite."

Jake raised an eyebrow. "What have you told them?"

Briggs ran his hand through his hair and looked down at his desk. "Not as much as I wish I could. Half of it is a lack of credible information, the other half is the recognition that my job is not to fix this problem for them but to reassure them."

"Keep the people happy?" Jake asked.

"Something like that. You know, when I joined the Navy, I had big dreams. Change the world, see different countries, help people. I did some of those things, but the older I got—the more involved in leadership I got—I realized that helping people from your perspective doesn't always look the same as helping people from theirs."

"What do you mean?" Eliza asked.

"Well, sitting behind this desk, looking out at an entire empire of bureaucracy, it's easy to think that what people want is a better system, a better way to handle the sorts of things we do. And in a lot of ways, that's true. Ultimately, that may be exactly what people want." His cheeks filled with air and he exhaled a long breath. "But I've come to learn that what people, individually, want is so much simpler. It may not be the best long-term solution for them, but it looks right in the short term. When I was overseas, on an early deployment, I remember thinking to myself that the place would be excited to have us there. I assumed they would be grateful for the help."

"You were protecting them, though," Jake said.

"No doubt. They knew it, too, but ultimately it wasn't not what they wanted in the moment. They didn't care that their government was going to be bolstered by US support. They didn't care that the United States Navy and a thousand seamen were going to massively boost their local economy, causing positive long-term change. They didn't care about any of that stuff because they couldn't *see* it. All they could see was what was in front of them: an enormous ship with a bunch of guns had just rolled into their port and started ordering them around. What was supposed to be freedom looked to them like the exact opposite."

"So there was a disconnect between what they *wanted* and what they *needed*."

"Yeah, exactly. People scream for justice and freedom and inclusion—all good things, and all things I want as well. But freedom and justice and inclusion for a single person is not the same thing as freedom and justice and inclusion for everyone."

Jake nodded. He had thought the same thing before, considered that people often claimed there was something wrong with society without realizing that society was just the people at large.

"It's impossible to please everyone," Eliza said. "I can't imagine your job is easy."

Briggs smiled, then shook his head. "No, I don't think anyone thinks their job is easy. Truth be told, I took this position because I was naïve. We all have big dreams and ideas, we all want to change the world. But what do you do when the world doesn't want to change? How do you convince people that what you want to do in the long term will be helpful, when it might hurt a bit in the short term?"

Jake knew it was a rhetorical question, but he felt obligated to answer. "You do what you can do, personally. Individually. You fight the battle you can fight."

Briggs' mouth turned downward as he considered this. "Unless your job is to fix the problem for everyone in an entire nation, all at once." He stopped and sighed, then placed his hands on the desk, one on top of the other. "I just wish we could start from a clean slate, start all over again from square one."

Jake shrugged. "Yeah, I guess it makes it a little more difficult that you're tasked with fixing the problem for an entire society."

Briggs sniffed and then looked around his office, signaling that he was ready to move on. "Anyway. Why are you two here?" he asked.

The question caught Jake off guard, even though he had anticipated it. If there were any chinks in this man's armor, Jake couldn't find them. He didn't seem to be hiding anything—on the contrary, he seemed far more open than Jake would have imagined the director of a major government organization being.

Eliza jumped in. "We… we need to figure out where this thing will go next. To make a battle plan in case we lose the facility in Dilley. If the parasite does get into the system there, can we stop the flow of detainees at the source?"

"Unfortunately, no. Not at the source. The 'source' is the border. In Texas, that's Mexico and the rest of Central America. It's too big, too long, and too expensive to completely halt immigration, even with something like an outbreak of infectious disease on our hands. That said, the federal government won't allow us to simply sit back and let people in. We have to do *something* to control the influx."

"Which means the Dilley center stays open," Eliza said.

"Exactly."

Briggs was about to continue when someone opened his door after a quick knock and popped their head in. It was a woman, in her mid-thirties, and she smiled at Jake and Eliza before speaking to Briggs. "Sir, you've got a call in about five minutes, and then your meeting with AEG in an hour. I'll have the car ready in forty-five minutes."

Briggs nodded and the woman disappeared, closing the door behind her. Without moving his eyes away from Eliza, he continued. "But we can slow the spread by slowing the resources and disabling some of the infrastructure. People get moved through our system using standard means of transportation—cars, trucks, and buses. I've already considered forcing a halt to all but major relocations, but there's a limit."

"What do you mean?" Jake asked. His mind was racing now, trying to solve the problem of where to put infected people once the spread got out of control. He could feel the sense of something nagging at him again, as if there were an answer just over the horizon, but as he drew closer, it stayed just out of sight.

"Since Border Patrol will continue to bring people in who cross the border, legally or illegally, they'll have to end up somewhere. That somewhere will become more and more overpopulated, the longer we shut down transportation between facilities. We are trying to stop the pandemic from starting, but I can't imagine that adding more people into the equation is the way to do that."

Jake felt his phone vibrate in his pocket, and he pulled it out beneath the desk and flipped it over. It was an email from Jorge.

Jake felt jittery, excited to finally know what his men had found. While Eliza engaged with Briggs, Jake glanced down at the screen as he read Jorge's words silently in his mind, listening to Briggs and Eliza at the same time. It didn't take long; the message was short and to the point.

He felt his stomach drop, a coldness settling into him.

The news wasn't bad. It was worse.

CHAPTER 54

The meeting had ended abruptly, with Jake standing and shaking Briggs' hand while trying to explain away his haste. Eliza had listened to him telling Briggs that he might have more information in an hour or so, but that he needed to "check things out first."

Briggs had needed to get onto his call and his next meeting anyway, so he had smiled and politely opened the door for them as they left.

Eliza could sense that Jake was holding something back—he had acted cryptically toward the end of their meeting. She didn't bother asking him until they were inside the elevator, riding down toward the ground floor once again.

"Jake," she began, "is everything okay? You seem… flustered."

Jake swallowed, looked out the glass wall at the back of the elevator, then spun around and faced her. He seemed agitated now, as if struggling with how to tell her bad news.

"Seriously, what is it? You basically ran out of the room back there."

Jake pulled his phone out and began clicking around on the screen. She wondered if he had even heard her question, but then he suddenly started reading aloud. "'Hey, Parker. Jorge here. Wanted to give you an update: we are still checking some of the last trucks to come through for the delivery, but we didn't find anything suspicious in the first seventeen shipments.'"

Jake dropped the phone back into his pocket.

"That's it?" Eliza asked. "They didn't find anything, and it has you this worked up? Jake, this is good news, isn't it?"

"No, Eliza, it's not. Shaw said there was going to be an incident there. He said it would happen—"

"Shaw's gone off the deep end, remember?" Eliza asked. "We can't trust him."

Jake was shaking his head. "We don't have to trust him. He saw it on a database meant to spread information across departments in the United States. It was verified and backed up, and I saw a screenshot of the report from another officer. Jorge must have known about it too, or he would have mentioned something already."

"Okay… so what? There was supposed to be an incident in Dilley, now there's not. That's still good news."

"It doesn't make sense, though. Jorge said all of the trucks were filled with office supplies—boxes of it, their weekly delivery. It was a dead-end, a red herring. Meant to keep us running in circles. The problem is, I can't figure out where this is all *actually* pointing us."

"Maybe it's not supposed to point us anywhere. You're a detective, so you are looking at this from a detective's standpoint. One thing points to the next thing, which points to the next thing… it's all a nicely laid-out puzzle, right? With pieces that fit together perfectly, eventually making a nice picture?"

"It's not that simple."

"That's exactly my point, Jake," Eliza said. "We have been assuming that there are clues that point to some larger answer. Maybe there isn't one. These attacks—the infections that have been happening at individual ICE facilities around the US—maybe they were organized by a central body, but maybe there was no larger 'master plan.'"

"Shaw seemed to think there was something bigger going on. It was big enough for him to kidnap you because of it. And Briggs—I mean, was it just me or did the guy seem to be completely bummed out?"

Eliza frowned as the elevator sailed down past the third floor. "What are you talking about? I thought his attitude was fine, if a little bit mellow."

"No, it was more than that. I didn't get the impression he was hiding something, but rather that he'd already failed at his job. That whole monologue about 'helping people the way they need to be helped' and his experience in the Navy... I mean, does that not strike you as the kind of thing a man who has already lost the battle would say?"

Eliza held a breath for a few extra seconds before letting it out. "I don't know, Jake. I'm no expert in human psychology. He didn't seem to be losing his mind or anything. Just a guy who's struggling with the reality of his inability to change the world for the better."

The elevator reached the bottom floor and dinged before the doors began to slide open.

Jake was already on his way out, but Eliza wasn't done. "He has an impossible job, you know. Trying to do right by the people he serves while also ensuring the safety of an entire nation? There's just no way he can please *anyone*, much less *everyone*. And it's not for lack of trying, either. I sent you the brief—the guy is a high-achiever no matter how you define it. He's on a call with one of his philanthropy missions right now—his secretary mentioned AEG—the Atlantic Enterprises Group."

They had just reached the metal detectors, preparing to leave the building, when Jake stopped short. He cocked his head sideways and looked down at Eliza. "What did you say?"

"About what? I was just saying that he's heavily invested in philanthropy, and—"

"No, about the company. Atlantic Enterprises Group. AEG."

"Yeah," Eliza said. "That's the one. It was in the documents I sent over last night. He's on the board."

She saw the light bulb go on in Jake's eyes.

Finally, Jake spoke. "Eliza, we need to get to a hotel. A coffee shop, anything. We've got some research to do."

Jake was halfway out the front door of the building, opening an app on his phone to call for a driver, when Eliza pulled him back. "About what, Jake? That company?"

Jake nodded. "Yes. They're a conglomerate, from what I've read. Involved with recycling and producing products from recycled materials, but also research and development for pharmaceutical companies."

"Okay, so, maybe there's something there, but—"

"When we talked to Dr. Edemza, he told us he hadn't administered any drugs to the Stermers, right?"

Eliza nodded.

"So we dropped that line of questioning, assuming that if he was telling the truth, it wouldn't make sense. Obviously, the parasite isn't being transferred via medication."

"Go on."

"But the reason we asked him that in the first place is because we discovered that his office *changed providers*, remember? It was a company called Pharland before, but now AEG—Atlantic Enterprises Group—is involved."

Eliza's eyes widened as she recalled exactly what Jake was referring to. "Yes," she said. "The same company Derek Briggs is involved with."

"Precisely."

"But I thought we trusted Edemza's story? That he's off the hook."

"No one's off the hook until the guilty party's in prison," Jake answered. "But I want to believe him. It could also be true that he didn't even know he was involved, that AEG somehow came into the picture and has been behind the infections."

"So what do we do? We look up their address, walk in, and see if there's anything labeled 'top-secret killer parasite' on one of their computers?"

Jake glanced sidelong at her. "No, not exactly. We find their offices and go in, ask around, see if there's anyone who works in or around the company that we trust. We can ping them for information. If not, and we're confident they're involved, we get the acronyms involved however we need to. Get a judge to issue a warrant, poke around their server room, hire a hacker—all of the above, maybe."

"The acronyms?"

"DEA, FBI, CIA if necessary. Anyone and everyone. Briggs wants to keep this quiet, which could either be suspicious or simply mean he's just trying to protect the information so it doesn't leak. We can use that to our advantage."

"How so?" she asked.

"Well, every federal agency is, by definition, working against every other one. So the DEA will gladly keep information from the FBI, and both will work in silos without reaching out to ICE."

"Seems counterintuitive and a waste of resources."

Jake smiled. "Welcome to the US Government."

CHAPTER 55

Jake and Eliza were in the back of an Uber, on their way to the nearest Starbucks. Jake was about to start looking up anything and everything about Atlantic Enterprises Group when he got another text from Jorge.

He read it out loud to Eliza. "'Jorge again. I'm sure you're going to hear about this in another hour or so, but I wanted to let you know, it does seem like there have been more cases of this bug you are trying to track down. Couple ambulances showed up at the Family Center about fifteen minutes ago—from what I've heard, people are complaining about stomach issues.'"

"Does he say how many?"

Jake shook his head, then slammed the phone down onto the leather seat between them. The Uber driver, a young blonde woman in her early twenties, glanced back at them in the rearview mirror.

"*Dammit,*" he said. "Shit. Eliza, how the hell did we miss it? How the hell did they not catch this thing when they checked all of the trucks? They must have missed one or two, maybe before they got there—"

Eliza held up a hand and Jake stopped talking. "Wait," she said. "Let's just think this through. What we know about the parasite so far is that it takes a few days to really start growing."

She's right, he thought. *She's exactly right.* "Which means that the 'incident' Shaw found out about wasn't at all the *delivery* of the parasite into the facility."

"Right," Eliza said. "It wasn't the delivery, the incident he was referring to was the *infection* itself. It's already in there, and whoever's gotten it has passed it around to others, and the symptoms are beginning to show."

"And it's the biggest facility in the United States, and currently just about at capacity. It's too late." Jake squeezed his eyes shut once again, as if wishing all of this would go away. He looked out the window. *I can't accept that we've missed our opportunity. That we've missed our chance to catch this and stop it.*

He felt Eliza's hand lower onto his. She squeezed it, gently. He looked over at her and saw her trying to smile.

He didn't remove her hand from on top of his, but he also didn't want to be consoled. "We didn't make it, Eliza. We didn't stop it before it got out of hand."

"Jake, we didn't stop *this* one. Sure, it's going to lead to major problems—probably more deaths than the facility can handle, and that's unforgivable. But we also know that unless a miracle of variables lines up perfectly, this infection can't leave the Dilley facility on its own."

"What exactly are you saying?" Jake asked her.

"I'm saying that I don't believe this is the only attack, the only incident that's going to happen. It might've been the only one Shaw intercepted, but whoever is doing this probably has more planned, and that means that there will be a way to stop *them*. And now that we know Shaw was involved in at least some part of it, how do we know he didn't just hand us the Dilley facility as a way to keep us occupied? That there aren't *many* other instances just like it?"

Jake nodded. "Okay, I can work with that. If the Stermers were a test run, we missed it, and we missed the first major attack. We're not going to miss anymore."

Eliza's smile brightened. "That's the Jake Parker I know," she said.

He couldn't help but smile back. It was true that going through a crisis with someone else brought those two people together faster than any other experience. He didn't feel like he knew Eliza very well, but he knew her well enough to know that she was going to stick this thing out to the very end.

"There's one thing I still don't understand," Eliza said.

"What's that?"

"Well, it seems like whoever is doing this wants to take down the weak and vulnerable of the population. We know most of the immigrants coming from Central and South America have sometimes traveled thousands of miles through terrible conditions to get here, so when they arrive, they are at their worst health-wise."

"Right, exactly," Jake said. "The system pretty much beats them down and wears them out, so getting sick is almost par for the course. Add in a deadly parasite and they don't stand a chance."

The Uber driver slowed and pulled up to a curb, and Jake could see the green mermaid beacon hovering over their destination.

"But what I mean is, if whoever is doing this wants to kill these people, why not just blow up the detention centers? Why not just get the job done quickly? As twisted as it sounds, doesn't that make more sense from their perspective?"

As he listened to Eliza's words, Jake suddenly had a flash of insight. Some of the pieces—not all, but some—began coming together in his mind.

Oh my God, Jake thought.

Eliza read the shock on his face. "What? What is it? What did I say?"

"It's what you *asked*," Jake said, working the app on his phone to tip the driver as Eliza opened her door. "'Doesn't that make more sense from their perspective?'"

They walked side-by-side up to the front doors of the standalone building. Jake opened the door for her and they entered, the familiar smell of coffee beans hitting his nose.

"I've been assuming that 'perspective' was one of a terrorist," Jake said. "But that may not necessarily be true. I mean, what they're doing is certainly an act of terrorism, but they may not be thinking like a terrorist thinks: fear for the sake of fear may not be their goal. If they're 'just' terrorists, then you are exactly right: there are far easier and faster ways to accomplish the goal of killing people and freaking everyone else out. The fact that it happened on American soil means it was targeted against America or Americans somehow, so we know they are trying to make a political statement at least."

The pair reached a table in the corner of the building, semi-isolated from other patrons. Jake could have used a caffeine boost, but his mind was now working overtime on its own. The coffee could wait.

"Okay, I'll bite: what *would* their goal be in this case?"

Jake chewed the inside of his cheek for a few seconds. "To 'start from a clean slate. To start all over again from square one.'"

Eliza's eyes shot up, boring into Jake's. "Wait a second. That's what—"

Jake nodded, smiling from the corner of his mouth. "Yeah, that's what Briggs said. Right to our faces. And I'm not sure if you noticed, but when we first entered his office, he asked if we'd just arrived from Boston."

"But we *did* just arrive from…" Eliza's voice trailed off as Jake watched the understanding dawn on her face. "We were in Boston," she said. "But we never told *him* that."

Jake nodded slowly. "I figured he's been keeping tabs on us like any boss would keep tabs on their employees, but I never thought he'd be scrutinizing our movements *this* closely. And I couldn't figure it out—the text message that seemed like it was coming from your phone? It was actually from Shaw's number."

Eliza frowned. "Shaw sent you a message that said 'Shaw,' trying to make it look like it was from *my* phone?"

"Well, that's what it seemed like," Jake answered. "But I've been trying to figure out why he would do that. If he was going to kidnap you, tell you things were 'moving too quickly' or whatever, why would he then send the message and have it spoofed, bouncing it from Eliza's phone only to make it look like it was actually from his own phone? Why make it *easier* for me to follow you both to Boston?"

Eliza gulped. "Because it wasn't Shaw at all. It was Briggs. He had someone spoof the message, in order to lead you right to me."

"But not to *save* you, Eliza," Jake said. "To get me out of the way. To keep us chasing our tails. To keep us off the *real* mission."

Jake changed his mind. He now strongly felt the desire for caffeine. He stood, and Eliza followed him to the counter to place an order.

Eliza paused for a long moment after ordering. "Holy crap. Jake, if what you're saying is true, if what Briggs told us in there is actually the reason why all of this is happening, it means we may have just found the person responsible for everything."

"That's what I'm thinking. It's not enough to take him in, of course. But it's the most important thing in the whole case."

"Which is?" Eliza asked.

"A motive."

CHAPTER 56

Eliza pondered what they knew so far. It did seem as though the motive behind Briggs' actions made sense. Briggs was a patriot, a man born to serve his country and dedicated to doing the right thing at all costs.

At all costs. Was this worth it, then? In Briggs' mind, was creating a parasite and spreading it through the population of a government entity he was in control of a worthwhile endeavor?

Briggs had said it himself. "Start from a clean slate, start all over again from square one."

There were still holes in the argument, but things were beginning to come together.

"He's a product of immigrants," Eliza heard herself suddenly saying out loud. "His mom and dad were from Scandinavia, right?"

Jake nodded next to her. "Yeah, something like that."

"It seems sick. Why would he do this to *immigrants* specifically? What the hell is he trying to prove?"

Jake shook his head. "No, it's not about trying to prove anything. Remember his motive: he wants to start over. To burn it to the ground and build it from the ground up, in his own image. That's why he's kept his hands relatively clean, maneuvering everything from behind that desk on the top floor of the building."

"Right, I guess," Eliza said.

"Look, he's not about *immigrants*, per se. He's about *immigration* at large. Society over the individual. The same stuff he was telling us in his office. The ends justify the means in his mind. He thinks he knows a way to do this properly, but it's impossible in the current system. There's no way—save for deleting everything and starting over—to build a new system the right way."

Their orders were called and Eliza grabbed the tea and handed Jake his coffee.

"He works for ICE because he's always been pro-immigration, but he wanted to fight the system from the inside out. He wanted to fix it. But he feels like he failed because he couldn't do it within the confines and constrictions of the system that already exists. So he decided to do something entirely different. Literally infect the system so much that there would be no choice but to start over."

Eliza started back toward their table, but Jake began walking toward the doors. "So where are we going now?" she asked.

Jake grinned as he opened the door for her. It was bright outside even though it was overcast. The temperature was hot and the humidity made things feel almost muggy. "Back to Briggs' office. I'll call an Uber."

"We need an Uber for that? It's like a few hundred feet away."

"Briggs has that meeting with Atlantic, remember? I'd like to see if we can follow him there, maybe get inside and confront him again."

Jake was on his phone hailing another Uber when Eliza finally noticed that he seemed different somehow. Almost as if he were relaxed. "What's up, Jake Parker? We've just discovered that the bogeyman has been in front of us all along, running us ragged and killing a lot of people in the process, and if I'm not mistaken you seem *happy* about it."

Jake laughed again as he answered. "No, I'm not happy, neces-sarily. I feel *successful*. It's been a long time since I've felt this way, honestly. I miss it. The feeling of finally figuring something out."

"Well, I hate to drop a stain in your petri dish, but we haven't succeeded yet. If Briggs is behind all of this, he's still walking around a free man, and there could be more ICE facilities ready to explode with new cases and deaths. And, you said it yourself, we still don't have enough to bring him in on."

Jake smiled at her. A true, genuine smile, probably the first one she'd seen since she'd met him. "But we've got enough pieces to see the big picture. It won't be hard now to find the evidence to fill in the little details."

"Fine," Eliza said, unable to stop herself from laughing along with him. She couldn't help but notice how cute he was at the moment, totally and completely absorbed in the thing he was best at. "But are you finally going to tell me what it is you've figured out?"

"Sure," he said as the Uber driver pulled up to the curb and he opened the door. "Still working on some of them, but there's one piece to all of this—the actual way the parasite is being spread—that I'm pretty sure about."

Eliza stopped before climbing into the vehicle. "Wait, really? You've figured out how the parasite is getting into the victims?"

Jake nodded excitedly from inside the car, motioning for her to enter. "I did, and it makes sense. I could be wrong, but…"

"What is it, then? What's the vector?"

He buckled his seatbelt with one hand, holding his coffee with the other. "500 Twelfth Street," he told the driver. "Immigration Customs and Enforcement Headquarters, please." When he was done, he looked back at Eliza with a cocky grin on his face. "Ink."

CHAPTER 57

"I don't get it," Eliza said.

They were on their way back to the Immigration offices. Jake didn't have a plan to approach Briggs—he wouldn't be prepared for an arrest, anyway—but he did know the man had to leave the office for his meeting with Atlantic Enterprises Group. There was an outside chance Briggs would leave via the back door of the building that led into the parking garage, but he remembered that the man's assistant had told him his car would be waiting. Jake took that to assume the car would be out in front of the building. If they were going to wait around and research AEG, they might as well do it from somewhere they could also keep an eye on their main suspect.

Jake had asked the Uber driver how much it would cost for them to just wait in the car for up to an hour; when he offered the driver a couple of hundred-dollar bills, the man simply thanked him and drove toward the downtown building.

Jake turned his attention back to Eliza. "Ink. Specifically, fingerprinting ink."

"I guess that technically could work," Eliza said, her eyes gazing up at the roof of the car. Jake could tell she was getting excited about how close they were to solving the case. "In its microscopic state, it would be pretty easy to add the parasite to the formulation."

"Fingerprinting ink is a pretty big deal in law enforcement," Jake said. "You can't just grab the first box of ink you see at the craft store. The FBI website even has a whole page on it. There's a process, but there's also a proper type of ink. One that doesn't leave residue, washes off of fingers but stays on paper."

"And because the government's buying it, I'm assuming there's a very specific formula for making it that suppliers must adhere to?"

"Yep, exactly. Only a couple suppliers they use, from what I remember. But they're big companies, the kind that make everything and can support a specialized division dedicated to producing just government- and law enforcement-quality fingerprinting ink. And remember the lady we spoke with in the hospital? Ms. Jenkins?"

Eliza nodded.

"She said her only job was to 'get their fingerprints and their names.' Who else would be prone to becoming a host than a woman whose job it was to deal with parasite-infested papers all day?"

After finishing the sentence, Jake couldn't help but think about their own experience at the ICE facility where they'd interrogated Dr. Edemza. They had both been asked to give their fingerprints. "A new database," the front-desk worker had told him. Jake believed that was true—he knew police fingerprint databases were always being overhauled, and asking for fingerprints of people who weren't already in the system was common practice. He felt a sinking feeling in the pit of his stomach. If what he was proposing were true, he and Eliza could be infected already.

But he quickly changed his mind. The parasite was being released slowly, and the cases they'd been tracking so far had been isolated to ICE detention centers, not broader ICE-related complexes like the one they'd been to.

They would find out soon enough if they had it, he realized, but for the moment there was no point in worrying Eliza about it. As a scientist, he had no doubt she had already considered the possibility.

"Okay," Eliza said. "So Briggs somehow tampered with the supply chain to swap out the normal fingerprinting ink with parasite-infested ink. How?"

"Well, I have a theory about that as well. I haven't done the research yet, but…" He stopped and typed something on his phone, then scrolled through the results.

The Uber driver pulled to the side of the road and found a parking spot just down the street from the government ICE headquarters. "Meter's going to let us hang out for a couple hours only," the driver said. "But we can move after that. Be right back—I'm going to pay the meter."

The driver got out of the car just as Jake found what he was looking for. "Here," he said. "Right on their home page." He scrolled up again and began to read. "'Atlantic Enterprises Group is focused on creating a better world and environment, through the research and development of sustainable, natural products based on recycled and recyclable materials. Our product lines include laboratory chemicals and byproducts of petroleum industry waste, pharmaceutical packaging and recyclable single-use medical instruments, and environmentally friendly office supplies and equipment.'"

"Office supplies and equipment."

"Exactly," Jake said. "And 'pharmaceutical packaging'? That's probably why we found AEG mentioned while investigating Edemza."

"Don't forget that the trucks carrying stuff to the Dilley facility were carrying *office supplies*. You think Jorge's guys might have found some fingerprinting ink pads?"

Jake snapped his fingers and his eyes grew in size. "Oh, man, that's *got* to be it. There was probably a delivery a week ago of ink pads, but another one—maybe even a bigger one this time. Jorge's team wouldn't have thought to examine the individual ink pads, and they wouldn't have found anything, anyway."

"The parasite has to be microscopic in order to transfer through skin. I've seen studies that prove some parasitic worm larvae can actually enter the host's body through the epidermis. Through the skin. So as long as the chemical compounds in the ink don't break down the parasite or otherwise harm it, that method would actually be a perfect delivery system."

Jake didn't enjoy her description of "a perfect delivery system," but he couldn't argue with it from a scientific standpoint. She was right; it *was* a perfect system.

"The scientist in me says we need a *lot* of testing to be able to prove this," Eliza continued, "but the human in me who wants to catch the piece of shit who thought this up says yes. Absolutely. This is how they're doing it, Jake."

"This is how *Briggs* is doing it, you mean."

She nodded, but there was a question on her face. "You think he could actually pull this off?"

Jake flicked through a few more pages of AEG's website. He stopped on a relevant article and read her the title. "'Press Release: Atlantic Enterprises Thrusts Forward with Waxworm Plastics Research.'"

Eliza raised an eyebrow. "Does that have anything to do with that discovery a couple of years ago that waxworms might be able to *eat* plastic?" she asked.

"Yes," he said. "That's exactly what it's about. And it seems like some of the byproducts of these little guys are very similar ingredients to what's in the formula for fingerprinting ink."

"How does that relate to Briggs?"

"Well, for starters, he's on their board of directors. Besides that, I'd bet that if we took a look around their laboratories, we'd find out that plastic-eating waxworms aren't the *only* type of worms they're studying."

CHAPTER 58

"There he is," Eliza said, pointing out her window to the front doors of the ICE building. "He's with his assistant."

Jake watched as Derek Briggs walked to the curb, where a long, black Chrysler sedan waited. His assistant opened the door and Briggs stepped into the vehicle. After the assistant closed the door, she turned and walked back toward the front of the building.

"Follow that car if you don't mind," Jake said. The driver glanced back at Jake through the rearview mirror, but Jake just smiled. "He's an old friend from work."

Jake didn't want to have to remind the kid that he had given him two-hundred dollars about ten minutes ago, but he didn't need to. The young man began driving, following behind the Chrysler at a good distance. They crossed over the channel, merging onto Highway 1 and passing the Jefferson Memorial. Thirty seconds later, they were on the other side of the small island and merged onto 395 and crossed over the Potomac.

Jake could still see the Chrysler through the front windshield, and he silently commended their Uber driver for staying a few cars behind. He doubted Briggs or his driver would be cognizant enough to be on the lookout for someone following them, but Jake also knew that government officials at this level rarely had the need for playing such spy games: there were probably NSA satellites watching him and Eliza at this very minute, waiting for him to approach Briggs with a threat.

Eliza held up her phone, and Jake looked at the screen. On it was a map of downtown Washington, D.C. Their location a blue dot slowly moving southwest down the highway. As he watched, she pinched her fingers together and zoomed out a bit, then scrolled around the screen with her thumb, eventually landing in a space that seemed to be ten or fifteen blocks away from their location now.

"What is it?" Jake asked.

Eliza pointed to a single building near the bottom corner of the screen, then zoomed in. She tapped on it and the title appeared: *Atlantic Enterprises Group, US.*

"So it seems our suspect is keeping to his schedule," Jake said. He passed the location information along to the Uber driver, who simply nodded and kept driving in the right lane.

They passed the Pentagon on their right and continued on for another five minutes, until they arrived at their destination. Atlantic had the tallest building on the block, and it was very clear that it was in no way a government-funded establishment. The building itself twisted upward, similar in shape to the Cayan Tower in Dubai, although far smaller. One entire façade of the slanted shape was glass, and the framing around the windows themselves gave the twisted wall the impression of being a single sheet of glass.

Eliza whistled.

"Yeah, looks like whatever product lines Atlantic is involved with have been paying pretty big dividends."

Jake watched the Chrysler turn around a corner and out of sight, and the Uber driver followed a few car lengths behind. He expected the Chrysler to turn left into the building's underground parking, but instead it kept driving for another block.

"Where is he going?" Eliza asked.

"Beats me, but I bet we're about to find out."

Sure enough, the Chrysler slowed and pulled over to the right side of the road, where it stopped and put on its hazard lights. Directly next to the vehicle, across the street from the massive headquarters of the Atlantic Group, was a much smaller building, this one under construction. Scaffolding had been built on the ground in front of it, and rose the five stories to the roof. Jake didn't see any construction workers out front though, and it seemed as though the building might have been abandoned while half-finished.

The Uber driver had pulled into a spot five cars behind the Chrysler, and they waited for about twenty seconds before Briggs exited the car. He closed his door and turned to face the uncompleted building.

"What does your map say about this building?" Jake asked Eliza.

She played with the screen for a few seconds, then pulled up the result. "All it says is 'AEG,' so possibly also Atlantic-owned."

"Well, I guess we're in the right place then," Jake said.

Eliza began to unbuckle her seatbelt and opened her door, but Jake stopped her. He looked out the window as Briggs entered the building.

Satisfied they would be able to proceed without being seen, Jake finally opened his door and got out. Eliza followed. She rounded the back of the car and began to step onto the curb, when something caught Jake's eye.

Oh, shit.

He squinted to try to see the newcomers in more detail, but he had no doubt who they were. The two grunts who had been following them. The two intruders who had broken into Eliza's house, and then the two who had nearly chased Jake off the road back in Boston.

Whether they were Shaw's guys or not, their master had redirected them to Washington D.C., and they had somehow found Jake and Eliza once again. The fact that they hadn't been sent to

Texas, where Briggs *thought* Eliza and Jake were headed, told Jake that they were more for Briggs' security than for tracking down anyone Briggs needed to keep tabs on.

Jake grabbed Eliza's elbow, tightening his grip on it and pulling her faster toward the front of the building.

"Jake, what the hell?" Eliza asked. She began to pull her arm away from his, but then looked at his face. "Jake, what is it? What happened?"

"Our friends are back," Jake said.

"Should we—should we call the cops or something?"

Jake nodded. "There's nothing like having a couple goons follow you around to different cities to tell you that you're on the right track. No, no cops. This is Briggs' world now, and we don't know we'll be able to trust anyone else."

He knew he could trust Eliza, and he knew she could trust him. But would that be enough? These guys had become more and more aggressive, and Jake wasn't entirely sure they were going to let them off easily this time.

As they turned right and began to enter the building under the scaffolding and hanging sheets of plastic, Jake got confirmation of that as, out of the corner of his eye, he noticed one of the men reaching under his coat with his right hand.

Here we go again.

CHAPTER 59

The interior of the building was in a state of complete disrepair, and it was surprising there were even lights on. But they were bright enough to see by, and Jake pointed Eliza directly toward stairs at the opposite end of the main lobby they had entered into.

Just as they reached the bottom stair, the two men entered behind them. "Stop! We will shoot!"

Jake muttered under his breath as he pulled Eliza along up the stairs. "Yeah, that's what they all say. Then they shoot you anyway."

They started to run, and Jake heard their footsteps pounding forward as they neared the stairs and closed the distance. He let go of Eliza—they could both go faster separately—and began taking the stairs two at a time, moving left as he ascended. Eliza followed next to him, and when they reached the top, Jake launched himself around the corner.

Eliza nearly fell as she ran around him, but both narrowly missed the first of the gunshots. One of the men had opened fire on them just before they'd reached the top of the stairs, and Jake heard the rounds thunk into the drywall on the back side of the hallway.

Jake pushed Eliza forward and together they ran down the hallway and took a right when it intersected with another stretch of hallway. Rectangular sheets of drywall had been hung in haphazard spots, framing beams and wood sticking out in-between them. They were in a hallway filled with unfinished office spaces, nothing but plywood floors and ceilings and open floor joists.

He hoped the floor beneath their feet would stay there as they ran, and he hoped the lights above their head would continue to illuminate their path.

They were running slightly faster than the two men behind them, but Jake knew there was nowhere they could stop. There were no actual walls to hide behind, no doors to shut and lock. They were in a maze of unfinished construction, and it was only a matter of time before they found a missing chunk of floor and fell through.

Worse, Jake was unarmed. The men had begun to fire at them, so Jake would happily have taken a few potshots back in return. He wondered if there would be anything lying around—tools, equipment, pieces of wood—he might be able to use as a weapon if it came to that. He had a feeling they were beyond talking, beyond being able to stop and turn around with their hands above their heads and claim innocence. Jake had approached Briggs on his home turf, and he had a feeling these men were here to make sure it didn't happen again.

And yet, aside from not wanting to be killed, Jake couldn't help but run through the possibilities of what they might find here. Jake had seen Briggs himself enter this very building. What secret meeting was Briggs about to join?

At the end of the hallway, Jake saw a light. It was brighter than the single dim bulbs hanging from the ceiling, and it appeared to be coming from the other side of a completed wall.

His money was on that being Briggs' destination. Possibly the only actual room in the entire building that had been completed, or at least fully formed. His hypothesis was confirmed when he realized the two men following them weren't shooting—every missed shot would simply punch through the wall in front of them, potentially hitting anyone inside.

It wasn't much of an advantage, but it was all they had at the moment.

The pair kept running, and Jake knew that if they were going to get to Briggs, they needed to do something about the two men behind them. Something up ahead caught Jake's eye just as he thought of an idea.

He kept his voice low. "Hard right up ahead," he said. "Duck behind that half-wall once you get in."

Eliza didn't respond verbally, but when the moment came, she veered to the right and jumped into the room like a trained athlete. Her body was lithe, catlike, and Jake couldn't help but feel impressed, though there wasn't time to dwell on it.

They needed to use the interior structure of the building as their weapon, and Jake had seen this opportunity and decided to act. He had calculated correctly. When they had passed a massive, square-shaped wooden tower—likely the site of a future elevator shaft—Jake knew they would have a couple of seconds when they were out of sight from the two men in pursuit. He had decided to duck into a room behind the elevator shaft and wait for the two men to pass.

He didn't have to tell Eliza to be quiet. She was already pressed hard up against the back wall of the elevator shaft in the tiny room. There was a half-wall protecting them and keeping them out of sight, but they needed to crouch and stay hidden until the men passed.

Or, Jake needed to be ready to fight them if they entered.

Thankfully, the two men passed right by the room without stopping to peer in. They slowed, now aware that they had lost their prey. They continued down the hall toward the finished room, and Jake could hear their footsteps turn and head in the other direction.

He hoped the building was big enough to keep the men occupied while he and Eliza snooped around, but he had no plans on staying very long. In and out. Get whatever information they could from here, then get the hell back to safety.

He wished he could call Shaw for backup. He wished he could text his friend and ask for his advice.

Not now, dammit. He needed to get through this alive—needed to get Eliza through this alive—and then he could have all the time in the world to focus on Shaw.

He turned to Eliza. "Ready?"

She was breathing quickly, but otherwise seemed to be okay. She nodded, and stood up.

Jake walked back to the hallway and peered in each direction. It was about a hundred yards to the end, where he thought Briggs might be hiding, and he hoped they would be able to get there without the two men finding them.

Rather than speed, Jake opted for stealth. He moved slowly, walking in the shadows and trying to keep his feet from making any sound. Eliza was better at it, and he had to continue checking behind him to make sure she was still there.

They made their way down the hallway and reached the wall. There was now more light than Jake had initially thought, spilling out from behind it. It seemed there would be two ways to enter the room, one to the left and one to the right. The light spilling from the left side was caught by the back wall of the building itself, which made Jake feel more comfortable. He didn't want to back himself into a corner, but being up against the walls would allow for them to remain out of sight more easily.

"There's definitely something back there," Eliza whispered.

Jake nodded. "Absolutely. I don't hear anyone, but there's a reason they've got all the lights on. Stay with me, and keep your eyes up. If you're able to, focus where I'm not looking so we can watch each other's backs."

Without waiting for a response, Jake stepped forward and snaked around the corner to the left. Eliza was right on his six as they rounded the turn and entered the light falling out from the room.

And what Jake saw inside left him completely stunned.

CHAPTER 60

Eliza pulled her hand to her mouth, covering it with an open palm. She wasn't sure what she had expected to see inside this room, but what was lying in front of her was beyond her comprehension.

The room itself was bare, the drywall screwed into place but still unpainted and unfinished. Fluorescent lights hung from the ceiling, shining brightly downward onto six rows of cheaply constructed tables, side by side. Eliza estimated twelve tables in all, placed in a grid throughout the room. The tables were also made of wood, likely thrown together by the same construction team that had gutted the building. And on each of the tables sat a rectangular tub and a cardboard box. The boxes seemed to be full of smaller, plastic boxes, and she could see stacks of them lying in-between the cardboard and tubs on some tables. Behind each of the tables stood a person, wearing a full hazmat suit and gloves. Eliza watched them work, trying to understand what she was seeing.

The worker closest to them, still unaware they were being watched, grabbed a plastic box from the top of the stack and opened it up, revealing a black pad inside.

Fingerprinting ink.

The worker then grabbed a Q-tip from a pile lying in front of him and dipped it into the tub. He swished around a bit, then withdrew it carefully and gently ran it over the top of the pad of ink. He rolled the Q-tip around to ensure he had administered the solvent across the entire surface of the pad, then he closed it and set it down onto a different pile of plastic boxes.

"Holy shit," Jake whispered. "He's doing it right here in Washington. I can't believe…"

One of the workers in a hazmat suit was walking a cardboard box of ink cases over to a stack against the wall, and they must have caught his eye. The woman stopped, tilted her head a bit, and Eliza could see her mouth begin to open inside her mask. Eliza noticed that she had dark skin and a dark complexion.

She pulled Jake back. "She saw us," she said. "Jake, she saw us. What do we do now?"

"Hey! You two!" Eliza heard someone yell from inside the room. "Who the hell are you?"

Jake turned to Eliza, his eyes wide. "We need to get proof. We need a picture. Have your phone ready, but also be ready to run. We don't know if they are—"

Two gunshots rang out and Eliza screamed. Jake pulled her downward, yanking her toward the room. He pulled her inside just as a hazmat suit-wearing individual came to the open space behind the wall, where a door would eventually go.

It was a man, but he did not have time to yell. Jake came up with both fists and hit him under the chin, knocking him backward and into a table. The table teetered, but the liquid inside the tub sloshed over the side and splashed onto the floor. Two other people inside the room jumped to the side, dodging the liquid.

Clearly whatever was inside the tub was not good.

Jake didn't stop moving. He was running toward the opposite side of the room, toward…

And then Eliza saw him. Briggs.

He was standing in the corner, calmly watching her and Jake. There was a computer behind him, likely a makeshift workstation where Briggs could control this project of his.

Briggs didn't react to the unfolding chaos, and Eliza wondered why—until a man standing next to Briggs, also not wearing a hazmat suit, lifted his arm and pointed it at Jake. The man's hand wasn't empty.

"Jake!" Eliza screamed. But it was too late. The man was holding a pistol and began to fire at Jake, completely unconcerned about the other people in the room.

The first shot smacked into the wall right next to Eliza's head. Jake jumped to his left, narrowly missing a worker and a table, and he kept running.

The shooter had to reconfigure, stepping in front of Briggs and opening his stance as he aimed again toward Jake. Eliza caught sight of Briggs working his way along the wall, toward the other exit.

He was going to make a run for it.

No chance in hell, Eliza thought. She picked up the first thing she could find: a food scale that had been lying on the table in front of her. It was lightweight, but it was all she had. She launched it through the air and watched it sail end over end toward Briggs.

Two more shots rang out, but Eliza was focused on her own target.

The scale was right in line to connect with Briggs' head, but at the last second Briggs noticed the object and yanked his head back quickly.

The scale smashed into a two-by-four and fell to the ground.

Briggs looked over at Eliza, then back toward the exit. He continued moving across the room, still walking but picking up his pace.

Eliza started running. She doubted she would be able to overwhelm him with force and keep him in the room, but she hoped Jake would be able to overcome his own assailant and help her.

She aimed for Briggs, and tried to line up her forehead with his side. She picked up speed across the long room and was about five feet away when Briggs finally noticed. He turned his head once again, and she spotted a look of surprise on his face.

He turned, but it was too late. Eliza crashed into his chest, knocking them both off their feet and back toward the hallway.

Briggs tried to keep his balance, but couldn't. He fell backward onto the plywood-covered floor, smacking his head hard against it.

Eliza was on top of him, and she began punching. She didn't know what to aim for, and she certainly didn't know if it would do any good, but she felt the anger flowing out of her as she attacked. She swung hard with her fists, bringing them down onto his face and ears.

Briggs finally registered what was happening and pulled his arms up, blocking his eyes. Another second passed, and he suddenly launched out with a right hook that completely took Eliza's breath away. He had directly connected with her ribs, and the pain was immediate and intense. She could tell in an instant that Briggs was far stronger than she had imagined, and she rolled off of him and held her side, trying to force air back into her lungs.

Every single breath hurt, in and out, and she thought she was going to die. If Briggs were going to attack her, she could do nothing to prevent it.

Eliza looked up at the ceiling of the hallway, staring at the single bulb. She knew there was just one, but it still seemed as though there were five, each circling one other. She blinked a few times, sensing that Briggs was now on his feet, standing over her. Eliza wondered what he was going to do to her, whether he would kick her or fall on top of her or something else entirely.

She saw Briggs pull his foot back, clearly aiming toward her head.

And then the man simply disappeared.

Something blurry sailed over Eliza's head and landed in Briggs' side. She heard him grunt in pain and then heard another impact as he landed farther down the hallway.

She forced her neck up and her head sideways against the pain, and looked to see Jake now fighting with Briggs. It wasn't much of a fight—Jake was pummeling the man's face, each blow smacking against the soft flesh of Briggs' cheeks, nose, eyes.

Some of the people who had been in the room were now out in the hallway, watching through their hazmat helmets. Eliza saw them, wide-eyed, their faces dark, watching as their boss was being completely destroyed.

And yet, not a single one of them ran over to help Briggs.

CHAPTER 61

Briggs felt himself being lifted up off the floor. He couldn't see—both his eyes were swollen shut. Blood dripped from his nose, staining his white Tom Ford poplin shirt. He tried to fend off the arms pulling him up, but they were rigid, sturdy and unwavering.

The attack had been unfair—he hadn't even seen Jake Parker coming. He had been standing over Eliza Mendoza, the bitch who had gone against his orders and initiated the investigation into the Stermers' deaths, ruining everything. She had forced him to speed up the timeline, to change the plan. There were a lot of variables at play, a lot of dominoes that needed to be stacked in the right order, and she had knocked one down in the middle of the line before the rest were ready.

He had chosen Jake Parker for a reason: Beau Shaw had affirmed Briggs' hypothesis that Parker was a by-the-book detective, the type of man who would methodically progress through a case, following all logical protocol in a perfect order. After recruiting Shaw to the case, Briggs knew the two men would come as a pair. He knew that having Jake Parker hire Beau Shaw to his team would only strengthen the case—it would seem as though Parker brought on Shaw, when in fact Briggs and Shaw had been working together all along. He'd targeted Parker early on, using the two things he knew the man wouldn't be able to resist: a good case and an ex-partner. Shaw was a perfect candidate, too. Emotionally unstable, needing only a solid motive and some direction.

But then Eliza Mendoza had ruined all of that. He didn't blame Beau Shaw for bringing her onto the case—there was no way they could have anticipated her actions—but it didn't make Briggs feel any better about it.

Parker lifted Briggs to his feet and held his collar, pulling his face close to his own. They were about the same height; Briggs had perhaps an inch on the younger man.

"This ends here, Briggs."

Briggs could barely see Parker's face; it was just a mask of white, a blurry, out-of-focus blob. "This doesn't end anywhere close to here," Briggs said. He sneered, hoping the message would come through on his battered face.

Parker pulled Briggs to the side, toward another unfinished room off of the hallway. The kid was incredibly strong, and Briggs knew he would have trouble fighting him even if he weren't brutally injured. Still, Briggs knew he could put up at least a bit of a struggle.

"What the hell is this, Parker?" Briggs asked through gritted teeth. "What are you doing here? Call the cops, have them come out and arrest me. Play it by the book, like you always do."

Instead of answering him, Parker turned to his left while still holding Briggs and kicked as hard as he could, sending the piece of plywood that had been nailed to the outside wall of the building flying away. Immediately the wind whipped into the interior of the construction site, and the cool air struck the wounds on Briggs' face and the searing pain began all over again.

He tensed, but Parker didn't release him. "Seriously," Briggs said. "What the hell are you planning? You going to—"

Parker suddenly swung him to the left, *over* the board at their waist and out of the building. Briggs felt the vertigo as he saw bright daylight up above. He felt his shirt slowly beginning to rip. His Tom Ford was the only thing holding his top half to the building.

"Why did you do it?" Jake asked. "All those people—how many of them were going to have to die for your plan to work?"

Briggs didn't answer. He stayed calm. He didn't owe this kid a response; he had handled far worse threats in his time. He knew Parker wasn't going to drop him from the building—it would ruin the detective's case. And Parker wasn't in a place of negotiating power, either. What was he supposed to do, drop the director of ICE backward out of a window? It would be a three-story fall, just about survivable, though Briggs would have to somehow make sure he didn't land on his head.

Still, he was willing to go through whatever pain this punk kid thought he needed to experience. He could handle whatever *anyone* could throw at him, much less what this washed-up cop thought he could do.

They hung there together for a moment. Parker had reached down and grabbed his sleeve to prevent him from falling, but Briggs could tell the younger man was losing his grip. The man's hands began to shake, and for a moment Briggs wondered if Parker would actually do it.

A voice called out from behind them. "Jake, no."

Eliza Mendoza. She was right there, right behind Parker now.

Jake made a low, grunting noise, then pulled Briggs forward and up. He tossed Briggs back into the room, where he fell in a heap against the wall framing.

"I asked you a question," Parker said. "How many people are going to—"

"Don't worry, the parasite is controlled. It won't leave ICE detainment centers." Briggs tried to focus up at the man and woman standing over him but couldn't. He coughed and felt a tooth become dislodged. "It was never going to get out. I made sure of it."

"Why?" Eliza asked. "You were just going to kill all of those people? Women and children?"

"Not all of them," Briggs said, shaking his head. He felt annoyed having to explain it, but at the same time he felt the pride in ownership over an idea he had birthed into existence. "*Enough* of them. Enough of them to make a difference. To let me start over."

"Enough people die, and suddenly the United States lets you burn everything to the ground and build it from scratch?"

Briggs knew his facial expressions weren't getting through the swollen mask he wore, but he tried anyway. "Son, how the hell do you think this country operates? What do you think happened after 9/11? You think we made some tweaks here and there? Slapped the airlines on the wrist and told them they better shape up, or else? No, we started over. The powers that be got to design the system they wanted all along. Sure, it took a little bit of fear in the right places and a few deaths to get the job done, but the result was the same: a brand-new system, one that works far better than anyone could have imagined."

"You think *this* is working far better than imagined?"

"I don't know, son. You tell me: how many planes have crashed into buildings since then? How many thousands of people have died on American soil at the hands of a foreign terrorist? Sure, there are outliers—American citizens who are so caught up in their own bullshit they commit horrible acts against other civilians—but, as I said, they are outliers. They're the exception that proves the rule."

"So what about this?" Eliza asked. "This *project*? What's it all about? What is your goal? You get to start over from scratch—what does it look like after?"

"Have you been in one of our detention centers? Have you seen the plight, the absolute devastation that registers on every single face of every single child that comes in? It's a travesty. No human should be treated that way."

He heard Parker scoff. "So you'll just have them killed, instead? Murdered from the inside by a horrifying parasite?"

Briggs took a moment to breathe. Clearly they weren't under-standing, and they weren't going to. People like them *couldn't* understand. They lived in a comfortable world of status quo, able to ignore things that were difficult. "Like I said, a few deaths and a little bit of fear. That's all it takes to change the game. I don't have to create a real pandemic—I don't have to kill *everyone*—the panic will do the rest of the work for me. The *panic* is the pandemic, and that will lead to change."

The pressure in his head was swelling, and Briggs knew he was going to have a hell of a time getting any sleep that night. Besides his face, however, he was still in good health. He wondered if he might be able to shift a bit, to get a leg out behind Parker's and then…

"Try it and see what happens, asshole," Parker said. "I know you can't see what I'm holding, so I'll help you out. That helpful little security guard you had in there? Let's just say he's no longer armed, and he no longer wants to be, either."

Briggs knew there were two other men in the building; he had assigned them to watch his back and keep an eye on these two for the past week. He also knew Parker and Mendoza knew of their presence as well. He needed to keep Parker talking, to keep him playing detective until his two guards arrived.

Thankfully, he had another tool in his toolbelt he could utilize to keep them here, to keep them occupied and focused on him. In all his years as a leader, he knew one thing for sure: everyone's favorite subject was themselves.

"Why do you think it was you, Parker?" Briggs asked. "Why do you think I chose you for this case?"

CHAPTER 62

Jake heard the question and had an answer prepared before Briggs was done asking it. "Shaw," he said. "He's been working with you for a while, hasn't he? There was no question he would ask me to get involved. And Edemza. Is he yours, too?"

Briggs was still laying at Jake's feet, and he saw the older man shake his head. "Close, but not quite. Dr. Edemza was just in the perfect position. Iranian, with enough connections back home that made it even easier to get him looked at by other agencies. And I started recruiting Shaw to my side shortly after I heard about your trial. Most of this has been in the works for a while now, but I needed the actual players. I needed you, and Shaw was a perfect vehicle for that."

"Okay, fine. Why *did* you choose me originally, if that's what you think happened?"

Briggs coughed again and Jake could see blood on the man's hand when he pulled it back from his mouth. He wasn't sure if Briggs had any internal injuries, but he also had a feeling his adversary was overemphasizing his weakness. The man was a fighter, used to having another card to play. Jake wondered what that card was.

"I needed someone who could do the job the right way. Slowly, methodically, turning over every stone but only in the order they were supposed to be turned over. I needed someone who followed the rules, someone I could point to when all this was over and say, see? I did it the right way. I got a great detective who wasn't tied to any political arena or any jurisdiction. A true third-party investigator."

"But you never expected us to go perform the autopsy on the Stermers, did you?" Jake asked.

Briggs shook his head. He lifted a finger, pointing it at Eliza. "That was all her, wasn't it? You, Parker, *never* would have done that."

"You're damn right it was her."

"I knew it. I knew I should have just had those assholes kill her the first time around. Doesn't matter," Briggs said.

"It *does* matter," Jake said. "Where'd you get them? They're not government."

Briggs shook his head. "No, of course not. Why would I hire government goons? No plausible deniability in that, is there?"

Jake knew he'd deflected, that he'd refused to answer the question. But it didn't matter—he could figure that out later.

"I'm burning this place to the ground, Briggs. Your little party up here is over."

Briggs didn't react. "You can't stop it now. We've got the parasite on the way to over fifteen facilities, and another twenty next week. Media attention is growing, the panic is starting."

Jake realized then that the Stermers—the entire family, really—had been a major part of the man's plan. And the kids: they weren't supposed to get sick; Briggs had rigged it so that the two young, orphaned white kids would feed a media frenzy. Jake knew it would have worked perfectly as well.

He wasn't sure exactly how Briggs had made it all work, but he realized that the family's unfortunate role in the whole mess had been premeditated from the beginning.

"This is all a game to you, isn't it?" Eliza asked. "You think it's you against the world?"

"Ah, see—*now* you're getting it. What had to be done, and the *way* it had to be done. Why it was the Stermers, and why it had to be controlled the way it was."

"I… I don't understand," Eliza said.

Jake squeezed his eyes closed for a second. "It was the color of their skin, Eliza. We talked about it in Albany, you even convinced me that it was about race. We—*I*—didn't understand how completely it was about race, until now."

"They were white."

"Exactly," Jake said. "They *had* to be."

Briggs grunted in pain, but smiled. "See? It's obvious, isn't it? Did you see the news articles about it? Their deaths aren't a secret now, and—because of what they look like—the entire *world* will be watching us as the parasite spreads, all controlled by the influx of the parasite into select areas and detention centers."

"Because it's not contagious, is it?" Jake asked. "It was never meant to be."

Briggs shook his head. "No, not really. In its most basic host-less form, sure. It's like yeast—small and easy to move around, and you could argue that it's *technically* contagious, but it's mostly dormant. But when it gets some sugar—or when the parasite gets into a host's body—all hell breaks loose."

"And you're controlling the spread by putting it on the ink pads and sending them to certain places. That way you can keep it controlled, keep it contained to your ICE facilities. Making the world think it's an *immigration* problem, specifically. And that's why it started with the Stermers."

"Of course. You think that level of media attention would be given to a *Mexican* family that's come across the border accidentally?"

"You targeted innocent people just to prove a point."

"Parker!" Briggs yelled, his voice gurgling. "That *is* the point. To answer my own question, *no*. The world doesn't care if a family with brown skin gets illegally detained. They don't care if they die. As a whole, as a society, it's always been about what we look like. Do they look like us? Okay, then they're more important. Do they look different? Speak a different language? Okay, then they can rot in a prison cell while we look the other way."

"That's not true, Briggs."

"You damn well better believe it's true, son. I'm the head of the organization that was built on this principle. Just last year we had a high-school student detained for over three weeks because they didn't believe that he had been born in Texas. He was stopped at a checkpoint one hundred miles north of the border. They didn't let the kid call his parents for God's sake."

"Why not fix *that*? That's just a policy change, right? Can't you type an email and in fifteen minutes solve—"

"It *isn't* a policy! Our policy—everyone's 'policy' is to let a person call their damn family. They didn't let the kid shower for twenty-three days, Parker. *Twenty-three days*. He lost twenty-six pounds while he was there, and when they finally let the poor kid out? They just shrugged and apologized.

"And again, three months ago, there was a deadly scare of scabies and mumps down in our El Paso center. The CDC had to quarantine an entire city block of refugees. And there were deaths. Did you hear about that? No, because it was hardly reported, except as a footnote in the *New York Times*. Even then, the mention was in an article that was actually about a family from Canada that was detained in 'terrible conditions' for 'two whole days.' A *white* family. For two days. But the country paid attention then—they wanted to hear *that* story."

"But this is *you*," Eliza said. "Briggs, *you* are ICE. This was *your* fault, and you should be held responsible for—"

Briggs screamed in rage, and spit flew from his mouth as he spoke. "I *am* holding myself responsible! Don't you see that? I can't fire everyone in the organization, all the way down, who's caused problems like this or allowed it to happen. No one cares—the article gets published, a few people comment about the sad state of affairs, then things go back to normal.

"Not anymore. With the Stermers' deaths, the world will wake up. They'll start to take notice. Two white people died of a parasite that's infected an entire system? They'll line up in droves to start tearing it down, piece by piece. There will be rioting on the streets if that's what it takes. If the problem is systemic, only destroying the existing system will fix it."

Jake shook his head. "It's too far, Briggs. You went too far. And you brought Shaw into it. He was a—"

"He was a what, Parker? A *good man*? He was a pawn. You know that, right? The man was as conflicted as you are, but he simply chose the right side. He bought into the cause even before I had to sell it to him. A perfect soldier, really. It hardly took any persuading at all to get him onto the project. I don't condone how he did it, and he's going to die because of it. But I didn't force his hand. I showed him the truth, just like I showed you, and he made his decision."

Jake thought about the man's words. He had to admit he heard truth behind them. He heard Shaw's words running through his mind. *How far would you go for something you believe in?*

It was unspeakable, what Briggs had done here, what he was planning. And was still planning.

Jake realized that they were wasting time. There was more of the parasite out there—more of the fingerprinting ink cartridges being shipped around the United States to ICE detention centers. They needed to move, to—

"Jake!" Eliza screamed.

He turned, saw the men charging down the hallway. They must have been on a separate floor; Jake had nearly forgotten about them.

For the moment, he ignored Briggs and ran toward the doorway, but it was too late. He heard the gunshot.

He saw Eliza fall.

CHAPTER 63

Eliza crumpled to the wood floor directly in front of Jake. He lunged over her prone body and toward the doorway, pulling up the pistol he'd been holding, the one taken off Briggs' guard in the other room.

These two men had antagonized them long enough. Jake was no longer unarmed, and he no longer felt it necessary to hesitate, to give them a chance.

He fired two quick shots. His body reacted involuntarily after the first, his habitual assessment through years of training and instinctual impulses kicking in to retarget for the second shot.

The first landed in the first man's chest, but the second went through his neck. His body immediately went rigid, and his partner nearly ran into him as he stumbled backward.

Jake wasn't finished, however. He fired again, clipping the second attacker's shoulder as the man jumped to the side, his own pistol flying upward as he tried to aim.

He knew the man was off-balance, and therefore didn't feel the need to duck or dodge. He wanted a clean shot, a straight shot. The second attacker was bleeding from his shoulder, and Jake could see, even in the dim light, that he was struggling with the pain.

Jake hadn't had time to check the weapon's loadout, but judging by weight alone he knew he had at least half a full mag, and this particular gun held a magazine of fifteen rounds.

Enough to do the job.

Jake calmly and quickly closed the distance between the dead attacker and the second man, who was still trying to catch his breath and fire a shot. Jake wasn't interested in letting him finish. He slid his pistol to the left, automatically adjusting his aim as he breathed, keeping the weapon's sights steady with the target. He pulled the trigger.

The round flew into the man's eye, and he stood still, momentarily shocked, the neurons in his brain still firing wildly to try to determine what the hell had just happened. Within another second, they shut off completely and the man fell.

Jake didn't even stop to see him die. He had his phone out and up to his ear, hailing help from local police. While there might be some in the ranks of Washington's police force on Briggs' payroll, he had to assume a 911 call claiming 'shots fired' and 'man down' would warrant at least a bit of proper attention.

He wasn't concerned with the backup; he only needed handcuffs.

"Hello? My name is Parker." He gave the address of the building they were in, told the operator what had happened, and then hung up, against their orders not to.

He walked back toward Eliza, who was lying on the ground face down, but moving her arm slowly, trying to position it near her side. Just as he reached her, he noticed that Briggs had pulled himself to his feet.

"I'm not dead, you know," Briggs said. His face was a mess of blood and swollen flesh, shining in the light from the overhead bulb.

"Yeah," Jake said. "I can see that."

"I can still walk. Run, even. So what's the plan, Parker? You going to convince me to wait here, to sit and hang out while the cops come to arrest me? Or are you planning to fight me again, to—"

Jake raised the pistol and fired another single shot. A hot round sailed through the air, through Briggs' side.

He looked down, then back up at Jake, a bewildered expression on his face. He placed his hand on his gut, the blood already seeping through his fingers. He stumbled, and behind Briggs, where he held the older man out the window, Jake could see a stain of blood against the dark plywood.

"You—you son of a *bitch*, Parker," Briggs spat. "You missed— was that supposed to kill me?"

"I don't miss. You should know that by now. It's a flesh wound, and you'll heal just fine, unfortunately."

"But what's the plan now? You've always got one, don't you? You think they'll let you off the hook for this? A detective, shooting the director of a government organization?"

He stumbled again and finally gave up, falling onto his rear end up against the same wall he'd been lying in front of before.

"No," Jake said. "I don't always have a plan. And I'm not a detective, remember? I'm carrying a weapon because you hired me to do a job, and I've got the emails and contract to prove it. What, you think they'll lock me up after all of this? Take away my license? I'm only here because you brought me in."

He pointed toward the room of ink and parasite-infested tubs. There were no more hazmat suit-wearing people inside; they had fled during the scuffle and gunfire.

"That whole room of funhouse horrors is on you, Briggs," Jake continued. "How will you explain that?"

Jake heard Eliza groan on the ground and he crouched by her side. He pressed one hand down tightly over the wound, knowing that it would cause immense pain but wanting to stop the blood flow.

Briggs chuckled, then shook his head. "This is a game, Parker. And I'm really good at playing it. You think you understand how this works, huh? You saw enough of it on the lower levels to understand it at the highest levels? Well, I've got news for you: all of this—everything around us—isn't *mine*."

Jake understood what he meant. AEG—Atlantic Enterprises—owned this building and their name was on the boxes of fingerprinting ink that were being shipped around the country.

"And hell, son, this is the smallest operation. I needed to keep my eye on the production, but I couldn't have all of it here, under one roof. That's insane. So you calling in the cavalry; you think they're gonna bust this up like a drug raid. Fine. We'll see. But it isn't going to stop any of this."

"I want to stop you, and I have," Jake said.

Briggs choked on a laugh, and Jake saw blood spilling out over his chin. "You… you think that's how easy it is. 'Stop the leader, and stop the whole thing.' Don't be naïve, son. I put this whole thing in motion, but I'd be damned if I had to be there the whole time to baby it, to see it through."

Eliza groaned again, and Jake reapplied pressure. "Shh," he said. "Help's coming. One minute."

Briggs kept talking, his voice growing more and more animated. "Hell, Parker, you think *I'm* the only one who wants this? Haven't you been around the block a few times, seen some shit? I'm not going to pay for any of this because they need this. The real power behind the closed door wants this to happen. It's plausible deni-ability, all the way up. Best of all, it solves a lot of problems for them they don't even want to know they have."

Jake nodded. "Maybe that's true, Briggs. I don't care anymore."

"Like hell you don't. You want me dead. You can't do it, because you know it won't help. So you're hoping that by getting me arrested, getting me due trial and all the other bullshit this country likes to hide behind, that somehow justice will be served. But that's not what will happen. You'll see."

"Will I?" Jake asked. He heard the sounds of sirens in the distance, knowing it was only a matter of seconds before they would arrive.

"You will," Briggs said, coughing. "You will. And by leaving me alive, I'll be there to watch it happen. To watch the recognition in your eyes when you realize that your own country will protect me—one of its own—far more than any of the people who may have died. I'll get a slap on the wrist. Not because it was wrong, but because I did what I did publicly."

Jake gently grabbed Eliza beneath her legs and back and lifted her up. She winced, but didn't make any noise. She placed her arms around his neck for support as he stood, carrying her, and started to turn away from Briggs.

"Good luck, Briggs," Jake said. "But I want you to know that just because I didn't have a plan then doesn't mean I don't have one now."

"What the hell is that supposed to mean?"

Jake smiled and walked out the door.

CHAPTER 64

Three Days Later

Eliza Mendoza awoke in a hospital bed, surrounded by flowers. Mostly from her students and faculty coworkers, but also some from her parents and sister.

One in particular—a single rose standing in an unassuming ceramic pot—sat on her tray table, where someone had hastily pushed aside some hospital-grade cafeteria food and a half-empty pudding cup.

She blinked a few times, assessing her state. She felt tired, but healthy. A gentle throb in her side, right between two of her ribs, told her she was still injured, and still very medicated. She remembered the incident, the feeling of helplessness as she fell to the floor, her ribs shattered and her lung punctured by the bullet.

She shook her head and rubbed away some eye gunk, then focused on the darker shape sitting against the far wall. Brown leather jacket, black jeans, aviator sunglasses hanging by a single arm from a white T-shirt.

"You look like James Dean," she said. Her voice was groggy, a few notes deeper than normal.

"I look way better than James Dean," Jake replied. "He's been dead for a long time."

She laughed, and the sharp pain in her side warned her against doing it a second time. "And how long have *I* been dead?"

Jake rose and walked over to the hospital bed. "Three days, give or take. Mostly surgery to repair your lung, but also to try to piece together a chunk of your ribs. How are you feeling?"

She shrugged. "I've been better. Probably would be a lot worse, if not for this extremely elaborate bouquet of roses you bought me."

Jake frowned. "How do you know it was from me?"

She cocked an eyebrow, and it was Jake's turn to laugh.

"All right, fine," he said. "Guilty as charged. But to be fair, I spent the rest of my per diem and most of yours on getting you here and checked in, and in paying your hotel balance."

"What happened to Briggs?" she asked.

"He's recovering, too. Actually, only a few rooms down from here. But he's on full lockdown. With cops who aren't being paid by him."

"That's… good, I guess. But what about after? I heard what he said. You think he'll get off scot-free?"

Jake smiled. "Don't worry about that. He's going to be looking at the inside of a jail cell for a long time."

"Jake, this is *America*. Remember what he said? This goes all the way to the top. If he's right, it means he's going to be protected. No American jury will be able to touch him with the protection of US litigation and defense attorneys, as well as the judge, backing him up."

"I have a plan. Don't worry about it. Jorge has been able to get local law enforcement and ICE leadership around the country involved to find the fingerprinting ink that AEG sent out. Already we're seeing only a couple of new cases, and there have only been four more deaths. We expect that to go down significantly over the course of the next week."

She didn't feel reassured, but she'd also learned to put a good amount of trust in Jake Parker's plans. As wild as they seemed at first, they also seemed to work.

"What about Shaw?"

Jake sniffed, then looked away. She had struck a nerve, but it was important they talked about it.

"He's—he's dying, not surprisingly. You know, I always had a feeling he'd consider doing something stupid. I mean he never showed any outward signs of depression, guilt, that sort of thing, but he was really broken after his wife's death. Had a therapist, like I did, but I know he was also seeing a doctor who prescribed him a lot of medications."

"I didn't know that," Eliza said.

"He hid it well. Hid it from me for a long time, too."

"But… you're a detective?"

Jake laughed, but she saw a tear fall from his eye. "Yeah, I'm a detective, so I guess it was only a matter of time before I put two and two together. Anyway, he wanted to meet me. By now he'll start to be feeling some symptoms—he won't want to move around a whole lot, so I think I'll go see him. Try to square things up."

Eliza nodded. "Punch him in the face for me, would you?"

Jake smiled and nodded. He pulled the armchair closer to her bed, then sat. He grabbed her hand, squeezing it a bit. "The parasite's still out there, but we know exactly where to look for it now. I got in touch with Jorge and he raised a flag down in Texas—just about every sheriff's office in the country is popping into ICE facilities and for-profit detention centers. They've recalled every shipment of 'office supplies' that have gone out over the past month, on the lookout specifically for boxes of ink."

"And AEG?"

"Yeah…" Jake said. "Sad story there. Their CEO was indicted yesterday on charges of terrorism and embezzlement of company resources. It's not her fault at all, but it'll take a long time to prove it. The company's most likely going bankrupt long before then—they weren't publicly traded, but their investors are running for the hills."

Eliza nodded. "All Briggs' fault."

Jake smiled again. "Like I said, I've got a plan. Don't worry about it—I'll fill you in next week."

"Wait," she said. "What's next week?"

"Oh, nothing. I set up a dinner with your parents."

Eliza's eyes widened. "You *what*? Parker, what the—"

Jake held up a hand. "Don't pop another lung, calm down. I merely suggested it; it was your dad who insisted."

"You… and me? At dinner… together with my parents?"

"Well, you know, they asked how you were doing, and I told them you were fine. Saved from an evil gunman and then nursed back to life by me, an Army veteran and world-class detective, who just so happens to be single, *very* good-looking, and—"

Eliza groaned loudly, then snorted as she tried to laugh. The snort caused Jake to lose it, and both began chucking uncontrollably. She was in pain with every expansion of her chest, and the odd rhythm of trying not to take deep breaths while laughing hysterically was almost too much for her to handle.

A nurse knocked, then entered, giving Jake a stern look when she saw Eliza in her fit of giggles. Jake held up two hands in apology, tears now streaming freely down his face.

"I'll need to change her, sir," the nurse said. "Which means I'm going to have to ask you to leave."

"Yeah," Eliza said, her tone mocking. "Unless you want to see me naked."

The nurse didn't seem amused, but the comment caused Jake to laugh even harder. He stood and walked back over to the door, then turned and waved.

Eliza waved back, feeling a sense of warmth radiate through her.

"I'll keep our dinner date on the calendar," he called back. "And we can schedule the 'seeing you naked' part later."

He winked, then closed the door.

CHAPTER 65

Beau Shaw waited on the bridge. He was in pain, barely able to walk on his own without the help of the cane he now carried with his right hand. He squinted as he heard footsteps, barely able to make out the shape of a man walking up the pathway toward him.

He knew who it was. Parker knew Shaw would want to meet here. No need to share details, there was only one place on the planet Shaw would want to meet for something like this. And there was only one other person who would know that place, but she'd died years ago.

His text to Parker had been simple: *Meet? 7pm?*

There was a date, and that was it. He'd responded: *Yes*.

Parker stopped short, about six feet away. He was wearing a brown leather jacket over a white T-shirt.

"Parker."

"Shaw."

Shaw didn't move, and Parker didn't offer his hand. They stood there, ex-partners and ex-friends, on the same bridge where Shaw had proposed to his wife. A lifetime ago.

He, certainly, had changed.

Had *been* changed.

"Why'd you do it, man?" Parker finally asked.

"Do what?"

"Kill yourself?"

"I ain't dead yet."

Parker laughed. "You got, what? A day? Maybe less?"

"Maybe." Shaw sighed, then worked his cane to the side and shuffled around so that he was facing Jake. "I wanted to change things. I needed to change things."

"There are other ways to change things, buddy."

"Yeah? How? What should I have done?"

"For starters," Jake said, "you shouldn't have pulled Eliza into it. She was innocent, always has been. She didn't deserve to—"

"She investigated the Stermers, man! We couldn't let her get away with—"

"'We?' Listen to yourself, Shaw. You found her for the case, and you were the one who called in those thugs to scare her off. Don't go pass this off on someone else. No one to blame but yourself."

"They were Briggs' men. I just asked if they could—"

"I blame you, Shaw."

Shaw stopped. Sucked his teeth for a second. He understood. He'd known Jake Parker long enough to likely have been able to spell out exactly how this conversation would go from the moment Jake arrived.

He nodded. "Okay, fine. I didn't think it would work, man. She was good, but I thought—hell, I *knew*—you were better. I knew you wouldn't be able to give in that easily, to betray direct orders and perform an illegal autopsy."

Jake shrugged. "Guess I'm not who I used to be."

"Guess not."

"And you're not, either. The Shaw I knew wouldn't be here right now. Wishing for it all to have gone differently, gone the way that turns you into some kind of hero or martyr."

Shaw clicked his cane and started toward Jake, but Jake was already there. Right in front of him, like a flash of light. He felt Jake's vice grip hand tightening around his own wrist.

Jake pulled him close, close enough that Shaw could feel his hot breath mixing with the cool Boston air. He whispered to Shaw. "You didn't need to do this, man. You got a battle to fight, that's fine. I like battles. But you chose the easy way out. The wrong battle. There's a problem, and you identified it, but then you went and aligned yourself with Briggs."

Jake released him and took a step back. He shook his head.

"I thought I knew you, man."

Shaw couldn't tell, but it seemed as though Jake had tears in his eyes. Shaw's own eyes felt moist, but he felt a lot of things right now. He thought he could even feel the parasites growing inside of him, wriggling and moving and—

"What about Briggs?" Shaw asked suddenly. "He was right, wasn't he? He's going to get let off easy? Maybe a year in federal, then back to the top of the food chain?"

Jake paused, then looked over the bridge into the water. Finally, he turned back up and focused on Shaw. "No, actually. He's not."

Shaw frowned.

"That's what he wants, sure. And as long as an American-controlled trial happens on US soil, that'd be the outcome."

"And?"

"And so I made sure that's exactly what won't happen."

Shaw pressed his tongue onto the roof of his mouth. He wasn't following.

"Briggs had a plan that seemed to be working. He knew all the details of it, inside and out. Since he was waiting for people like the Stermers to slip up and make a mistake, we can assume he'd been ready to move on this thing for a long time. He even knew the legal side of it, how the US judicial system would respond, from the top to the bottom. Guy like that doesn't do anything haphazardly; he knows the court system here better than anyone but the code of law itself."

"What are you getting at?" Shaw asked.

"Well, that was his only mistake, but it was a big one: he knew how the US system would respond. But he wasn't just dealing in US-based assets. He was killing immigrants—citizens of *other* countries."

"But the crimes you're bringing against him happened *here*."

"Well, sure," Jake said. "But unfortunately for him that's sort of a moot point. See, I reached out to some friends who work in international affairs and do some overseas paralegal-type stuff, and as it turns out, there are a lot of non-US entities ready and willing to try him in international court. I started the proceedings a few days ago, and I've got a list twenty names long—legal staff interested in helping out. We'll get it pushed through, and then the US will have to allow the investigation to take place at the United Nations Security Council, as part of the terms of our UN covenant."

Shaw swallowed. He was hearing the words Jake was saying, parsing them as they entered his brain, but he wasn't fully understanding. "But, how… I don't—"

"It's okay," Jake said. "Briggs had about the same response when I brought it up to him in the hospital. There was more 'Navy-this,' 'war hero-that' sort of talk, but the gist is simple: he won't be protected by American courts and powers-that-be when he's brought to trial. Any and all citizenship and US attachment will be on trial as well."

Shaw wanted to scream, but the pain of doing so wasn't worth the effort. He knew he only had hours left before the parasite would tear away at the inside of his body enough to hospitalize him, and then it was only a matter of time. He'd failed—he was *not* going to die a martyr for a cause. Few, in fact, would even know his name. Thanks to Jake, he was merely a victim, not the hero Briggs had promised him he would be.

"Kill me, Parker."

Jake looked at him. "Come again?"

"Just do it. Kill me."

"You think you're a martyr for some cause, is that it? You hoped you'd die before all of this came to light, that you'd be painted as some sort of hero? 'A man who gave it all for what he believed in,' and when the truth *really* came out, you'd be too far dead to care? Your death would save you from the humility of it?"

Shaw closed his eyes. "No, it's… I thought I wanted this, and now… I don't know. Just… can you do that for me? Just toss me over the side. The water's deep enough, and I can't swim like this." He looked into his friend's eyes, pleading. "Just kill me."

Jake looked around at the beautiful scene. Shaw had taken in the beauty as well, hours ago when he'd arrived, before it had gotten dark. The summer-tipped leaves of the great trees surrounding the park, the water itself, still and unmoving, reflecting none of the turmoil that existed up above.

"I would, friend," Jake said. "But I can't." He turned to leave.

"Why not?" Shaw watched as Jake Parker walked a few steps back toward the edge of the bridge, then stopped and looked back.

Jake stuffed his hands into his pockets. "Well, Shaw, because you can't kill a man who's already dead."

A LETTER FROM NICK

Dear reader,

I want to say a huge thank you for choosing to read *Containment*. If you did enjoy it, and want to keep up to date with all my latest releases, just sign up at the following link. Your email address will never be shared and you can unsubscribe at any time.

www.bookouture.com/nick-thacker

As an author constantly working to reach a larger readership, one of the best things you can do for me is leave a review. I'd love to hear what you think, and it makes a huge difference in helping new readers discover my books for the first time.

I love hearing from my readers—you can get in touch on my Facebook page or my website.

Thanks,
Nick

AuthorNickThacker

www.nickthacker.com

www.nickthacker.com/free-books

ACKNOWLEDGEMENTS

This book is far from my first but it's most likely my best. I've been writing novels like this one for about eight years, but it's the first project I've taken on that I can confidently describe as "a team effort."

I truly believe this effort is the reason for it being the best of my books to date. Hands-down, it is the most solidly researched, edited, and carefully vetted book of mine, and I believe those elements elevate the finished product to one that I will always be proud of.

However, none of this "elevation of craft" is due to my own skill—it's down to the talents and hard work of the team at Bookouture. To Emily Gowers, the editing team, and all the rest who took part in this project to create something incredible, this book is equally *yours* as it is *mine*. You took a decent idea and promising outline and helped me turn a rough draft into the most polished, professional, and (I believe) well-written piece of fiction I have ever completed.

I truly hope the results speak for themselves; but no matter the outcome, I feel incredibly blessed and humbled to be able to count myself among your ranks. Thank you for your time and effort working with me.

I can't mention the team's help at Bookouture without also mentioning my team here at home. To Emily (my wife), this project would not have been possible without you. The initial concept for this book and its main premise was based on a conversation we had almost a year ago, and you helped develop that thread into something marketable and (hopefully) entertaining to read about. More importantly, you have been with me through the many ups and many (terrifying) downs in my author career, and it has been your constant and never-ending support that kept me pushing forward. I love you.

Finally, to all the friends and acquaintances who sat with me, worked with me, laughed with me, and drank beer with me—this 'writer life' is no walk in the park. Thank you for helping me through it, and I only hope to be able to return the favor one day.

9 781838 887162